Love at First Con-Flict

JANET LEIGH

Also by Janet Leigh

The Jennifer Cloud Series

The Shoes Come First

Dress 2 Impress

3 Ways to Wear Red

In Style 4 Now

Keeping Time (A Between the Clouds novel)

After 5

Denim, Diamonds & Deep 6

Stilettos & Secrets on the 7 Seas

For Eryn, who loves Star Wars as much as her mama.

Love at First
Con-Flict

Janet Leigh

Chapter One

Jade

Being a twin can lead to an identity crisis, and God knows I'm a VIP member of the crisis-a-day club.

The elevator pinged, notifying me I had reached the main floor of the San Diego Marriott Marquis Hotel. I stepped to exit, barely avoiding a collision with two Comic-Con patrons dressed as Nintendo characters Mario and Luigi.

"Your Iron Man costume is real good." Mario gave me a thumbs-up and they crossed into the elevator.

"Thanks." I was shocked by the deep, mechanical sound of my voice due to a voice-altering gadget installed in the mouthpiece of my costume. "Yours is cool too."

They waved and the doors closed. I walked toward the large convention center of the hotel, my armor clanging like a metal wind chime with every step. Other cosplayers joined me on the way to the best Comic-Con in the world. I would have been stoked at attending my first Con, except for the idiotic promise I'd made to my sister.

I cursed Raylynn, my older sister by a mere eight minutes, for the tenth time this morning for suckering me, again, into one of her "must-attend" events. Then I cursed myself, also for the tenth time this morning, for answering the phone two days ago.

"Jade?" My sister's voice had cut through the other end of the line like a screeching hawk. Sharp and focused on her prey.

"Yep." After pulling a double shift at Shadycade, the bar/vintage arcade where I worked, it took a full minute for my eyes to clear and recognize the moonlight streaming through my bedroom window. "Did someone die?"

"No. Why would you think that?" I could almost hear her mouth twisting into an impatient smirk.

"Because it's four," I squinted at the time on my Pokémon alarm clock. "No, five a.m."

"You know me. I never pay attention to the time." A beat of infuriating silence followed her indifference. "I need a favor."

Uh boy.

"Your favors are always the same. Can you do this one little thing for me? And that one little thing usually involves me pretending to be you and doing something I despise."

"You're right. I need a twin swap, but Jade, you're gonna love this one."

Doubtful.

My parents, Ray and Lynn Sayer, named their firstborn a combination of their names. The second bundle of joy, the medical sonographer told them, was a boy. Surprise! I wasn't. Yet I still got the previously chosen name of Jaylynn after my grandpa Jay and my mom's namesake, grandma Lynn. Thankfully, my mother nicknamed me Jade because the only thing entirely mine was the color of my eyes, a fierce jade green.

My eyes, now hidden behind brown contacts to fool the small handful of people my introverted sister had seen in person, itched from the unfamiliar layer of plastic stuck to my pupils.

Growing up in Dallas, I fought hard for my identity—tantrums against matching clothes, dying my brown hair in various colors, and piercing my nose. In seventh grade, just before I spent the money for an illegal tattoo that would mark me Jade forever, I figured out Raylynn got the brains, and I got dyslexia.

Having a smart sister take your tests in school was worth returning my dyed fiery-red hair to boring brown.

With school, Texas, and tests long behind me, the search for my identity had returned along with my red hair. I'd spent a week's tips at a bougie salon to get the perfect shade of red. I accepted doing Raylynn's "favor" but refused to dye my red hair back to its dull birth color. I'd only heard a hint of hurt in my sister's voice before informing me I'd be in costume, so it wouldn't matter.

Raylynn's instructions had me meeting her publicist bright and early, before the day's events began at the San Diego Comic-Con. The numero uno reason I agreed to play switcheroo with my sister was her agreement to cosign on a loan for the bar. She'd also dangled the best Comic-Con in the history of Comic-Cons in my face, knowing I loved gaming. I loved comic books. And I loved anything in the Marvel Multiverse.

I'd always wanted to attend a Comic-Con but couldn't afford it. Now I'm in for free. And not only that, but her publishing company put me, or technically her, up in a deluxe room with a view of the San Diego Bay.

She also mentioned the cast of Guardians of the Galaxy would be making an appearance and promised me at least a Chris Pratt sighting.

I stepped outside, into a courtyard. No sexy Star-Lord. No gorgeous Guardian of the Galaxy. No Chris Pratt. But I had an Olympic-size swimming pool, comfy lounge chairs, and giant palm trees with I'll be dammed, real coconuts.

I pictured myself lying by the pool, reading the current edition of *Game Informer*, and listening to Billie Eilish's powerful soprano croon life's mysteries. "Later." I promised to reward myself for my "favor" later.

The sun, which I normally worshipped on vacation, reflected off the pool and heated the metal on my costume like an unregulated furnace.

"Ohmigod, it's hot." A breeze swished the leaves in the trees, but I couldn't feel it inside my prison.

My instructions were to meet Jerry Cheng, my sister's best friend, stylist, publicist extraordinaire, and apparently costume designer, outside the coffee kiosk, poolside. He'd be dressed as Wong, Dr. Strange's sidekick-pre-Blip.

I'd known Jerry since we were kids, and I recognized him immediately, even in costume. He waited, fidgeting by a large palm tree, a to-go cup of coffee in each hand. I hated lying to Jerry, but Raylynn insisted impersonating her was top secret. Even to Jerry.

"All right, Jade," I whispered to myself and approached him. "Transform into Raylynn. If you can fool Jerry, you can fool anyone."

He did a little two-step. "Raylynn, you look fabulous!" He extended one of the cups toward me.

"Yep, here I am." I took the coffee and stood back for his inspection.

He tucked a strand of dark hair behind his ear and turned me around so he could see my ass.

"Jeez, Jerry, who would have thought you'd be checking me out? Did you and what's his name have a fight?"

"Me and George are fine." He fumbled with the thingy on the side of my thigh. "I had a little trouble with the battery pack thruster, but I think it looks realistic."

"I have to give you credit. I look f'ing authentic. It's the bomb. If I were taller, everyone would think I was the real Iron Man."

"My awesome creation and that voice changer gizmo will have you onstage for best costume."

"Gre-aaat." I loaded that word with fear. Raylynn would hide in the bathroom stall before stepping onstage in front of at least a thousand Comic-Con attendees. Her phobia of crowds was the main reason she paid me for the occasional twin swaps.

My sister, New York Times bestselling author R.D. Sayer, wrote romances that I never read. All those false hopes of love. False promises. False people. A wealthy billionaire falling in love with a barista? I mean, get real.

I lifted the plastic face shield and took a much-needed jolt of caffeine into my bloodstream. My lips puckered as the sugary-sweet concoction sat on my tongue. I didn't do sugar in my coffee. I had forgotten

Raylynn doctored her mocha lattes with enough sugar to wake the dead, but Jerry hadn't forgotten.

I forced it down and made a sour face at the cup.

"Damn, she did it again." Jerry's eyes shaped into suspicious slits.

"What are you talking about?" I kept my tone archangel innocent but knew by the look on his face that I'd failed my top secret sister swap in less than five minutes.

"Jade." He knocked his fist against my helmet. "I don't know why Raylynn thinks she can get away with this shit. I've known both of you since first grade. You don't take sugar in your coffee. You don't fool me."

"I had to swap, she's on a deadline."

"She's not on a deadline. She's avoiding the crowds, the public, her fans. Why do you do this for her?"

"You know why. Because of her agoraphobia." I gave an I-surrender shrug. "And besides, it's the San Diego Comic-Con. I might meet Chris Pratt, or Nick Fury, or"—I placed my hand over my Unibeam in the chest piece containing my imaginary Vibramium Arc Reactor core—"Thor."

"Calm down, impostor girl. Raylynn's fear of crowds will be the end of both of us." He glanced around, probably checking for a sneaky, eavesdropping gossip vlogger.

I frowned down at my coffee cup.

Jerry sighed. "Here, take mine. It's a skinny, no sugar." He traded cups with me, took a long gulp, swallowed, and then eyed me. "Did you even read her latest novel?"

"Of course not."

Jerry tsk'd a finger at me. "I'll have to get you up to speed. Raylynn's on a panel at the end of the conference."

A sudden cramp formed in my ass. "Raylynn didn't say anything about a panel."

"She didn't know. She wouldn't have come. And not only that, but the world-renowned critic who sent Raylynn's last book spiraling off the Top 100 Best Books will be on the panel too."

Jerry paused and scratched the scruff of beard on his chin. A thing he did when he was worried. "Jean-Claude Cabaliér didn't have nice things to say about Raylynn's last book. I bet money the Con set it up to spur some drama. There are two other authors on the panel. All have been the butt of Jean-Claude's bombastic reviews."

"It could give Ray the chance to defend her work." I took another sip of the coffee and let the caffeine fuel my foggy brain.

"The panel is destined to end in tears—hers, and mine. I'll call and try to talk the queen bee into coming out before the grand finale. In the meantime, enjoy yourself. I'll send a copy of the book to your room. Read it. Know it. And be ready to defend your plot to the evil reviewer if the real R.D. Sayer chooses not to leave her hivey-hole."

"Chubby chance in hell getting Raylynn to show after she finds out about the panel and the critic." I'd have to spend my valuable gaming time reading a stupid romance novel.

Jerry gave me a once-over. "Maybe having you here isn't all bad. At least you have balls."

"Gee, thanks?" I wasn't afraid to stand up for myself, but supporting one of Raylynn's bodice rippers was a different story. "I can do this," I heard myself say as I watched a sexy guy dressed as Black Panther cross the courtyard. "And who knows? Maybe I'll meet a few developers and get a heads-up on the latest software."

"Isn't your arcade vintage games? Like Pac-Man?"

"Yeah, but I'm working on a plan to update the bar." Jerry sent me a good-luck-with-saving-that-dive look.

"Raylynn's publisher wants a book tour to promote the new series. The review killed book one, and book two is being announced at the panel this week. She needs to be here. No more hiding behind the cute emoji she uses in all her publicity photos. If this goes bad, it could mean both of us get the cut."

"Both of you?"

"Of course. Who wants to be represented by a publicist who can't even lure his own author into the limelight for book signings, Instagram photos, TikToks, or Facebook Live?"

"You have a point. I'll do my best."

"I know you will. But promise me one thing. In case Raylynn doesn't show, for heaven's sake, don't let anyone know you're not her."

"Cross my Unibeam and hope to be vanquished to the outer rim." I crossed the light thingy on my Iron Man costume.

He winged up an eyebrow, indicating that was a flawed promise.

"Die sounds so wrong," I said.

"It does indeed. Just like my career if this thing goes south."

"Where do I go from here?" The gold stretchy pants I wore under the Iron Man costume didn't have pockets, so I'd tucked my cell phone and lip gloss in the arm laser glove. No room for anything else.

"You're free until the panel on Saturday afternoon. Here." He reached inside his impeccable suit jacket and handed me a lanyard with a clear plastic badge holder attached.

"Thanks." Jerry's company logo was visible in place of the name badge. I flipped it over. The schedule was printed on the opposite side. Jerry had highlighted events he wanted Raylynn to attend.

"I've already checked you in. The cast of *Throne* has a panel interview in about twenty minutes." He took the lanyard from me and slipped it over my head.

"I love that series."

"I'll walk with you, but I have a meeting with a prospective client." The worried look on Jerry's face told me new clients were hard to come by.

If I didn't pull off being R.D. Sayer, it affected Raylynn's credibility, Jerry's reputation, and I'd look like the court jester. I shook off the gravity of my situation and followed him to the session.

Giant banners of the most recent blockbuster sci-fi fantasy film covered the wall in the atrium. The film's characters, displayed in life-sized posters, wrapped the massive columns.

We crossed the mezzanine and walked toward the conference rooms. Clank, clank, clank.

"Jerry, I love this costume, but it's a little noisy." I paused as a Stormtrooper passed me, pretending to fire his blaster in my direction. I sent him a fake energy blast from my palm repulser, which glowed and buzzed thanks to my battery pack disguised as a thruster. He stumbled back, gripping his chest plate. This was the fun I was looking for.

"Doll, that costume screams fantastic on you." Jerry tilted his rose-colored glasses down his nose at me. "These cosplayers should be so lucky. Here we are." He stopped in front of a large display with a scene from *Throne* showing all the characters in action. "I bid you adieu for now." He gave me a don't-fuck-this-up gaze. "Please, keep a low profile. Just in case."

"Just in case my sneak of a sister doesn't show," I said to Jerry's back as he walked away. I got in line behind a couple of *Walking Dead* zombies for the *Throne* panel. A trickle of sweat slid down my back and pooled in the valley above my butt crack.

Raylynn owed me big-time.

Chapter Two

Luke

I adjusted the lightsaber secured on the belt at my hip and glanced across my exhibitor booth. My dad, Steve, had been dragging me to the San Diego Comic-Con every year since he adopted me at age six. His love for Comic-Cons outweighed mine tenfold. Twenty-one years of dressing up like Luke Skywalker. I was so fucking over it.

Dad swiped away a bead of sweat at his receding hairline. "Luke, how many more comics are we unloading?"

"Sorry, this is the last of them." I'd been waiting on the printer to deliver the latest issues of *Cronman*, and they finally arrived just as the Comic-Con opened its doors. Now, with Dad's help, I frantically tried to sort them.

"The Con's more crowded this year than last year." I noted the steady stream of people who walked by, some dressed in cosplay, some not.

"Looks like another exciting event." Steve, sporting his usual Darth Vader costume, caught sight of another Vader and double-checked his costume in comparison.

"Yeah, real exciting." I tried to sound enthusiastic, but after attending so many Cons, all I really wanted to do was get drunk.

Steve entered my life as my uncle Steve until my mom bailed and he took over. For the last few years, he proudly helped me work my booth at the Comic-Con.

I reached for one of the bins of comics from my hand cart. A group of middle-aged men dressed in green tights and Mutant Ninja Turtles cardboard shells bumped into me, sending the bin toppling and my comics fanning across the floor.

The turtles wore giddy smiles of newbie Con fans and apologized profusely for the clumsy bump. They attempted to help pick up the mess, but their costumes made them unable to bend down.

The turtle nearest me shrugged. "Sorry, man. No flexibility in the shell. My wife made them."

"No prob. I've got it. You guys go have fun." They left with another round of apologies.

I gathered my comics and handed the last stack to my dad, who sorted them into the correct bins. Marvel, DC, Image, Dark Horse, and...mine. "Thanks for helping me out again this year."

"I'm always willing to help my son on his life journey." He grinned when I sent him an exaggerated eye roll. "Besides, I love all the nostalgia that surrounds these Cons. Plus, I heard Wonder Woman is signing autographs."

"Wonder Woman? I didn't think she was your type." My two dads had been together since I was born. They married shortly before my mother decided she had better things to do than raise me.

"You know Paul has a thing for Chris Pine. Heard he's signing too." Dad grinned again, reminding me too much of my birth mom.

My other dad, Paul, whom I called Zaddy until I grew hair on my balls and shortened it to Zad, helps when he can. Paul's an orthopedic surgeon, extremely good-looking, dresses like a GQ model, and women actually cry when they find out he's gay.

"When is Zad getting here?" I flipped through a bin and grabbed a Wonder Woman comic.

"Should be here soon. He had a late patient but promised he wouldn't miss Wonder Woman."

I handed the comic book to him. "She can't sign your forehead. I mean, she could, but it wouldn't be recognizable in a few years."

He shuddered, and I laughed at my meticulous, neat freak father, who washed his hands almost as much as he cleaned the kitchen.

We unloaded the last bin of comics, and Dad organized them. I placed flyers about my bookstore on a table with freebie pens and superhero stickers. "I don't know why I do this every year."

"Because you're a fantastic artist and amaze everyone with your snarky dialogue and three-dimensional characters."

"Snarky, huh? I always thought of my superheroes as clever."

"They're witty and smart-assed and will drive the win home for you at the awards ceremony." His eyes cut to something behind me, and he frowned. I turned to see Jean-Claude Cabaliér, my business partner and frequent pain in my ass, heading in our direction.

"I don't understand why you keep ghostwriting for that egomaniac." Dad sent a chin thrust in Jean-Claude's direction.

"The money's good, and he's an investor in my bookstore. One day I'll buy him out. I'll stop ghostwriting. Stop living his dreams. And stop letting him rule my life."

"We could loan—"

"You know I don't want your help. I need to do this on my own."

"I get it. But that guy's a step away from smarmy villain." Dad tucked the Wonder Woman comic under his arm and grabbed the handle of the cart. "I'll take this back."

"Catch you later."

Dad made himself scarce just as Jean-Claude stopped and picked up one of my comics. He held it between his thumb and finger, as if it contained a contagious virus. "I see you're still pumping out the comics."

"This is a *Comic*-Con." *You dumb fucker*. I snatched the *Cronman* comic from him.

Jean-Claude gave me a look that seemed to say he was the important person, I was a toe fungus, and he didn't give a shit about my desire to have my own career.

"You should spend more time writing for me and less time writing for you."

My blood pressure, already on a slow climb to the high dive, rocketed off into an out-of-control quadruple. I tucked in before I landed a belly flop. "I've kept your book review blog up to date, posted clips on your social media channels, and finished book six in *your* sci-fi series. I barely have time to work on my own comics." *Much less get laid.*

"You work for me, and I need a new review of the R.D. Sayer novel."

"I gave you my take on it. What more do you want?" He'd twisted my words around, but technically they were all my words.

"I want another review up ASAP. I want it more critical than the last one. I want Sayer to suffer."

"Why Sayer? Don't you want every author to suffer, except you?"

"R.D. Sayer is attending the conference."

"For real? I didn't think Sayer made public appearances. Maybe your bad review brought the recluse out to punch you in the face." I chuckled at my joke, but Jean-Claude didn't join in.

"I'm on a panel with that unicorn, and I need some dirt. I need to know who this Sayer person is. Man, woman, or unidentified. I need to know what it eats for breakfast. I need to know who I'm dealing with. I need more fuel to back up my critique."

The asshole meant my critique. "Jean-Claude, I'm not a detective. How am I supposed to get you the dirty details on an author no one has ever seen?" I gave him a pissant shrug. I wasn't wasting my time. "It's an impossible request. Sayer uses a unicorn emoji for author photos and profile pics. And most of the people at the Con are in costume."

He tapped a finger to his vampire-sharp chin. Another villain characteristic. Along with his dark, slicked-back hair, wiry frame, and pretentious attitude. He had all the makings of the perfect bad guy.

I thought about the villain in my graphic novel. I'd have him tapping his chin in just that way.

Jean-Claude's words interrupted my mental sketching. "You know the loan you owe me for that unproductive bookstore? It may come due sooner than you planned."

My jaw dropped and I fought the urge to land an upper cut right on that pointy chin. "You can't do that. I have a contract."

"I can and I will. You're the creative one. Get creative and find Sayer for me."

He walked away, then stopped and turned back toward me. His eyes wide and round like he'd had an idea. But not the bright, shiny kind. A black light moment. "You know, if you do this for me, I might be inclined to add your name to the next book in my series."

I had just recovered from the threat of losing my store. Now, he dangled the one thing I wanted more than anything. Credit for *my* work. "And 50 percent of the royalties that go with it?"

"Absolutely." His matter-of-fact tone made me want to check behind his back for fingers crossed.

"Is that a promise?" Skepticism clung to my words like overcooked fettuccini.

He wielded that villainous smile at me. "Right under mine, smaller, of course."

I looked around for a pen and paper to get the promise in writing, but I was sidetracked by Jean-Claude saying hello to a woman pushing a stroller. A boy clung to her side.

Jean-Claude smiled at them, and I wondered—does he realize all my villains are pieces of him?

The way his mouth creeps into an evil grin. His sinister laugh that makes my flesh crawl. I've even occasionally caught him picking a wedgie, which made Wedgie Man a particular favorite in my middle-grade comics.

"Consider my offer." Jean-Claude walked away. I stared after him, surprised he didn't leave in a cloud of smoke like some nefarious sorcerer.

"You're the writer, right? This is your picture?" I blinked at the woman. She was holding my comic book and pointing to my author photo on the back. "And which woman is the villain? You've dangled three beautiful possibilities, and I can't figure it out."

"You'll have to wait to find out." When she looked upset at my plot tease, I followed with, "It releases next week."

"C'mon, throw me a bone here. I've got three kids under six. Who knows when I'll have time to read it?"

"I'll give you a hint. She's a redhead."

"That's my husband's favorite bad girl." She gripped the handles on the stroller. A toddler slept inside. I knelt next to the little boy clinging to her skirt and held up two stickers. "Cronman or Black Dart?"

"Cronman!" The little boy shouted.

"That's the spirit, dude. Nobody likes a bad guy." I stuck the sticker of Cronman on his T-shirt. "Except for Venom. He was one of my favs."

I looked up at the woman. She stared at something behind me. Her eyes softened, and her lips pulled into a dreamy smile. I turned and spotted Zad standing there in blue scrubs, *Dr. Paul Schroader, MD* embroidered above his right breast pocket.

Zad slapped a hand on my shoulder. "Venom isn't a bad guy. He's an anti-hero." He nodded at the woman and boy. "Hey, there. I see you're team Cronman. Good choice."

"Hey, Zad." I stood and waved goodbye to the boy. His mother pushed the stroller but turned back for one last look at my handsome dad. I couldn't blame her.

"How's it going?" Zad flashed a full-on movie star smile at me.

"Finished setting up just as the first wave rolled in." I spotted the red cape draped over his back, and a Jaeger-LeCoultre watch on his wrist. The watch Steve had given him for Christmas. "Dr. Strange?"

"Yep. Steve's going to pay. He bet me I wouldn't dress up."

I nodded my praise of his costume. "How much did you bet?"

"A massage at the hotel spa." He tapped the plastic lightsaber hanging on my utility belt. "I see you're Luke Skywalker again this year."

"Who else would I be?" Steve was a huge fan of Star Wars. When I was born, he convinced my mom, his sister, to name me Luke Sky Walker. My mom, being an I-don't-give-a-shit sort of person, told him to name me whatever the fuck he wanted.

With my real dad out of the picture, Steve became my dad and my hero.

"Hey, do you mind watching the booth until Dad gets back? *Throne* is doing a panel, and I'd like to see it."

"No problem. As long as you're back in time for me to see, uhm... Wonder Woman."

"Yeah, right. Wouldn't want you to *Pine* for her autograph."

He grinned and sent me a six-shooter, you-got-me, gesture. "Later, son."

Chapter Three

Jade

The line for the *Throne* panel was long but filled with people in amazing costumes. One dressed as Thanos from *The Avengers* had to have taken hours to put together. Occasionally, event employees wearing headsets and the Con T-shirt rushed by, probably making sure the event ran smoothly. The smell of coffee wafted by me. Most of the line held plastic cups with branded coffee collars, similar to mine.

I drained the cup and wished I had another. Closing my face shield, I tossed the cup in the trash bin a few steps from the line. A colorful 3-D display of the *Throne* cast was next to the trash bin. I took a minute to salivate over my favorite character. Sighing heavily, I took my place back in line. Men like that didn't exist. He was handsome, had a witty sense of humor, would die for his queen, and never lied. His honor was his weapon.

I pulled my phone from the laser glove on my Iron Man costume and texted Raylynn.

Sorry, didn't fool Jerry. And you have some panel thingy on the last day that sounds super important. Get your antisocial, crowd-avoiding, sister-swapping-ass here, Ray-Ray.

I thought using my nickname for her might entice a response, but I got nada. No little bubbles with a possible *I'll get on the next plane.*

I was used to waiting on Raylynn. If she was writing, it could be days before she'd respond to a text. Until she completed her manuscript, she kept her door locked. Her phone on mute. And her attitude bitchy.

I tucked my phone back inside my laser glove and scanned the crowd in front of me for Chris Pratt. The possibility of meeting the Star-Lord of my dreams sent a thrill through my core. Attending the Comic-Con was a score for Raylynn, even if I did have to pretend to be her.

All around me people talked of gaming and comics. Two of my passions. A couple in front of me dressed as avatars from Minecraft discussed the cliffhanger ending of this season's *Throne.* Which characters they predicted to be killed off next season.

Another cosplayer dressed as a Star Wars Stormtrooper walked toward me, stopped suddenly, yanked out his blaster, and pointed it at someone behind me.

My helmet had zero peripheral vision, and I had to turn completely around to see who was in his line of fire. A guy dressed as Luke Skywalker in his Tatooine days, taller and more buff than the actor who played the renowned hero, stood behind me. Eyes as blue as the ocean in the travel sites I lusted over, destinations I'd never be able to afford, stared down at me.

My yum-o-meter pitched right into the oh, yes, please, red zone.

It had been a light year since my thruster had been activated. Before my last semi-serious relationship with the loser doorknob, I'd had a string of men who snuck out in the middle of the night. No more one-night stands for me. A Comic-Con hookup was not happening. I needed to focus on finding new ideas for the bar. Theo, the current owner of Shadycade, was making noises about selling the place. My goal to buy him out had become a dream after my last boyfriend stole my life savings. He was a real piece of shit.

The Skywalker wannabe cocked his head as his eyes took in my costume. Was he checking me out?

I reset my meter to Not Interested and turned my back on tall, sandy blond, and yummy. No more men dragging me into their lying, stealing, sex on the patio table world. I stepped forward and the Stormtrooper moved closer to his target.

Chapter Four

Luke

Damn. Jean-Claude could smoke my pole—finding R.D. Sayer in this crowd would take a freakin' miracle. I adjusted my lightsaber and checked out the cosplayers standing in line for the *Throne* panel.

The Iron Man in front of me was a little short. Not that Robert Downey Jr. was tall, but the one in front of me couldn't be more than five-four. A Stormtrooper heading my direction caught sight of me. He halted, whipped out his blaster, and pointed it at me.

Iron Man turned around and looked my way. If it wasn't for the dark shield masking his eyes, I could have sworn the dude was checking me out. Not my thing, but I respected love. Too bad it didn't work out for me. Maybe someday I'd meet a woman who wouldn't lie to my face or fuck my best friend. Sure, it was after we'd broken up. After the cable guy incident but come on. There's this thing called gap time before you move in on your best friend's ex. He did ask me if I was cool with it. And like an idiot, my ego shrugged it off and gave the green light.

Stormtrooper pushed me, trying to engage me in battle. "What d'ya got, Luke Skywalker?"

"This is not the battle you seek." I waved a hand at him, Jedi mind-trick style.

He spread his arms welcoming wide. "Give yourself to the Dark Side. The Dark Side is the only way you can save your friends."

"Wrong line, dude. That one belongs to Darth Vader, but thanks for playing."

"C'mon, let us battle for the best lightsaber show." The guy holstered his blaster and pulled out a lightsaber. A red light beamed through the plastic tube. A small crowd began egging us on. Iron Man turned back around as if the cosplay was a nuisance.

"You shouldn't wield a weapon that's above Stormtrooper ability." I whipped out my saber. It had seen a few fights, so his brand-new one might take mine down.

"I could be Vader in disguise," Stormtrooper lunged at me.

I lunged back. "Doubtful." The crowd opened up around us.

We did the whole bash against each other. The guy was getting into it. I gave him a go-easy-man glare, but he kept coming at me. I didn't want to bump into Iron Man, so I took my eyes off the guy for a minute, missing the foot planted in my chest. I stumbled back into Iron Man, righted myself, pushed off, and heard a yelp, then something snap.

Stormtrooper came at me again. I didn't have time to apologize. I ducked, somersaulted into a full twist, popped up, and slashed my weapon into the air. With a grand finish, I plunged my lightsaber into his heart, the plastic cone scaling up inside itself and winning a round of applause from the now not-so-small crowd around us.

"OK, dude, you win." Stormtrooper panted, hands on his knees.

"I'll never turn to the Dark Side." I shook hands with Stormtrooper and bowed to the enthusiastic fans. When I turned around, Iron Man was getting up off the floor assisted by another Con attendee. He turned toward me with hands on hips. I could feel the irritation radiating through his face shield. A piece of his costume lay next to me on the ground. It looked like a...I squinted at the penis shaped object. Yep, it looked like a giant dick.

I scooped up the shiny piece of metal. It buzzed and vibrated in my hand.

"Sorry, man, I think this..." I looked down at the broken thing. "Belongs to you."

Iron Man yanked off his helmet. Thick auburn hair framed wide, angry brown eyes and full, luscious lips. She pushed the hair behind her shoulder, leaving it to fall down her back in glorious waves.

My mouth dropped open. "Fuck me." I managed to say in place of moaning at the sight of her. I stood speechless. Enchanted.

"Yes, fuck you." She snatched the metal thingy from my hand. "You should be more careful."

"I'm sorry, I broke your...uhm...vibrator."

"It's my thruster, you idiot."

"Your costume is fantastic. It vibrates like a real thruster." I sounded like a starstruck fan, fawning over her. "I never expected you to be a chick...er, I mean, woman." Another thick-witted remark. I couldn't stop myself. *Shut your mouth, dude.*

Dark brows pulled into a frown over eyes I could lose myself in. "I didn't expect you to be a klutz. What happened to using the Force?"

Damn, her voice held that bit of rasp like a soulful blues singer. I could listen to it all day. "Uh, that only works with CGI?"

The line moved forward, and I followed her inside the conference room for the stars of the *Throne* panel. Although the voice in my head told me I was taking a break from love, I wanted to know more about this petite, feisty Iron Man. I took the seat next to her, and she groaned.

She placed her helmet and the broken thruster on the empty chair to her right and crossed her arms over her chest. Those full lips pressed together in a frustrated pout.

"So, you come here often?" I added a chuckle, not an overconfident I'm-hitting-on-you chuckle, but a low, humble, please-forgive-my-stupidness, I'm-a-fun-guy laugh.

Silence.

"Hey, what are you doing after the panel?"

She ignored me.

Not a good sign, Walker. "What if I make up for my bad behavior by taking you to lunch?"

She turned to me. "No."

"Ah, c'mon, it was harmless fun. I didn't mean to break your vibrator."

She sucked in some air. "Thruster. Do you always hit on women you knock down with your LARPing?"

"It was cosplay, and you'd be my first casualty."

"Imagine that. And here I thought Han Solo was the Jackass in your entourage."

I couldn't help the wide, stupid grin that spread across my face. She had that quick comeback I worshipped in women. One that could hold her own against any heckler.

"You're right. I'm the nice guy. The Good Samaritan. The safe farm boy who'd like to repent for his sins by buying you lunch at the best place in town."

She looked at me. "I don't do fancy."

I almost did a victorious fist pump but caught myself. She was hovering on the possibility of a free meal. Maybe that's all she wanted, but I'd get the chance to hear that sultry voice and look into those eyes for at least an hour.

"No." I shook my head. "Not this place. It's caz, but the food is great. Best pico de gallo this side of Me-hi-co. So, we can meet, say around one?"

"I'm not interested in your pico." She leaned back and studied the schedule. I stared at her. "Game over," she added with a huff.

I wasn't giving up that easily. Interlacing my fingers, I cracked my knuckles.

She glanced over at me.

My player character was leveling up for round two.

Chapter Five

Jade

This guy was a pain in my Iron Man ass. First, he breaks my costume, and now he hits on me. Not that he wasn't eye candy, but picking up a guy at a Comic-Con wasn't in my plan. There would be no fling with Luke Skywalker or anyone else. Eyes in front, Jade, stay focused on the mission. Do not get lost in those blue eyes or that sexy voice.

"What if we start over? I'm Luke. Luke Walker." He held out his hand.

Was this guy for real? He didn't bother to tell me his real name. Then it dawned on me. I couldn't tell him my real name either. And I wasn't supposed to have my helmet off. Jerry was going to kill me.

"Again, not interested." I twisted my hair into a top bun and plopped the helmet on my head. There. That should keep my gaze forward and send a don't-bother-me message.

"Do you have a boyfriend?" Skywalker shifted closer to me.

"Definitely not." I glanced at him and gave myself a mental head slap.

"Girlfriend?"

I huffed. This guy could not take a hint. "No. And not that you need to know, but I like men. Just not you."

"Ouch." He rubbed his muscular pecs like my words caused an ache deep in his chest. An obviously unhappy end to his pursuit.

I did my best to keep my lips pressed together and fight off the smile. Thankfully, the emcee began introducing the cast members of *Throne*, saving me from those seductive blue eyes.

The actors entered one at a time, waving at the crowd. My heart did a little tap dance when the lead actor entered the stage and I straightened in my chair.

"Well, Sith spit! I can't compete with that." Luke shifted uneasily next to me.

I told myself to ignore the Jedi wannabe and focus on one of my man crushes. The other being Chris Pratt, who I hoped to see and smell during the Con. I bet he smelled like vanilla and love.

The lead actor looked so different without the dreads he wore for the show. Now, his dark hair was cut short, and he was more attractive yuppie than badass knight of the round table. I couldn't decide which one was more appealing, the real-life man or the character on the screen. Both could warm my sheets anytime. "Dammit."

"Did you say something?" Skywalker leaned even closer. "Your voice thingamabob muffles your words."

"No," I snapped, followed by a silent curse. Stop thinking about warm sheets and who's between them.

I tried not to notice the casual way Luke Skywalker's knee touched mine. Was it my imagination, or did I feel erotic tingles through the metal of my leg armor?

I moved my leg, losing the direct contact of sex tingles, and focused on the actor. I'd read on a movie blog that he had initially been killed off by the writers in season three but was kidnapped by some crazed fan. The writers changed the storyline until they found him, then he married the kidnapper. With all the press he received, the producers insisted he stay on the show. Good for him, saving his career. Good for me, I got to fantasize about him at least once a week.

I hoped to be as lucky in my career. If Theo sold the bar, I didn't want to resort to a kidnapping. Maybe the new owner of Shadycade would allow me to run the bar. Or worse than being sold, what if they tore it down and built a swanky office building, or God help us, apartments?

The heroine of the show wore tight skinny jeans and FMPs. She flipped her sheet of blond hair, strutted across the stage, and wiggled into her seat.

"Are you a big fan of *Throne*?"

Ugh, he was speaking to me again in that sexy voice with just the right amount of gravel—like he'd recently rolled out of bed and was bringing me a steaming cup of coffee.

"Yeah, but a bigger fan of the video game. You?" Why was I encouraging conversation? Repeat head slap.

I felt his excitement over my revelation that I was a gamer. He exhaled slowly, as if trying to control his enthusiasm. "The series was all right. The plotlines are a bit weak, and after the first season, they totally screwed up the hero's character arc."

"His what arc?"

"You know. His storyline. What happens to him in the overall scheme of things. He should have died at the hands of the evil warrior."

"In the game, I make up the character's story." Stop talking to him, Jade. Just stop.

A guy dressed as Link in the row in front of us turned to shush me.

Luke waved his hand at him in some sort of Jedi move.

"That doesn't really work," I said. "You're not Luke Skywalker."

The guy wrinkled his nose at Luke, pressed his middle finger to his lips, and returned his attention to the front as the moderator introduced the rest of the cast.

The journalists and bloggers fired questions at the stars.

The lead actress adjusted her low-cut blouse before answering a question. I had the video game that came before the movie, but the creators had leveled up her avatar after the series became popular. She had super cool magic powers I utilized to outwit my opponents.

I wondered if Luke Skywalker played any video games. Then another mental head slap for thinking about the annoying guy. Of course he played video games, it was practically written on his forehead. And were those calluses on his thumbs? Luke Skywalker, loser, LARPer and low-down costume wrecker. I'd stay far away from him.

Luke shifted in his seat. The guy could not sit still. Was that a hint of vanilla in the air?

Chapter Six

Luke

My arm ached slightly from my battle with the Stormtrooper. It had been a while since I'd wielded my lightsaber. I rubbed my shoulder, trying not to look like a total douche.

A young blogger asked the lead actress an inappropriate question, and she answered with a sweet but brilliant comeback. Her blond hair wasn't braided and tied back with rope like in the show but hung straight as a waterfall. When the guy kept asking annoying questions, she tossed it behind her shoulder and lit into the guy.

She was a total hottie, but nothing compared to the woman next to me. When my knee touched her costume, I felt sparks ignite between us. I wanted more sparks. One of the journalists asked a question about dragons and drew my attention.

I focused on the dragons, but when they started talking about the romance, my thoughts wandered back to Iron Man. "Have you watched the entire series?" I tried to make conversation with her. "I was a fan but lost interest after the fourth season when it started getting all soap opera-y."

Nothing. She kept her eyes on the panel, but I thought I saw her brows furrow at my question. I tried to get her attention by waving my hand at her, and one of the panelists thought I was raising my hand.

"It seems we have a question from an enthusiastic fan in the middle row." He pointed at me, and with a very British accent said, "Just there."

The audience turned and looked in my direction. I gave them a finger wave.

A perky panel moderator slid her way down my aisle, microphone in hand.

"Luke Skywalker, what's your question?" She held the microphone in front of my lips.

Damn, I needed a question, maybe just a compliment. "Umm... I'm a fan of the show. The writers are great."

"Fantastic." The British accent came from a short, balding man sitting next to the leading actress. He balanced his chin in his hand and stared at me inquisitively. "Who's your favorite character?"

I didn't recognize them out of costume. If I said the actress, Iron Man might label me a playa. "You, of course."

Out of the corner of my eye, I caught Iron Man turn and look at me. The audience laughed. Iron Man shook her head.

"I'm the director." The man chuckled along with the audience, who some might call their level of laughter a guffaw.

I wanted to redeem myself, but I couldn't shut up. "The plot was spot on until that mess with trying to hide the actor you were trying to kill off and redeem him as some sort of holy guardian. I've only seen the first few seasons. I lost interest after the dragon died."

A gasp from the crowd made my stomach clench and my breakfast burrito threaten an ugly return.

"What question did you have then, Nonfan?" The director, his tone caustic and critical like all the eyes staring at me.

Question? I glanced at Iron Man and a thought bubbled to the surface. She might not like it, but what the hell. Ride or die, right? I took a deep breath and threw the dice.

Chapter Seven

Jade

My trip down the rabbit hole of my favorite series suddenly derailed, and I realized Skywalker was standing next to me and all eyes were on us. He mistook the director of the film for one of the actors. Amateur. I was mortified at his embarrassing blunder.

"Give the guy a break," the lead actor spoke up. "He can't know every actor, and we look different without our makeup artists and costume designers."

Luke let out a swoosh of air. I almost felt bad for him.

"Actually, my question is for you." Luke spoke to the lead actor. "I wondered if, in your realm, you have ever had an altercation and used your magic powers to ask forgiveness?"

Frozen strawberry margaritas! What was Skywalker up to?

"I forgive her every time she forgets her lines." The lead actor received a scowl from his co-star, the main actress.

The actress ran her eyes over Luke. "Who wouldn't forgive Luke Skywalker?" Her voice purred like a panther on the prowl. "He's got such an innocence about him."

"That's why I need your help. I'd like to ask Iron Man out to lunch, but she won't forgive me for a minor altercation that was totally not my fault." Luke hiked a thumb my direction.

The crowd looked at me, and I shrank deeper into my metal hideout.

"Maybe she's avoiding you." The actress tapped a long nail on her water bottle.

"Most definitely, but I'd like to convince Iron Man I'm worth the trouble."

The actress's ruby-red lips twisted into a pout. "Well, if Iron Man doesn't take you up on the offer, I sure will." The crowd hooted with laughter. "He's got the Force, honey. You should take advantage of it."

A simultaneous cheering began from the audience. "Luke, Luke, Luke." They stared at me with hopeful expressions, waiting for me to say something.

"Fine!" I shouted and hoped to put an end to Luke's quest and draw the attention away from me. My synthesizer reverberated like Darth Vader on steroids.

"Awwwwwwww." The star placed her hand over her heart. The crowd applauded.

Luke bowed and sat down next to me, casually putting his arm on the back of my chair.

"That was ballsy, but embarrassing," I said.

"Yeah, but it got me a lunch date with you."

Jeez. An entire room full of people knew I had a lunch date with Luke Skywalker. Way to be discreet, Jade.

After the panel, Luke turned toward me. "I'm working a booth in the exhibition hall. I could come by your room around one?"

"Nice try, Skywalker. You're not getting my room number."

"I meant to escort you to this great little Mexican restaurant. It's on the hotel property. You won't need to bring a bodyguard."

"Afraid I won't show?"

"I hope you will. I'd like to get to know you better and make up for my altercation." He shrugged a shoulder. "But if you don't, I get it."

"I always keep my word. Why don't I meet you at the restaurant?" I suggested. His boyish good looks, that deep dimple in his chin, and the easy way he bantered with me killed all the excuses I'd thought of to break the date.

"That'll work," Luke said.

"There's one condition." I squinted my deal-breaker eyes at him.

"Name it," Luke's eyes twinkled at the prospect of a challenge.

"You can't ask my name." If he ditched our date because the weird woman didn't want to reveal her name, then no loss. But I sort of wanted to get to know him now.

"Why not?" He leaned in and lowered his voice. "Are you a spy?"

"I have my reasons."

"You're not married, are you?" He looked around. "There's not a giant brute about to rip my head off, is there?"

"No. No husband. No boyfriend. But no name. That's the deal." I shrugged and turned to leave. He grabbed my arm.

"All right. I won't ask your name." He glanced at my badge. "What should I call you?"

"Whatever you want."

He reached up and tugged on a strand of hair that had escaped from my helmet. "I'll call you Red."

I watched Luke saunter off. His backside was almost better than his front, broad shoulders, confident stride, and what looked like solid muscles under the farm boy Luke Skywalker, pre-Jedi costume.

Jade, Jade, Jade. I mentally cursed myself for caving to his so-called Force. I shouldn't be admiring his attributes. I shouldn't be having lunch with him. And I shouldn't be wishing I could strip the farm boy and check out his real weapon.

I shook my head, freeing myself from the hormone overload overtaking my brain like the Imperial Army snatching the galaxy.

Focus, Jade. You will not fall for this guy. He had a lot of nerve asking me out in front of a room full of people, including my favorite stars of *Throne*.

I pushed the upcoming lunch date aside and checked my schedule. Jerry highlighted a session for Raylynn, a panel discussion led by some famous entertainment guru. I figured I'd attend. I mean, why not? There wasn't anything I wanted to see until the gaming demo at 4:00 p.m.

The urge to return to my room and log in to my favorite game, Dragontoon, threatened. Nope, not going to happen. I'd spent way too many hours trying to beat the game's notorious hacker, the Python. I wasn't going to let that self-righteous PC ruin my Comic-Con.

Chapter Eight

Jade

Walking toward the session's room seemed to take eons. The conference wasn't a small venue. I was sweating like a hippo on a treadmill. By the time I found room 24ABC, my pits were squishy. Jerry flagged me down like runway patrol to the empty seat next to him.

"Hey, doll. How was *Throne*? Did the costume designer salivate over your Iron Man?"

"I didn't meet the costume designer, but I did meet someone." I pulled off my helmet, and Jerry sucked in some air. "Sorry, Jerry, this costume is frying me like an egg on a Texas summer sidewalk. I don't know if I can wear it the entire day."

"Put the helmet back on. If anyone sees you with me, they'll ID you as R.D. Sayer."

"Isn't to be R.D. Sayer the point?" I wiped my brow, twisted my hair into a topknot, and pulled on the helmet, but flipped the face shield open.

"Not yet. I'm still hoping the real Sayer will arrive." His lips twisted into that disappointed frown I'd known since elementary school. The frown that made me want to climb mountains for the little boy whose parents didn't understand why he wanted to play with Barbies instead of Matchbox cars. "If you must change, there are eight more costumes in your room."

"Eight?"

"Yes, Raylynn wanted a different costume for each day, with a few backups in case she didn't like one of my designs. As if." He wafted a hand in the air and rolled his eyes heavenward. I understood. Many times, I'd had the same response to Raylynn's demands.

"I had them delivered to your room while you were in the *Throne* session. It took me all night to finish the last one. But of course, Iron Man is my crème de la crème."

"Raylynn wanted costumes for a Con she wasn't attending?"

"Oh, you know her. She plans big, then at the last minute, she freaks out and spends the weekend in bed with a cold cloth on her head."

"Did you talk to her?" I gave him a hopeful sideways glance.

"No, I tried calling, but it goes straight to voice mail."

"Yeah, I tried too." I blew out a long, should-have-seen-this-coming sigh. "If she doesn't show, I'll do my best to give vague answers to any questions about her book. I've been playing Raylynn for a long time. It shouldn't be a total catastrophe."

Jerry patted my hand as if to say *bless your heart*. "Who did you meet?"

"What?" I asked.

"Earlier you said you met someone."

"Oh, yeah. Some guy asked me out. Get this. He was dressed like Luke Skywalker."

"I heard the Force is strong with that one." Jerry laughed at his own joke.

"I'm meeting him for lunch, but only because he put me on the spot, and I couldn't say no."

"Jade, you've always let people manipulate you."

"I don't."

"You do. What about your last boyfriend, Girlie Cocktail?"

"Big Mike?" No forgetting that loser. "You call him Girlie Cocktail?"

"Raylynn's nickname for him. He drank those drinks with the little umbrellas. I hope he was called Big Mike for other reasons."

It certainly wasn't the size of his brain.

Jerry nudged me. "You know you didn't want to add all those exotic drinks to the menu. The cost of the pricey liquor alone cut into your overhead. Theo was beside himself when that asshat took off with the weekend's earnings."

And all my savings. "Yeah, the prick caught the first plane to Mexico and hasn't been seen since. I'm glad Theo didn't fire me."

"Mike manipulated you into those flashy menus. And let's not forget how Raylynn always manipulates you into playing twinzies."

"Yeah, well..." I didn't know what to say. He was right. I let people muscle me into things I didn't want to do, like my upcoming lunch date. Maybe I should stand Luke up. That would teach him.

"Was he cute?"

I pulled out of my self-indulgent rant and stared blankly at Jerry.

"I asked, was he cute?" Jerry huffed at me.

I couldn't stop the devilish smile that stole across my face.

"You should meet him. It's only lunch, and you haven't had a date since Girlie Cocktail."

I hated to admit, but those blue eyes had me wanting to know more about Luke Skywalker, what he did for a living and how good he was at using the Force.

"Maybe I'll go."

"Oh dear," Jerry said, sending me a sideways glance.

"What?" I looked around as best I could.

"That man over there." He nodded at a man in black sitting in the front row. "That's Jean-Claude Cabaliér. He's the critic that gave Raylynn that horrible review."

My sister shield sprang into action. I mean, nobody can bad-mouth Raylynn except me. "Why does anyone care what that prick thinks?"

"He may be a prick, but he's a well-established, influential, prolific prick. He's written over a dozen bestselling books on the craft of writing romance, sci-fi, and fantasy. His recent graphic novel is on the *USA Today* and *New York Times* bestseller list. The world looks to his blog

34

before buying a book. His rave reviews have turned many authors' novels into movie deals."

"Huh. Big deal." I lifted a shoulder, then slumped back into my seat.

"Remember, I told you he's the critic on the panel. The prick knows his shit!" Jerry almost rocketed off his chair. "You need to read the book. I'll send you a summary, but it won't be enough. He'll string you up like dirty thongs on a clothesline."

"Calm down. I can handle him." It might take all night to read Raylynn's book. How bad can it be? I've pulled all-nighters in college. My dyslexia made reading a novel slow and painful—especially one about love. I was more of a comic book type of girl. I mean, how many ways were there to have sex in the shower? Raylynn's last romance novel was entertaining, just not my thing.

A hush fell over the room and the session began with a panel of three, the entertainment guru, an author of a bestselling sci-fi novel, and a screenwriter of a recent Netflix movie.

The guru, a feisty, fifty-something woman had a beehive of blond hair and perfect pink painted on lips. She explained marketing strategies using examples from the author's branding and the screenwriter's movie.

Jerry made a few notes on the complimentary hotel stationary. The author went next explaining his plot, and I almost fell asleep. Until Jean-Claude stood and interrupted the speaker.

"Wouldn't you say your storyline is merely a retelling of Shakespeare's *Othello*?" Jean-Claude asked the thin, sallow-faced man who hadn't seen the light of day for, oh, I'd guess about ten years.

I craned my neck to see the author's reaction.

"No. It's nothing like *Othello*." Sallow face's tone was as bitter as the look on his face.

Jean-Claude pointed out a few similarities, quoting actual lines the author stole from *Othello*, while the screenwriter and guru looked like they were afraid they'd be next.

"OK, I guess maybe there might be some coincidental parallels." The author seemed to shrink in his chair.

Jean-Claude continued to ream him until the guy lifted his water bottle and downed the contents like it was vodka. Maybe it was.

Smirnoff Shitbuckets! A surfer sized wave of nausea crested in my stomach at the possibility I could go cute-snub nose to pointy-wicked-witch nose with this prick on the author panel for Raylynn.

"I see what you mean," I said to Jerry. "This guy's the tallboy of jerks."

"Does my neck look red?" Jerry scratched at his neck. "Am I getting hives?"

I looked at his neck. Was that a red blotch? I couldn't be sure. Why worry the poor guy? He had enough on his mind. "Nope. Looks good to me."

"You need to read Raylynn's book. Don't get busy with the Force and forget. I'm going out into the hall to call your sister again."

He left the room, cell phone in one hand and scratching furiously at his neck with the other. I turned my attention back to the panel. Now, the crowd fired questions at the author about his plagiarism of *Othello*. If they'd had rotten vegetables, the author would be a tossed salad.

Jean-Claude glanced over his shoulder at the angry crowd. He wore a smug expression I'd like to smack off his face. The session ended with the author stomping off the stage.

I glanced at my phone. I had about an hour before my railroaded lunch date. Jerry mentioned I had other costumes in my hotel room. I closed my face shield. A costume change was in order. One that would make Luke Skywalker sweat bullets, or in Star Wars land, blaster bolts. *Oh yeah.*

Thirty minutes later, I put the finishing touch on my Harley Quinn makeup, including the tiny, temporary heart tattoo below my left eye. I had to give Raylynn credit. Her costume choices were frickin' awesome, and Jerry's designs were over-the-top.

The costume gave me an idea for the bar. I could host a theme night. The Barflies, my BFFs since I moved to Sacramento, would love it. Jerry could design a few costumes to keep on hand for those who can't afford them. I sighed. Who was I kidding? I couldn't afford them. I shook my head. I'm not going to think like that—only positive thoughts from here on out.

I squeezed into the über tight short shorts. Ugh, was Raylynn forgetting to eat again? I'd have to go easy on the enchiladas. I slipped the T-shirt that read Daddy's Lil' Monster over my head and attached a leather dog collar around my neck. The six-inch mock tennis shoe boots gave me the height I needed to look Luke in the eyes without getting a crick in my neck.

After positioning the blond pig-tailed wig with pink and blue tips, I smiled at myself in the bathroom mirror. "Payback time, Luke Skywalker."

I'd give him something to remember for putting me on the spot. I thought about those blue eyes, broad shoulders, and how I might be missing a night of wild sex in order to seek my revenge.

I told my reflection. "You're not going to get all melty over Luke Skywalker." Top priority is making this guy suffer for that embarrassing scene he created in the *Throne* panel.

I picked up Harley Quinn's weapon of choice, a Louisville Slugger baseball bat with the words *Good Night* stenciled on the side. Between my makeup and the wig, no one would recognize me. Not with my boobs stacked up to my neckline and my ass eating these shorts. I'd never wear an outfit like this, and neither would Raylynn. I preferred loose-fitting shorts and T-shirts. And Raylynn? I hadn't seen her out of yoga pants in years. Jerry had been over-the-top optimistic on this one.

I glanced one last time at the sexy villain in front of me and pointed my bat at the mirror. "Eat shit and die."

Oh yeah, this guy was going to suffer. He'd remember 'Red' for many Cons to come.

Chapter Nine

Luke

Damn. Not knowing Red's name was seriously seductive. On my way back to my event booth, I ran over reasons why she wouldn't want to tell me her name, nixing my first thought that she was Jean-Claude's mystery writer. This girl didn't know a plot from a character arc.

Maybe she was a movie star—one on a Netflix series or a Hallmark movie. An image of her kissing some romancy stud with those tantalizing lips of hers caused my jaw to clench. Man, I needed to get a grip.

Red didn't give off the vibe of someone in the industry. Maybe she was just a fan here to enjoy the Comic-Con, but she had a nervous energy about her that screamed movie star.

I arrived at my booth. Zad was bagging up an action figure for a customer and Dad gave me a questionable scowl at my tardiness over the tub of pens he refilled on the promo table.

"Sorry, I...got a little caught up," I said.

"You're late. We're going to be at the back of the Wonder Woman line," Dad said.

"Don't worry, Steve. I'll make sure we get those autographs." Zad looked at me with a knowing smile, the kind he used to give me in middle school after a party that included spin the bottle. "By that dopey expression on Luke's face, I'd say our boy has met a girl."

Dad stopped straightening the pens and stared at me. "Really?"

I rolled my eyes at the thought my dads might ditch Wonder Woman to be involved in a matchmaking scheme. "Don't get all riled up. I just met a woman at the panel, and I'm taking her out to lunch."

"Did you hear that, Paul? He's doing lunch. There's hope for him, yet." Steve placed his hand over his heart.

Oh brother.

"You guys go bother Wonder Woman. Thanks for watching the booth." I shooed them away.

"No problem." Zad picked up Dad's Darth Vader helmet and handed it to him. "Do you need us here during lunch?"

"Nah, Marty, the college kid I just hired is coming after his classes."

Dad tugged the helmet on. "Are you taking her to the Mexican restaurant?" A Vader voice synthesizer amplified his voice.

"Yeah, it's the most convenient, and if she orders the top-shelf margaritas, it won't break the bank."

"That's my boy." Dad breathed the words through his iron lung mouthpiece using his deep Darth Vader voice. He tugged Zad's shirt sleeve. They headed in the direction of the north tower.

I called after them. "Don't let Wonder Woman get your secrets with her magic lasso."

"No way." Zad gave me a thumbs-up.

"You have secrets?" I heard Dad say before they rounded the corner.

Was I ready for a relationship like that? After I caught my last girlfriend naked on my pool table stroking the balls of my cable guy, I swore off women. She blamed me, stating I wasn't relationship material. I worked too many hours. I didn't like loud dance clubs or dancing. Her idea of dancing was more like public gyrating that embarrassed the hell out of me.

I preferred a local sports bar with decent food. A game on the television. Or, gaming into the early morning hours. All things she hated. Maybe I should cancel my date with Red.

Screw it. It was just lunch. Not a date. I'd have a good meal with a pretty girl, hopefully good conversation, and return to my rented apartment alone to write a good review for Jean-Claude. He wanted it in his inbox by ten p.m. And I could make that happen.

But the thought of Red, naked on my bed, flashed in my mind. The latest selection of comic books spread out under her, because that's what is covering my bed at the moment and, of course, we wouldn't have time to move them. I felt myself stir south of the border like some pubescent sixth grader scrolling through his first *Playboy*. That's what I get for focusing on work and putting my sex life in dry dock. *Jesus*.

I arrived at the restaurant before her. At least I hoped I had, and she wasn't ghosting me. The Mexican bistro was busier than usual. A few patrons, dressed as their favorite characters, sat at tables and booths. It felt like the Multiverse crashed into Mario World.

I waited in line for the hostess, and the smell of fajitas caused a loud gurgle from my stomach. The protein smoothie I'd had for breakfast was long gone.

"Two," I told the hostess, and she led me to a corner booth near a window with a good view of the door. I slid onto the seat, and she handed me a menu, then placed the other on the table. I'd eaten here many times before, but I held the menu in front of me and kept an eye on the door.

A bombshell walked in dressed as Harley Quinn from *Suicide Squad*. She headed toward my table. I leaned to my left, glancing behind her, hoping Iron Man wouldn't stand me up. The woman stopped next to me and poked me in the shoulder with her bat. "You here all alone?"

"I'm waiting on someone." I kept my eyes on the door. I didn't want Red to see me talking with this woman and ditch.

She smacked the barrel of her bat against the palm of her hand. "Maybe you're waiting on me."

This girl had the Harley Quinn voice down. I blinked up at her.

Bright green eyes sparkled down at me. Her full lips pulled into a slow sexy smile.

"Red?"

"Yeah," she blew a giant pink bubble and slid into the booth. Her bat hit the table leg, and she banged her hip against the table edge. "Yeow."

"Sorry, would a table be better?"

"Nope. I'm in, and I'm starving."

"Wow, your costume is...well...wow." I sounded like a lusty loser.

"Thanks. Iron Man was making me sweat." She laid her bat on the booth next to her.

"I knew you had a boyfriend. I'm no match for the Joker."

"That old clown? I left him in the dust last movie." She spit her gum into a cocktail napkin and grinned at me.

The server brought two glasses of water and a basket of chips and salsa. She downed half her glass.

"Thirsty?" I didn't hide my smile. My play on the word was unintentional, OK, maybe a little intentional. Making this girl banter with me was fun.

"Yes, but not in the way you're meaning, naughty boy. The Iron Man costume was friggin' hot, and I didn't have time to hydrate between sessions."

I sent her an innocent look. She ignored it and studied the menu. We reached for the chips at the same time.

I dunked mine in the salsa and ate it in one bite. "What if I guess your name?"

She stopped a salsa-loaded chip halfway to her mouth. "You've already broken your promise." She ate the chip, swiped her hands together, brushing off the crumbs, and by the look on her face, me as well, then picked up her bat. "I'm leaving."

"No, stay." I cuffed her forearm with my hand as she tried to slide out of the booth.

"You never told me your name, either," she shot back.

"I did."

"You're lying, Luke Skywalker."

"No, I told you. Luke Walker. That's my name."

"Seriously?" She raised a cynical brow but stayed in the booth.

"Seriously. My dad is a huge *Star Wars* fan. He named me Luke Sky Walker."

"My condolences." She grinned that slow, luscious red lipstick smile and scooted her sweet ass back across from me.

A server carrying a sizzling skillet of fajitas passed by the table and Red looked them over like she was checking out a hot guy.

Our server returned, and Red ordered a house margarita on the rocks.

"Good choice."

"It's never too early for a cold 'rita, right?" She batted thick lashes over those sultry green eyes.

"Right. I'll have the same," I told the server, then looked over at Red. "I recommend the enchiladas. They're muy bueno."

"Sounds delicious. I'll have the same."

The server gave me an incredulous glance and left.

"Moooey Bwano." Red chuckled out the words. "That had to be the worst Mexican accent I've ever heard."

"I admit I'm a California boy, born and raised." I scooped up another chip. "What if I ask where you're from. Is that allowed?"

"Do you usually start a sentence with what if?"

"Only when I'm trying to get to know a beautiful woman who wants to run from me like I'm a zombie in the *Walking Dead*."

"Originally, I'm from Texas, just outside of Dallas, but I live in Sacramento now."

The server returned with our drinks, and Red lifted her glass. "To what ifs."

I clinked mine to hers. "What ifs."

"Since you won't reveal your name, my guess is you're a princess who's run away from her bodyguard to attend her first Comic-Con."

"Nope. Guess again."

"You're an actor trying to keep a low profile?"

"You'd be wrong." She sipped her drink and studied me with those erotic eyes.

Damn those eyes. If I could wake up to them just one morning, I think my life would be fulfilled. But the color had changed. I was sure of it.

"I could have sworn your eyes were brown."

"Contacts. The brown went better with my Iron Man costume."

"Is this mesmerizing shade of green contacts too?"

"What if my eyes are purple?" She made a hammock with her fingers and set her chin on top, leaning toward me with earnest eyes. "Would you still want to have lunch with me?"

"Now who's starting with what if?" I sent her a disapproving faux scowl then answered her question. "Only if you landed here from another planet to make me your sex slave."

She threw her head back, and a deep, seductive laugh erupted. Man, she was sexy.

"These eyes are all mine. The brown contacts were itchy. I didn't want to walk around the Con with a vat of eyedrops. For all you know, I could be a host for an alien lifeform."

My hand covered my heart. "My dream girl."

She gifted me with another laugh that made things stir below the belt again.

Thankfully, the server returned with our meal.

"Holy Mango Margaritas! That looks good." Her eyes went from her plate of food to my stunned expression. "It's a thing. I tend to use alcohol related expressions."

I watched her devour a plate of enchiladas like a starving truck driver at an all-you-can-eat diner. No girly bites or pushing the entrée around on her plate like so many dates I had in the past.

"What?" She waved a fork at me.

I couldn't stop the film playing in my head. Me and Red drinking cold 'ritas on a beach in Mexico.

"You're staring at me." She took another forkful. "My alien hasn't eaten all day. She's famished."

This got a laugh out of me, and I joined her in devouring the enchiladas.

Chapter Ten

Jade

Luke watched me with that intent gaze like he could see my deepest, most intimate thoughts. I hoped he couldn't because I'd just imagined us rolling around on this table. Naked. Calm down, Jade. Not gonna happen. Finish the meal and call it a day. Nice to meet you, Mr. Walker, but gotta run. The gamers are calling me home.

"OK, Luke Walker. What do you do with your life?"

He waited while the waitress refilled our water glasses. "Currently, I run a bookstore. It's mostly comics."

"Like Stuart in *The Big Bang Theory*? But you don't look nerdy at all."

He chuckled, a husky rumble. "What a relief to know my five a.m. workouts are paying off."

"Five a.m.?" I mimed stabbing my eye with my fork. "I don't roll out of bed until noon."

"If you're not an actor, what do you do?" he asked.

I chewed my lip a minute and decided the truth wouldn't hurt with this guy. I mean, what is he to Raylynn? "I run a bar."

"A bar?" His eyebrows shot up like so many of my first dates. A woman managing a bar didn't match most men's image of the future mother of his children.

"It's a vintage arcade bar with video games from the eighties and some unique pinball machines."

"Like Pac-Man and Space Invaders?" His face softened, and he sounded genuinely enthusiastic.

"Yes, we have those. Most of the time, when I tell a date what I do, they frown at the idea of their girlfriend working in a bar and sour at the relics, preferring online gaming like Minecraft, Fortnight, or Grand Theft Auto."

"Your bar sounds cool. I love the online stuff, but I also love those old games. Like, I kick some serious ass at Galaga."

"Yeah? It's one of my favs too." Our eyes met and held for a moment. A moment that sent my heart ping-ponging like the steel ball in my favorite pinball machine.

I broke contact, continuing my unintentional spill about my bar. "I host pinball tournaments. It pays the bills, but I'd like to add some things to draw the younger crowd."

"Do you have a gaming room?" I could tell by his expression he was interested in my bar.

"I'd like to start a gaming room and hold small competitions, but Theo, the owner, is die-hard old school. I'm hoping to bring home a few ideas from the Con."

"I'd like to check it out sometime. I have a gaming room at the store. Maybe I could come and offer a few suggestions, and while I'm there, kick your ass at Galaga."

"Doubtful." Way to go, Jade. Too much info. Time to go.

"Never doubt my mad skills." He confidently crunched another salsa-loaded chip.

"This meal has been lovely, but I don't want to miss the Comic-Con." I wiped my mouth with the napkin.

He stared at my mouth, and I knew I'd missed a spot. I brushed the napkin over my lips again. My insides turned warm and doughy, but my alerts were dinging at me to run. I liked him. I couldn't continue sitting here with him, or I'd be toast. I needed to make a fast getaway. Where was that Suicide Squad when a girl needed them?

He sent me a sly smile. A smile slow, sensual, and oh so eager.

My chest constricted like I needed a shot of albuterol to inhale. He's about to ask me to dinner. I've played this game before. Dinner tonight, and with the electricity sparking between us, afterward, there would be sweaty sex and possible cuddling. Oh, yeah, he looked like a cuddler. I imagined lying tucked in next to Luke, wrapped in those arms. My girlie parts tingled. Don't go there. No kissing. No cuddling. No hooking up. No way.

Luke

S he wiped that full mouth with her napkin, and I felt my manhood harden. Again. Before I could stop myself, I was inviting her to dinner. "What if you join me for dinner later?"

"I...umm..." She ran the corner of her full lip between her teeth. Damn, she was so cute when she felt uneasy. Like she struggled between doing what she wanted and something else. And what was I doing? I was stuck writing Jean-Claude's damn review that would take me most of the evening, but I couldn't stop wanting to spend more time with her. "You have to eat, right?"

She placed her napkin on the table and leaned back against the soft vinyl booth. Her curious stare made me smile.

"You're not bad looking. Why don't you have a girlfriend?"

"Gee, thanks. I had one. We broke up last year. Just not a good fit."

"What was wrong with her?"

"Nothing." *She fucking lied and diddled the cable guy.* "She's in publishing, works for one of the biggies. Her job brought her to the West Coast for a short time, but she always planned to go back. Her family is on the East Coast. She wanted to live there. I didn't. My family and store are here, and I wasn't willing to leave." I was uncomfortable talking about the details of my relationship with my ex. We didn't leave on good terms, and she was Jean-Claude's editor.

"Guess she wasn't your perfect avatar?"

"Long-distance relationships never work." I grumbled the words and changed the subject. "How about another drink?"

"No thanks. One at lunch lets me have more at dinner." She fidgeted in her seat. "As for dinner, I'm previously engaged, but thanks for the invitation, and thanks for lunch."

I held up my hands. "I surrender. I'll quit with the annoying invitations, for now." I signaled the server for our bill. I wasn't mistaken. There was a connection here. I'd make a point to find her at the Con and talk her into another date. I might not be able to win her over, but like the great master Yoda would say, "Do or do not, there is no try."

Chapter Eleven

Jade

Luke held the door open for me to enter the hotel's conference center. The guy got bonus points for manners. I tucked my bat into my belt and walked past him.

"I'm heading for the exhibition hall," I said over my shoulder, taking one last, long look at the gorgeous Jedi. Too bad I was currently off men. With my bar in danger of closing and the whole sister-swap thing, I couldn't waste my time on a fling. I might have liked a few days and possibly nights with him.

"Me too." His words jolted me from my wistful pining.

"What?" Was this man a mind reader?

His mouth pulled into that crooked little smile that held a bit of badness. "I'm heading to the exhibition hall, also."

"Oh, right." I turned my back on him. Jade, you idiot.

We entered the exhibition hall, passing booths filled with collector's items, memorabilia, and games for every device in existence. I took a right, and he kept my pace. I was about to end his stalking with another *thanks again for lunch* and go away before your Force breaks down my shields when a large trailer wrapped with a colorful banner caught my attention. Escape, the banner read.

A couple exited the trailer via a ramp at one end. "That was super cool," the woman said through snorted laughter.

"Yeah, I thought we were going to land that sucker and then," the guy made a nosedive with his hands, followed by crashing noises.

A rather stout Wonder Woman stood at the entrance to the trailer. She whipped a rope in the air, cowboy style, and tangled Luke and me in her lasso of truth.

"Next in line," she said in a deep voice that explained her midday five-o'clock shadow. She gathered the slack out of the rope until she stood in front of us. "I've got two players for ya, Davey."

A man wearing a Starfleet uniform peeked out from behind a curtained doorway. "Fabulous."

I looked over at Luke. He shrugged. No help there. And the boyish grin on his face told me he might enjoy being tied up.

"What is this?" I asked.

"It's an escape room," Davey announced, using Vanna White arms to acknowledge the word stretched across the side of the trailer.

"Ever done one?" Luke asked me.

"No."

"I did, back in college. It was fun." Luke glanced at his watch. "Want to give it a go?"

"No, I don't think so. I need to get back." I tried to lift the gold plastic rope over my head, but Wonder Woman gave it a hard tug, cinching me in tight next to Luke. My hands pressed against his chest. He smelled so good. Too good. Like Raylynn's descriptions of the heroes in her romance novels, Luke actually did smell like a spring rain or a dewy Sunday morning. I probably smelled like tequila, tortilla chips, and pico de gallo.

"You're not telling the truth," Wonder Woman crowed. "My lasso says you want to go inside with the strapping young man."

"You're wrong," I said. But she was right.

"Afraid you're not smart enough to escape?" Luke's raised eyebrow gave me just the taunting I needed to accept the challenge.

"I'm not afraid." I wiggled out of the lasso and strutted up the gangplank toward the man. He collected ten dollars that Luke insisted on paying, more good manners, then stepped aside and pulled back the curtain. We entered a small foyer with a flat-screen mounted on a wall painted like the interior of a spaceship.

Davey held out vests and headsets, indicating I exchange them for my bat and crossbody.

"Put on your space gear." He motioned toward the flat-screen. "Your instructions will come on the monitor, then the door will open, and you proceed inside."

We did as we were told. Davey exited, likely to round up more unsuspecting Con attendees.

"Testing one, two," Luke's voice came over the headset.

"Copy that." I grinned at him. OK, this could be fun.

He grinned back before looking down at his vest. It had a badge of four stars embroidered on it.

"I'm the captain." He tapped my badge. "That makes me in charge, Lt. Commander."

I looked down at mine. Three stars. "Hey, I want to be the captain."

"You can't be the captain."

"Why not?"

"Because your badge only has three stars." He held three fingers in front of my face and chuckled at the obvious. "And you should address me as 'sir.'"

I rolled my eyes as an intergalactic message scrolled across the monitor, interrupting my demand to be captain. Attention crew.

A polished, gray-haired man in uniform appeared on the screen.

"Hello, space fleet." His stern voice broadcast into my ear. "I'm your commander for this mission. The starship *Interferon* is hauling medicine for humans to earth, but it has been taken over by aliens. You are locked outside of the main deck. It's up to you to break onto the bridge, open the control panel, and land the ship. When the entrance to Deck 1 opens, you must choose different paths to arrive at the bridge. Captain, you are top of your class."

Luke smirked at me.

The commander pointed at Luke as if he knew where he stood. "You must lead wisely." He turned his attention toward me. "Lt. Commander, your gift with weaponry is second to none in the galaxy. You're an asset to the team. Only by working together will you land the ship safely. You have twenty minutes until the aliens take over the bridge. Good luck, crew."

"Did you hear that? I'm good with weapons." I returned his smirk and added a confident chin lift.

"I heard. Lucky me."

The commander signed off, and a door on our right slid open. We walked inside. The door shut behind us. No handle, no knob, no way out. I sucked in some air, but Luke's scent suffocated like an ether-soaked rag. Being this close to him, I was doomed.

He scowled at the three hallways forked out in front of us.

"I'll go right," I said.

"OK, I'm up the middle," he said.

"Why not left?" I asked.

"Left is for sissies."

"Alrighty then." I followed my hall to the end and found a locked door. Five buttons flashed colored lights from a panel attached to it.

"Lt. Commander, this is your captain, copy?" Luke's voice came over my headset, startling me.

"Ten-four, Captain Jackass." I almost had an orgasm at the deep, sexy chuckle that followed. Jeez. How long had it been since I'd done the deed? I mentally counted backward, almost a month before Girlie Cocktail took his leave. And he left six months ago. No wonder my hormones were dog-hungry.

"Tell me what you see." His voice took on the steely tone of a man in charge.

"I have five flashing lights. You? Bossy boss."

He paused, and I swear I heard him wrinkle his nose. "I have instructions to play Simon Says."

I quirked my lips. "What's the first one?"

"Simon says, look up."

"What's up?" I asked, glancing up at my white ceiling.

"Nothing but a blue ceiling."

"Mine is white. I'll press the blue button. What's next?"

"Simon says, bend over. The floor is red." His words lifted with a burst of enthusiasm. I pushed red.

"The next line says look right. The right wall is yellow.

"I'm not pushing yellow," I said, determined.

"Why not?"

"Simon didn't say."

"Oh, right, got it." A smooth-as-silk *hmmm* flowed through my headset.

"What's next?" I asked.

"Simon says you should go to dinner with Luke."

I huff-snorted. "Sorry, previously engaged, remember?"

This time, a long pause preceded his response. "Do you have a date?"

"If I did, it wouldn't be any of your business. The clock's ticking, Captain." My tone was more huff than I intended, but I had to end this for Raylynn's sake. If Luke found out I was a fraud, he'd ditch me in a heartbeat. I had no intention of telling him my name and I didn't think he was the kind of guy who would have sex with me without knowing my name. At least I hoped he was that kind of guy.

"Got it," he said, not sounding the least bit discouraged.

"What does Simon say now?" My passion for winning urged me forward.

"Simon says do a disco dance like John Travolta in Saturday Night Fever. What the F...?"

"Simon says." I giggled. Shuffling sounds vibrated in my headset, and I would have given anything to see what Luke was doing on the other side of the wall.

"Hey, purple confetti just rained down on my head."

"Must have been some dance to get the confetti."

"Push the button, Red." Bossy Captain Luke barked in my ear.

After I pushed the purple button, my door opened. "Doors open."

"Mine too," he said. "Good work, Red."

"You too, Captain."

We met at a door centered in a hallway. Little bits of purple paper peppered his hair.

"That's a good look for you." I stopped my hand before it could reach up and brush away the loose confetti.

He caught my indecision, then smiled and ran a hand through his hair.

I stood on tiptoe and peeked through the barred window in the door. Inside, the room simulated the bridge of the Star Trek *Enterprise*. A wall-to-wall screen mimicked the window to outer space. It showed a dark sky filled with stars, spinning chunky asteroids, and distant planets. A control panel blinked at us from a commander's island in front of the faux window.

Luke tried the door. Locked. "We need a key." He pointed to an old-fashioned keyhole.

"'ello? Is anyone oot there?" A voice laced with a thick Scottish accent came over the headset.

"This is Captain Luke Walker." Luke spoke into his headset and sent me a cocky smirk.

I rolled my eyes and listened to the voice in my ear.

"This is Lt. Commander Hamish Scott, the engineer. The alien bastards have taken over the engine room on C-Deck. Locate the—" His words cut out in static. "Find the—" More static. "Unlock the tools, then look north to locate the key." My headset went dead.

"Did you get any of that?" Luke asked.

"Something about looking north, I think." A metal box with a combination lock hung on the wall to my right. A digital clock above it counted down the minutes. We had fifteen left. "Maybe the key is here, but we need a combination." I ran my hand around the box, searching for a clue.

When I came up empty, I noticed Luke studying the bridge. "Look at the control panel. Those lights are flashing in a pattern."

I counted three, then five, and seven.

The flashing stopped and restarted. We counted together. "Three. Five. Seven." I twisted the dials on the lock until the numbers matched the flashing lights, and the lock clicked open.

"You might be a genius." I removed a bag from the box.

"Careful, you just gave me a compliment. Next, you'll want to have your way with me on the bridge."

"The only thing I want is to win this game." I dumped a compass, a tape measure, and a pen into Luke's open palms. No key. A cuss word escaped from my lips.

Luke handed me the compass and the tape measure. "Someone has a competitive streak." He looked down at the pen and clicked it a few times.

"If you're not first, you're last," I said, reciting my favorite movie tagline.

Luke's head snapped up. "Did you just quote *Talladega Nights*?"

"Maybe." More bonus points for recognizing a quote from one of my favorite movies.

"It's one of my favorite movies," he said.

And with that, he achieved the grand slam of bonus points. Damn. What were the odds I'd find the perfect man at the worst possible time?

He tried to jimmy the door with the pen.

"Stop. You'll break——"

The pen shattered in his hands.

"You broke it." I stomped my foot.

"I didn't break it. The door broke it." He sent me a frustrated frown.

We were both frustrated. The time ticked away like a bomb in the room, promising impending failure. We stared into the bridge. There had to be a reason to have a compass and a tape measure.

"The Scot said to look north." I handed him the tape measure and pointed the compass north. We watched the dial stop a little past northeast. I looked through the bars in the direction the compass pointed.

He leaned in and looked over my shoulder. His body immensely close to mine. His neck within kissing distance.

My lips puckered, heading for the soft tanned skin behind his ear, when a shiny object caught my attention and distracted me from committing a mortal sin.

"There it is." I pointed to a shiny brass key hanging on the far wall.

"You're right."

"How are we going to get it?" I asked. "It's across the room, and we can't get in there."

"There has to be a way." Luke looked all optimistic.

Irritation with myself for almost making an inappropriate move on him and with him for being so, so sexy snowballed. I lashed out at his ray of sunshine attitude as the clock knocked off another minute.

"All we have is this stupid tape measure and a pen. Or had a pen, which you broke opening the door."

"Hey, I was doing my best."

"You ruined our chance to win."

He got in my face, breathing heavily. "You need to calm down and think."

"Me? Calm down?" Maybe I was a little overzealous about our quest. The thought of those minutes ticking by crawled under my skin. I knew I was overreacting, but I couldn't control myself. My competitive nature was getting the best of me. I wanted to land the ship. I wanted to win. And I wanted to keep him at a distance.

"Why are you such a...a...dick?"

"A dick?" He looked surprised.

"Yeah. You didn't think to ask me before you used the pen, the same way you didn't think before you asked me out in front of an entire audience." I stabbed my finger into his chest. "So don't tell me to calm down!"

"Jeez, Red. You have a temper."

Before I could respond, his face split into a grin. "That's it."

"Wait. What?"

"The measuring tape. If we extend it across the room, we can grab the key."

He pulled out the tape measure and touched the end to the bars in the window. It stuck. "It's a magnet."

"And you figured this out because I called you a dick?" Now my face split into a huge smile. Men. Geesh.

He stuck the tape between the bars and extended it toward the key. About halfway across the room, a loud snap made me jump. The tape measure bent and clanged to the floor.

"Damn." Luke dropped his head to his forearm.

"Don't worry. It happens to a lot of men." I gave him a reassuring pat on the back.

"You're funny." He retracted the tape measure and tried again. This time, holding it up slightly and extending it slowly.

"Steady, steady," I coaxed using my seductive tone.

He cut his eyes at me, then focused, extended the tape slowly, patiently. Somehow this made me excited. The damn tape measure was turning me on.

The tip of the tape measure tapped the key, and it stuck to the magnet. "Bingo!" He gave me a sideways glance. "Just needed to slow down a little."

"Reel it in. Slow. Steady." My wispy words released with a held breath.

"Careful, you're turning me on."

"I'll try to control my sex kitten." I rolled my eyes at him, but the reality was, he turned me on too. No matter how much I wished he didn't have that effect.

I plucked the key off the end of the tape measure and shoved it in the keyhole. The lock tumbled open.

"We did it!" I did my favorite Fortnight dance move, the floss. "Oh yeah, oh yeah. He's got the touch."

Chapter Twelve

Luke

R ed was doing some sort of wacky dance I'd seen playing Fortnight. Damn, she was cute. I couldn't help the wide lopsided grin that covered my face. I wanted to kiss her but instead, I held up my fist, and she gave me a knuckle bump.

A voice came on the headset. "Aye, ye did a fine job, but the aliens are coming for ye. Land the starship and arm yerselves for battle."

We'd wasted so much time. Only a few minutes left before we crashed.

We raced onto the bridge. Red searched the command center and I took the blinking panels that lined the far wall.

A door to my right opened a crack, and a one-eyed monster peeked in at us. "I'm going to eat your brains."

"Great. Now my brains are dessert." Each minute that ticked by, the door opened another inch.

"I don't see any clues. This isn't working." Red slumped down into the captain's chair.

"Keep looking." I moved to the next panel, pushing buttons and knocking on wall panels. I pushed up the sleeves of my costume, revealing my tanned, muscular arms and heard her exhale a sexy groan. I smiled to myself.

"Luke *Skywalker*, what would Captain Han Solo do to save the *Millennium Falcon*?" She asked.

"He'd land the ship somewhere safe," I said.

She pushed a button labeled intercom. "Land the ship on that green planet."

"Command doesn't compute." A robotic voice echoed into my headset.

"Why the hell not?" she yelled into the speaker. The entire room shifted, and I fell to my right.

"There must be hydraulics under the trailer." I steadied myself on the navigator's desk attached to the wall panel. The room jolted again, shaking us around like a carnival ride.

The alien's door opened a little wider. "Evacuate or be eaten."

"Mayday, Mayday. You're going to crash. Evacuate the ship!" the robotic voice announced.

"Dammit vodka martinis!" Red punched the arm of the captain's chair. "I'm sorry to say, you're going down with the ship. I mean, *you* are the captain."

I puffed out my chest. "A very gallant captain, but I'm not giving up."

"What should we do?" She sounded upset.

I wanted to wrap her in my arms, console her. Was I going crazy? This was only a game. My internal hero took over. It's now or never, Walker. It might be your only chance to taste those full lips.

In two stumbling strides, I reached her. I jerked her up from the captain's chair, pulled her toward me, and kissed her senseless.

God, she tasted so good. When I let go, she blinked away the dizziness. Steadying herself, she touched her lips. "Why did you kiss me?"

"It seemed appropriate." My mouth kicked up in a shy grin. I tried to read her. Did she like it? Was she mad?

"Uh...uhm, that was an amazing display, captain," the engineer's voice spilled from the headset. "But ye still need to land the ship or save yerselfs by escaping before the ship crashes."

I checked the clock. Two minutes left. We were going to lose.

My heart ticked-tocked, tick-tocked along with the rocking of the ship. The door slid open another inch. The alien monster had its tentacle inside the room, grabbing at the air.

"I'm not quitting!" She slammed her palm on the console. A secret panel opened. I reached inside, removed a laser gun, and eyed the monster.

"Why can't I land this ship?" Red fumbled with the controls again. The ship remained on its course of destruction.

"Are you willing to give me a chance?" I asked, the question bigger than landing a fake spaceship in an escape room.

"Maybe." Her eyes narrowed, curious.

In one swift move, I twirled her away from the captain's chair and shoved the laser gun at her. "You're the weapons expert. If he gets in, shoot him."

She grabbed the railing for support. The ship seemed to rock harder. I sat in the captain's chair, pushed the intercom button, and commanded the spaceship to land on the green planet.

"Command accepted. Destination planet green," the automated voice of the spaceship announced. The rocking and thrusting slowed to a smooth vibration.

Red held her arms up in a *what the hell?* gesture. "I did that! Why didn't it work for me?"

My face split into a full-on smile. "Like I told you before, you're not the captain."

"Eesh!" She huffed. I stifled the laughter that threatened to explode from me.

Red hated that I'd figured out how to land the spaceship and win the game. The room tilted and shook again. The monster burst into the room. Our mission wasn't over. My heart raced, stealing the blood from my brain.

I couldn't think. The fear of losing this game seemed real. Or was it the fear of losing the girl due to my screw up. Was I an anti-hero?

Red blasted him with the laser gun. *Pew, pew, pew.* The monster crumpled to the floor. She was a badass. The tilted room settled and our time was up. I wanted more time. More time to get to know this woman.

"Congratulations, space fleet. Your mission was successful," the robotic voice said.

I stood. Red leaped into my arms. I swung her off the floor—and spun us around.

"We did it!" The tiny heart tattoo under her eye tilted upward with the lift of her cheeks. "We saved Earth."

I hugged her tight and inhaled the scent of her. "Yep, we won." I put her down and kissed her again. A warm rush flushed my body as she moaned into the kiss.

As quickly as it began, she pushed away and held me at arm's length. "Sorry. I umm...got excited over our win."

I stepped back. "I did too." And I still wanted more.

Davey entered the room removing his headset. "Congrats! You're the only couple who made it all the way through." He looked despondent about our win. "And that was quite a peep show." He fanned himself.

Red blushed crimson. "I didn't know you were watching us."

"I'm the escape room host." Davey dug inside the pocket of his Starfleet uniform.

"And it was just a victory kiss." Red glanced at me like she was checking my reaction. It wasn't just a victory kiss.

"Anyone can tell you two are lovebirds," Davey said.

"Not us." Red tapped a hand on her chest and then motioned at me.

"We just met." It was more than a victory kiss. So much more.

"Here you are. Two complimentary tickets to tomorrow's Star Wars trivia at the tequila bar." Davey handed the tickets to me.

"Thanks." I looked down at them, then handed one to Red. We stood looking at each other, unsure of the next step. We moved toward the exit.

Red stopped and turned toward Davey. "What was the pen for?"

"Yes, weel." He scratched his chin speaking with the accent he used for the Scottish engineer. "It should have opened the secret panel to the laser gun, but you used your brute strength and managed to pop the lock. I'll need to fix that, I imagine."

We exited the escape room. "That was fun." Red pointed toward the hallway leading out of the exhibition hall. "My next session is thataway."

Was this the last I'd see of her? A sudden montage of our escape room played in my head with a cliffhanger voiceover from my comic writer subconscious. "Was this the last time the hero would see the stunning Red? Would he break free of his personal issues and ask her out again? Tune in tomorrow. Same time, same channel."

"Hello?" Red waved a hand in front of me. "There you are. Thought I'd lost you for a minute."

"I'm this way." I motioned toward the right, my brain firing thousands of neurons trying to come up with the words to convince her to see me again. When nothing manifested, I gave up. Coward. You really are an anti-hero, Walker. "Well, it was fun, Red."

"Yeah, it was." She smiled at me, and her eyes lingered on my mouth.

Never hurts to try. My anti-hero would give it one last shot.

"How about you meet me for lunch tomorrow at the trivia game bar?" I held up my ticket. "We already have tickets."

"Luke, I…"

"C'mon. It's only lunch. I'm not going to kidnap you and take you away in my spaceship. I just don't like eating alone." I sent her my best suck-up Star Wars hero face.

"OK." She twisted her lips, then gave a wry smile. "I'll let the fates decide. If you recognize me, I'll share my table with you."

"Sounds like a challenge." With that body, those lips, I'd recognize her anywhere.

"You'll have ten minutes to find me at the bar. Your time begins when you cross the threshold. If you don't recognize me, then you'll be eating solo, my friend. And you can't ask me out anymore." She said the last words with what sounded like trepidation.

"Challenge accepted." I held out my hand, but she ignored my handshake, giving me a half shrug instead followed by a sly, secretive grin.

"Tequila bar. High noon."

Chapter Thirteen

Jade

Daaaamn. This guy could kiss. I left Luke standing in the hallway next to a booth with paintings of quirky, Picasso-style caricatures. The faces in the paintings looked exactly how I felt—sad and twisted inside, but with a spark of something magical, something exciting. Dating Luke would be like opening Pandora's box and releasing a curse. A curse that would expose my lies and ruin my sister's credibility. And something I shouldn't pursue.

That kiss. My fingers went to my lips. I'd never been kissed with such power, but there was a seductive tenderness when his mouth took mine. He was like the Warner Brothers' Acme super magnet pulling my Iron Man toward him with a force I couldn't fight. Maybe he did have Jedi skills. Good thing I traded my Iron Man costume for Harley Quinn. She was more my style anyhow.

I took a left and stopped at the gaming booth I'd read about in the program. The company hosted gaming competitions, and I wanted information. I didn't want the bar to pay their outrageous fee to host, but I thought maybe I could get a few pointers to start events of my own.

"Hello, pretty lady." A guy who reminded me of Fez from *That '70s Show* waved me into his booth. "I am Rez."

What are the odds?

"Hi, I'd like some information about the gaming competitions." I moved inside and went wide-eyed at the equipment required.

After chatting with Rez and only hearing half of what he said because my thoughts strayed to Luke, I thanked him and moved on to a live gaming session. I'd play for a short time, then retire to my room. I could work on my notes from Rez, then start reading Raylynn's book. If I ordered room service, I nixed the chance of running into Luke again. Good. My focus was back on Shadycade. Exactly where it needed to be.

I spent way too much time playing the beta edition of Dragontoon only to have my high score squeezed out at the last minute by that damn game-hacker, username Python. The new graphics sucked me in, and when I came up for air, thoughts of Luke returned with a sledgehammer pounding away on my heart. I touched my lips, where his kiss still lingered. He was a great kisser, maybe even fantastic. Definitely the highest skill level I'd ever encountered.

"Where would this lead anyway?" He doesn't even know my real name.

"Pardon?" A short, balding man on my right asked. Startled by the strong, frustrated, East Coast accent, I realized I had voiced my question, and I had gotten on the elevator. Thinking about Luke was apparently like driving while intoxicated, not that I ever had, but I couldn't remember walking to the elevator.

"I'm sorry?" I replied to the man.

"What's ya floor?" The man's finger hovered in front of the massive rows of buttons, waiting on my answer.

"Twenty-two, thanks." I reminded myself to be present. Focus on the mission. Pretend to be R.D. Sayer.

I let myself into my room, dropped my crossbody bag and my bat in the chair, and flopped down on my bed. How did I get myself into this mess? Oh yeah, Raylynn. I pulled out my phone and stared at it. Only one message. From Jerry.

Read the book.

"I know you're ignoring me, Ray." I thumbed to her number and texted her again.

Where are you? Did you die? If you're not dead, I'm going to kill you. You have a signing and appearance at the end of this thing, and if you're not here, yours truly will have to stand up there and take it on the chin. You don't want me screwing up your personal appearance, do you?

No little bubbles of response. Nothing. I tossed my phone aside. Raylynn's latest book called to me from the nightstand. A sticky note reading "ASAP!" sat on the cover of a man and woman, lips locked and half dressed in what I'd call spacesuits. I'd read the book, but first, I needed a shower.

I ordered a club sandwich from room service and took a long, hot shower washing off the Harley Quinn makeup. The shower, another perk. My shower at home lost hot water when the neighbor above me flushed his toilet or ran the dishwasher.

After towel drying my hair, I wrapped myself in the complimentary hotel robe. It was soft and fluffy and decreased my anxiety over the Luke thing with the faint scent of lavender fabric softener. I added Pond's moisturizer to my face and neck. My mom always did that. She applied a thick layer and let it soak in.

Mom. Raylynn took care of her. She was diagnosed with multiple sclerosis four years ago. If it wasn't for Raylynn paying for her top-notch care, mom would be in a nursing home.

I secured my damp hair in a bun on top of my head, pulled on yoga pants, and shrugged into a T-shirt. A knock sounded on the door. For a second, I worried Luke had found me. Was I ready for whatever followed that kiss?

"Room service," the voice on the other side of the door announced.

Releasing a disappointed sigh, I wrenched open the door to a rosy-cheeked woman in a hotel uniform. "Hi." I stepped aside allowing her to enter. She took a few steps and stopped, waiting for further instructions.

"Place it there." I pointed to the credenza.

"Sure thing, Miss Sayer." She sat the tray down.

I handed her a five, hoping it was the current rate for tipping room service. It didn't matter. It was all the cash I had. I thanked her and shut the door behind her.

I removed the plate cover and sighed again at the sight of the thick, perfectly made club sandwich, fresh fruit, and dill pickle slice. Also on the tray were two chocolate chip cookies and the only thing I loved from Texas, an ice-cold Dr Pepper.

I moved the plate of food to the bed, picked up the DP, and sat criss-cross applesauce. I took a sip of the soda, flipped open the book, and spit the soda in a spray across the dedication page.

For my sister, Jade, my twin, my first best friend, and my inspiration.

Jeez. Now I really couldn't tell Luke my name. It was right there in black and white. If Luke saw this book, he'd know what a big liar I am. But what were the odds? A comic book guy reading a romance book. Never going to happen. He wasn't exactly a man of mystery. He'd practically told me his life story on our first lunch date. And wiggled out part of mine. But the books would be passed out at the panel, and if he happened to get his hands on one...

I put a finger to my lips and remembered how his kiss weakened my knees. I laughed out loud. Raylynn would love my romancy thoughts. Weak knees. Ha! But it was true. If he kissed me like that again, my knees would melt like gum on a hot summer sidewalk.

I blew a long, wistful breath and moved on to chapter one. Raylynn introduced the heroine, a sassy redhead with no family and a string of bad relationships, a woman stuck in a rut. I took a bite of the sandwich and chewed as the image became crystallized in my head. This heroine sounded familiar. In fact, she sounded a lot like me.

Dammit, Raylynn, anyone who knows us could recognize me. Maybe I wasn't so unhappy it got kicked off the bestseller list.

The heroine worked in a coffee shop. She loved the job, but a corporate broker was buying out the shop, and her job was on the line. She had a rough life. Always the one cleaning up the messes. Did Raylynn mean coffee spills or the character's messy life? Or did she mean my messy life?

An image surfaced: me with a dishcloth wiping down the bar after closing. Me, scrubbing off the sticky residue left over by spilled drinks and heavy-handed pours. Me, constantly cleaning up for Raylynn when she committed and then no-showed.

I finished my sandwich and took a long drink of soda. Kept reading. She desired wealth. She desired adventure.

"Oh, brother." I flipped the page. She desired love.

"Wrong. I'm not looking for love, Ray. I want the bar. That's my true love."

I ate the fruit and finished the chapter. "OK, Raylynn, who rescues me from my boring life of despair?" I imagined the hunky guy on the cover, and then the hero suddenly had Luke's sparkling blue eyes with that hint of playfulness. I hurriedly turned the page.

Chapter two. In walks said hunky man that Raylynn describes surprisingly like Chris Pratt. My sister knows my secret crush. He smiles at the lonely, despairing barista. She looks hopeful and writes her number on the coffee cup.

I rolled my eyes. "Jeez. Raylynn. That's so cliché. I'd never do that."

I stretched out on my stomach, waiting for the hunky hero to ask the barista out. After several, and I mean several, pages of whining about her miserable life, he calls. They meet for coffee. He tells her he's not an average guy. Is she willing to accept the strange circumstances that surround his life? Is she willing to take a chance on love?

As I read hunky man's words, I saw Luke's face. I heard his voice say *Red, are you willing to give me a chance?*

Take a chance on love? Take a chance on Luke? I shut the book in frustration. This wasn't my life. My life wasn't dull. I loved working at the bar. I loved the Barflies. They were my family. And I wanted to keep the bar for them. For me.

Where would Marjorie and Stew go if they couldn't come to the Shadycade every night? Chili's? Applebee's? Or, for God's sake, a Red Lobster? Who would make their favorite cocktails and referee when they had Pac-Man throwdowns? Or give them Monopoly money to purchase little trinkets I had collected from bargain store bins when they got high score? Not happening at Red Lobster.

Raylynn had it all wrong. I loved my life.

With a growl, I opened again to chapter three and woke up with drool on the page. The last thing I remembered was the hunky hero whisking the barista away on his spaceship. Jeez, Raylynn. Where was the buildup? She ran off with the guy on an adventure, but she hardly knew him. How could she trust him not to sell her to the Dark Side? Was she so starved for affection that she hopped into the first spaceship that came along?

Then I remembered all my past boyfriends and how quickly I fell for them. Was Raylynn making me an example? I'd show her. I wasn't going to make that mistake again. Luke and his most awesome kisses be damned.

I pushed the book aside and glanced at the clock—11:30 p.m. I couldn't read anymore tonight. Tomorrow I'd find out how Raylynn redeemed my miserable, disparaging life.

Chapter Fourteen

Luke

When I arrived at the tequila bar, it was packed. Way to go, Walker. I'd purposely waited a few minutes past the time of our lunch date. They were the longest few minutes of my life. I wanted to meet her. Hear her smoky laugh at my ridiculous jokes. Ten minutes late might have been an oversight.

I adjusted the lightsaber tucked into my Jedi Knight utility belt and scanned the room. A woman in a Queen Amidala costume sat alone at a corner booth. I zeroed in on her. The costume broadened her shoulders. She looked up, caught me staring, and sent me a shy smile. Not my cosplay queen for sure.

Another woman in a Mario costume balanced on a stool at the bar. Legs crossed, she had her back to me, and I almost approached but was sidelined by another Nintendo character scooting next to her and kissing the mustache off her face.

This might be harder than I intended. I mean, how many women had a mouth like Red's? Full. Sensuous. And bonus level, she tasted like warm honey.

I licked my lips at the reminder of yesterday's kiss, slid onto a barstool, and scoped out the place.

"What can I get you?" a meaty bartender with a spider tattoo on his neck asked.

"Beer. Whatever you've got on draft."

While waiting for the beer, my watch ticked off the minutes I had left to ID my date. Maybe she was late too? No, she wouldn't cheat, and she wouldn't make it that easy. She was here. I could almost hear her laughing at my difficulty in identifying her.

I took my beer, paid my tab, and left the bartender a few bills. I walked outside, checking out the tiki hut tables surrounding a fire pit. Only a few held a single person. None seemed right.

I moved back inside and scanned the room for anyone looking smug. At the far end of the room, a table of three included a couple dressed as Captain Marvel and Deadpool. A horrible match, I thought, but by the way they cozied up to one another, they'd overcome their differences.

I glanced at my watch. Five minutes left.

The third person at the table held up a menu, engrossed in its contents. The recognizable buns of Princess Leia poked out from behind the menu. The galactic princess lowered it an inch, saw me checking her out, and jerked it back in front of her face.

Gotcha.

"Mind if I sit?" I asked the couple so absorbed in each other that they barely shook their heads.

I sat across the table from Princess Leia. The menu stayed vertical, shielding its reader.

"Princess," I said, tipping the menu down and exposing knitted brows and full, pouty lips. "You owe me lunch."

"Damn." She smacked the menu down on the table. "I didn't think you'd spot me that quickly."

I tapped my watch. "Six minutes and thirty-four seconds. And I bought a beer."

"You almost went for Queen Amidala." She huffed out a sigh. "When I walked in and saw her, I have to admit, I did a victory dance. We have the same build."

"Celebrating too early is a jinx and a surefire sign of imminent anni-hilation." I took a long, victorious drink of my beer and set the glass on the table.

"All right, you win. I'll buy you lunch." She tapped the menu. "I'm craving a thick, juicy burger."

"You're making things difficult," I said.

"Why is that? I'm fulfilling my end of the bet, buying lunch, and having a second date with you."

"Your costume. I can't be seen kissing my sister. It could cause an intergalactic battle." I leaned back and took in her Princess Leia costume.

"I see you've become a Jedi Knight. Congratulations."

"Is dressing as Skywalker's sister your way of keeping me at a distance?"

She leaned close to me. "Is it working?"

I inhaled her perfume. "No. Do you want me to keep my distance?"

"I might be into a little nepotism if the mood strikes me."

Before I could tug her into my lap and persuade her to make good on her words, her gaze shifted over my shoulder.

I glanced behind me at the couple sitting next to us. The woman went wide-eyed, staring at Red.

"I'm only kidding, we're not related." The prior sizzle in Red's tone was replaced by a nervous laugh.

"Aren't you the author of *Midnight in Space*?" the woman asked, her voice on the edge of exuberant.

Red's face looked shocked and then fell into a grimace. She shook her head. "Sorry. I'm Princess Leia Organa, leader of the rebel alliance with a soft spot for scoundrels." She sent me a self-righteous grin.

Captain Marvel laughed, gave her Deadpool companion a sideways glance, then shook her head at Red. "Sorry. I saw a picture of R.D. Sayer a long time ago in one of those trash talk blogs, and I thought you looked a little like her. I heard she was going to be here. I'm a huge fan. I love her books."

The guy with her shook his head, discarding his Deadpool mask on the table. "She's already asked at least half a dozen women if they're the famous author. She's obsessed." He hugged her into him.

The girl squirmed, then relaxed into his arms. "I want to meet her, is all. She's the best. And her new space romance is better than *Star Wars.*"

I grabbed my chest and sent her a horrified expression. "You must be mistaken. There's nothing better than having your father chop off your arm with a lightsaber, leading to his imminent demise."

The woman giggled at me. "Maybe not, but it's a good book no matter what that stupid critic Jean-Crap says."

I laughed into my beer. Nice to know my critiques earned Jean-Claude a new nickname.

An announcement for Star Wars trivia was made, and the couple moved on, leaving the table to us.

I hadn't seen a picture of R.D. Sayer. I rarely had time to look up all the authors Jean-Claude wanted to run into the ground, but it was good to know the super-secret author was a woman. If she looked as amazing as the woman sitting next to me, it might be tough to watch Jean-Claude twist my critiques and tear her work to pieces. I'd have to search Google for the old photo and see how much Red resembled the author. I took another drink of my beer and realized Red didn't have a drink.

"Ready to order?"

"Yes." She perused the menu again. "I'm starving. I'd love a cheese-burger and one of these." She tapped at a picture on the menu.

I motioned to a server and ordered Red a Tropical Thunder, her drink of choice, and two cheeseburgers.

"I got here early," she said. "I wanted to snag good seats for the trivia. I have a no blood, no foul attitude when it comes to compe-titions."

"Poor dumb bastards." I waved a hand at the crowd around us. "They don't know who they're playing against."

"We might have some competition." She pointed at someone behind me.

I turned to see a group of five dressed as the main cast of *Star Wars,* including a giant Chewbacca but minus Skywalker.

"They don't have Luke Sky Walker."

She laughed that deep sexy laugh, and it was all I could do to keep from cozying up next to her and pressing my lips to her delicious neck.

She caught my look and focused on the fruity drink the bartender placed in front of her.

"This looks delicious." She plucked the cherry off the top and popped it into her mouth. A few seconds later she presented me with the stem tied into a perfect knot.

I stared down at the stem in my hand, then up at her. My focus centered on her tongue. *Slow your roll, Walker. You don't want to embarrass yourself. I mean, you're basically wearing pajamas, and that's not going to hide the giant boner this girl causes if you continue to think dirty thoughts about taking her to bed.*

"What's on your mind?" she asked.

"Huh?" I shook the lusty cobwebs from my head.

"You were staring at me like I had chocolate at the corner of my mouth. Like you couldn't decide whether to lick it off or hand me a napkin."

"Umm." I took in the I've-got-your-number look on her face, and regrouped. "Just thinking about how you look more like Padmé than Leia. Not Queen Padmé, but the fresh-faced rebel in disguise."

"This is one of the costumes Jerry designed for—uhm—me." She tucked her bottom lip between her teeth like a child caught in a fib.

Who was Jerry? Finally, a glimpse into her secrets.

"Jerry?" I asked, trying not to sound too curious, or jealous.

Her face contorted like she didn't want to tell me.

"Jerry's the guy who gave me a ticket to the Con."

"Oh, right. Is he my competition for your affection?"

"Don't worry. We've been friends for years. We went steady, once, in fourth grade, then figured out I wasn't his type."

"His type?" I ran a finger down my beer glass. Was the guy a moron? "In fourth grade, he had a type?"

"Yeah, Jerry's gay. We've been besties ever since."

"What a relief. Now I only have to battle the other five thousand single men attending the Con."

She chuckled, glanced at the three people sitting at the bar, and let out a small sigh.

"Penny for your thoughts? OK, that was cliché, but you sighed like you wished you were somewhere else, and I tell you, my ego took a hit."

"I was thinking about my friends back home. I call them the Barflies. I miss them."

"Barflies?"

"Yeah, they hang out at the bar every night. There's Marjorie. She's a pistol and a real fighter. She had cancer last year, and I'm proud to say she's in full remission. I drove her to her chemo treatments. She never complained, and all the nurses loved her. She only wears animal print."

She raised her glass to her lips and sipped, making a yum sound that sent my insides bubbling up like the foam in my beer.

"Marjorie has one of those low, sexy voices like a movie star. You know?"

"Yes, I do." I did know because the woman across from me also had one of those voices.

"Stewart's an old hippie. He used to be an accountant before he retired. He loves the sixties. We have a jukebox, and I switched out the more modern records for artists from that decade. His wife died a few years ago, and he's alone." Her face drooped into a melancholy wistfulness but lifted as she sipped her drink and continued.

"Then there's Ed. He drives a school bus. Comes in after his drop-offs in the afternoon. He's trying to quit cussing because of the children, so I make him put a coin in an old moonshine jug I keep on the bar every time he slips up. It's about half full." She laughed, and I smiled at her love for her bizarre friends. "We're going to run off to Tahiti together when he fills it up."

"So, I do have competition." I grinned.

She waved me off. "Only if you consider a sixty-eight-year-old man a threat. I don't know what will happen to them if Theo sells the bar to a corporate chain. He wants to retire, so I can't blame him for selling it. I just wish I had the money to buy it."

"You could get a loan."

"There's that optimistic Skywalker again." She shook her head. "No down payment. I had a crappy boyfriend. He worked at the bar and convinced me to make some pretty expensive changes. I allowed them because I thought I was in love. Come to find out, I was in lust. He was an ex-con, stole my life's savings, and I learned my lesson."

"Whoa, that's a real bummer."

"Yeah, sorry, I didn't mean to tell you my sad little story."

"It's obvious. The guy was a dick," I said as my internal ass-kicking gauge flipped from a punch in the face to barely breathing. My loathing of the ex was interrupted by the server placing two juicy burgers in front of us.

"Yum," Red said, taking a big bite out of the stacked burger. She chewed and made sounds I'd prefer she saved for me, naked. "Just the fuel we need to take home the trivia prize."

She'd moved on from sharing her story so I did the same, but the hurt that lingered in her eyes when she mentioned her ex-boyfriend gnawed at my gut along with the greasy burger.

Chapter Fifteen

Jade

Damn. I didn't know when to shut my mouth with this guy. Now I'd told him about the Barflies, my ex-boyfriend, and my financial problems. Why didn't I just spill out all my secrets like the pitcher of beer the drunk guy at the next table spilled all over the floor?

"Dang, it's only noon. Some guys don't know when to quit." Luke hiked a thumb at the table behind us.

"Yeah, seems sort of early to be spilling things." I nodded, agreeing with my own words. I took another bite out of my delicious burger and plucked a fry from the basket we shared.

By the time we finished our burgers, the tequila bar had scaled down to the trivia junkies. A Con emcee stood at the front of the bar. He announced that trivia would begin in five minutes and gave instructions on how to log in on our phones. He would ask a question, and our team captain would type the answer in an online chat box.

Luke pulled out his phone and sent me a lopsided grin.

"Fine, you can be captain," I said, stealing another fry and soaking it in ketchup.

"I was pretty good at it in the escape room." He logged in to the trivia game site.

"Since it's Star Wars trivia, and you're Luke Sky Walker, we should win, right?"

"My dad is the huge fan. I've seen these things end in a brawl. Star Wars fans are like extreme skiers. They know the minute details."

"Do you game much?"

"Yeah, when the store is slow and I can't wrap my head around my writing."

"Your writing?" My *oh shit* moment caught and held with a fry stuck in my throat. I forced it down with a hard swallow of my drink.

"Yeah, I write comics. Do a little ghostwriting for an author." His face fell like it might be too much ghostwriting.

"Are you published?" I asked, my worrywort-o-meter increasing at the possibility that he might know my sister.

"My comic books are published. Ever heard of *Cronman*?"

"Oh my gosh!" I reacted without thinking and punched him playfully in the arm. "I love that one. The redhead is definitely the bad girl."

"Jeez, did I make it that obvious?" He rubbed his arm. "Red, you pack a solid punch."

"Sorry," I gave him a pitiful grin. "But the way she stands up for Cronman even though he's taken command of her spaceship makes me think she's got secrets, and she's attracted to him. It's what I would have done. That's why I picked her."

"Yeah, she's got secrets." Luke's insinuating gaze made me squirm. He looked down at his phone, then up at me with brows furrowed. "We need a team name?"

"How about team Cronman?" I suggested.

He smiled and typed it into his phone.

"Who do you ghostwrite for?" I asked.

"I can't tell you. I'm under contract, but I'm hoping to cut ties later this year." His eyes clouded and the lighthearted Luke I was growing fond of showed a glimpse of the dark side.

"Right." I nodded. Luke had secrets too.

His face brightened as the emcee came over the microphone and began the game.

"First question. Who killed the younglings in the Jedi temple?"

"That's easy," I said. "Darth Vader."

"Nope. He wasn't Darth yet." Luke typed in Anakin Skywalker.

"Oh yeah." I finished my Tropical Thunder and felt the rum relax the muscles in my neck. I contemplated another drink but needed to keep my wits so I motioned for the server to bring me a glass of water and Luke held up two fingers.

We answered more questions. The emcee announced the Cronmans and the Han Solos were tied for first place. I high-fived Luke and received a growl from the Chewbacca guy at the next table, the same one who spilled his beer earlier.

Chewie didn't take the news of his tied status well. He catcalled the server and heckled the emcee.

The emcee rolled his eyes at the guy and stated we'd take a short break.

"Whoa, Chewbacca needs to chill out," I said.

"Yeah, it's guys like that who give us cosplayers a bad name."

I laughed at his cheeky grin. "How long have you been ghost-writing?"

Before he could answer, a guy dressed as Darth Vader stopped at our table. "Luke, I am your father."

Luke shrank under the table. If a six-foot-two guy could do that.

"Hey, Dad." He motioned to me. "This is Red."

"Like Little Red Riding Hood?" Darth looked me over. "Your costume is all wrong."

A man in a cape came up behind Darth Vader. "Sorry, Luke, I told him not to come over. We were sitting outside at the patio tables and Steve spotted you."

Darth Vader removed his mask. "I'm Steve. Luke's dad." He held out a hand my direction.

"Nice to meet you." I grabbed his hand and shook it. They had the same eyes, except Steve had those adorable crinkles at the corners. And a contagious smile.

"Wait, he really is your dad?" I asked.

Luke waved a hand at the other man. "And this is my other dad, Paul."

I raised a questioning eyebrow.

"Yep, these are my dads. Steve and Paul."

I shook hands with the tall, handsome man that reminded me of Dr. McSteamy from *Grey's Anatomy*.

"Are you playing trivia?" I asked Steve. "Luke told me you were a huge Star Wars fan."

"No." Steve shook his head and frowned at Paul. "We were too late to enter."

Paul grinned sheepishly. "My massage at the hotel spa ran a bit late."

"Late?" Steve crossed his arms over his chest. "You added an extra thirty-minute seaweed body wrap. That's the last time I make a bet with a massage as the prize."

"We're tied for first place." I beamed up at them.

"Never doubted my boy. He's been brainwashed since birth." Steve smiled and his eyes crinkled again.

"I'll see you guys back at the booth?" Luke's voice held a gentle nudge.

"Right, nice to meet you, Red." Steve sent Luke a goofy grin.

Paul nodded at me. "A pleasure, please stop by the booth later." He gave Luke a squeeze on the shoulder I didn't miss and steered Steve, babbling good luck wishes, away from our table.

"Two dads, how cool is that?" My words poured out like melancholy wishes from my own life. "I would have loved to have one dad."

"What happened to your dad?" Luke's voice held a curious empathy.

"He died when I was two. Left my mom with twin girls and a mortgage." For the love of Pete, I'd just admitted I had a twin sister.

"You're a twin?" Luke stared in awe. "Now it's my turn to be amazed."

If he only knew the half of it, he wouldn't be so amazed. He'd probably think I was mental.

"Identical?"

"For the most part, but our eye color is different, so that makes us fraternal. My mom raised us, but I would have loved a fun dad like I assume you have."

"Yeah, they're great. I'm happy to share. They've always wanted a daughter."

"I can see the resemblance in Steve, so you're not adopted, right?"

"Wrong," Luke said, leaning to the side as the server refilled our water glasses. Luke picked up the last fry, scooped it in the ketchup, and popped it in his mouth. "There's a story there, but you'll have to commit to another lunch date to find out the ending."

I blew out a regretful sigh. The guy didn't give up. "I guess I'll leave it at a cliffhanger."

"Your loss. My life story is a fascinating tale. Better than the real Skywalkers."

Thankfully, the emcee returned, stalling Luke's shot at another lunch date, and bombarding us with a lightning round of questions. In the end, we were still tied with the Han Solos.

"The final question will be the tiebreaker between the final two teams. The first team who answers correctly wins the prize," the emcee said.

After a loud, throaty gurgle from the Wookiee that sounded like something between an elephant and my granny Sayer's snoring, and nothing like the real Chewbacca, the emcee called out the question.

"What is Jabba the Hutt's full name by those who respect him?"

Luke blinked at the screen. "I don't know this one."

"It's a trick question. I mean who respects the Hutt except for his slaves." I held out my hand for the phone. I typed in His Excellency Jabba Desilijic Tiure of Nal Hutta, Eminence of Tatooine, and handed the phone back to Luke.

Luke stared at the phone in disbelief. "How did you know that?"

"Uhm...was in a book I read." I recalled reading the reference to the famous Hutt in my sister's book last night.

"What book?"

I paused. He probably wouldn't even know my sister's book. The server removed our empty plates and I debated how to answer my slipup.

"I promise not to laugh if it's one of those alien erotica books." His lips curved playfully at the rim of his glass.

I took a long sip of my water, and mumbled, *"Midnight in Space."*

His eyebrows shot upward. "Are you an R.D. Sayer fan?"

I cringed. He knew the book. "I don't normally read romance, but I feel a strong pull toward her work." I skirted around the question.

"Her romances are good, but her sci-fi book missed the mark." He leaned back and gave me a long, contemplative stare.

This guy reads romance? Missed the mark? I didn't know which question to ask first, so I stammered out the first thing I could think of. "What do you mean?"

Before he could answer, the emcee held up a gold trophy with the words *May the Force Be with You* emblazoned on it. "The winner of Star Wars trivia is the Cronmans."

The crowd applauded as Luke stood and accepted the trophy.

Chewbacca booed us and made lewd gestures from his seat at the next table.

"We should go." Luke signaled the server for our check. "Sounds like Chewie has had too much to drink."

I agreed. I didn't want the big ape to make a scene.

The server brought the check over. Luke tried to grab it, but it was my debt to pay. I snatched up the slip and dug around in my purse for my credit card, then paused. I couldn't use the card Raylynn had given me to use when I impersonated her. It had R.D. Sayer on it. My own credit card had my name on it, and it was maxed out anyhow. I couldn't risk exposing my secrets. Luke would find out I was Raylynn or broke. I didn't know which was worse.

I opened my wallet and prayed I had enough cash to cover the bill. Luckily, I had emergency money tucked in a side pocket. Enough to cover the bill and tip.

After saying a mental thanks to my mom who taught me to stash money out of sight out of mind, I put the bills and the slip on the table.

We stood and turned to leave. I led the way and Luke carried the gold trophy proudly behind me. Extra-large Chewbacca jumped to his furry feet and blocked our exit. "That's our trophy. You cheated."

"We don't want any trouble," Luke said. "We're leaving."

"Cronman's a pussy," Chewbacca shouted, followed by his guttural groan.

"You're a pussy," I shouted at him. I couldn't help myself, the guy was a jerk.

"Just like Cronman. Can't control the redhead." Chewbacca stabbed his furry gloved index finger into my shoulder.

"Shut up man. It was only a game." Luke stepped in front of me, obstructing my view of the Neanderthal.

I leaned around Luke and looked up at the idiot. "Yeah, a game you lost, dickhead." The guy made my blood boil.

I didn't see the punch, but I heard the crack of Luke's jaw and watched him crash to the floor. The trophy tumbled loose from his hands. Out of the corner of my eye, I saw Chewbacca's friends escort him outside.

"I'm so sorry." I dropped down on one knee. My big mouth just got Luke punched. "Are you OK?"

Luke massaged his jaw and grinned up at me.

"Why are you smiling?" I asked him.

"Chewbacca reads my comics."

Chapter Sixteen

Jade

Luke clutched the trophy to his chest as we waited for the elevator. His jaw was red and swollen. I couldn't leave him alone, especially since the altercation in the bar was my fault.

"Look. I feel really bad about what happened. Come up to my room and I'll get some ice and ibuprofen for your jaw." What the hell? He took a punch in the face because of my big mouth. It wouldn't hurt for him to see my room. There wasn't anything that would give me away. My driver's license and credit cards were in my purse. Nothing else had my name on it. It wasn't like I had a big *Thanks Jade for being such a fantastic sissy and pretending to be me this weekend* banner from Raylynn.

"You're not going to seduce me, are you?" His cute little grin that pulled at the corners of his mouth came and went as he opened and closed his mouth a few times, working out the stiffness. "I'm not sure I will be at my best right now."

"Nope."

"Maybe in a few—"

"Absolutely not." I shook my head in a way that showed I meant business. "I'm only offering a little TLC for the pain and bad experience."

His eyebrows drew together in a disappointed frown. "Ice would be great. My head feels like it hit a brick. I wasn't expecting the Wookiee to unleash on me. They're normally so cordial."

When the elevator opened on my floor, we were laughing. I tried to recall the last time a guy made me laugh and couldn't come up with one.

"Where's your comic bookstore?" I asked on the way to my room.

"Only a few blocks from here. It's Neverland Comics & Games."

"Wow. That's one of the major players in the world of comic bookstores."

"I like to think so. I've worked hard to make it something."

I flashed the key card at my door lock and Luke followed me inside, whistling at my deluxe room. He made a painful face and held his jaw between his palms. "Whistling hurts."

"Sit down over there and I'll go get ice." I motioned toward a paisley-covered armchair and picked up the ice bucket, glancing around the room for signs of me or Raylynn. When I was sure all was clear, I left Luke and walked down the hall for ice.

Good god. I had him in my room. All six-foot-two inches of yummy. I reminded myself to keep my distance. Ice the jaw. Give him medicine. Ride him like a wild stallion.

I leaned my head against the ice machine and let the chilled metal cool me off. "Now is not the time."

I froze when I walked back into the room. He had Raylynn's book open on his lap. Damn. I'd left the book on the nightstand.

"You're in the middle of reading R.D. Sayer's book." He glanced sideways at me and held his jaw while he thumbed through the pages. "That's why you recalled Jabba the Hutt's formal name. It's right here on page twenty-five. I'd forgotten the reference."

"Uhm, yeah. Well, you know, I heard she was going to be signing so I figured I'd get an autograph. Maybe resell it on eBay." I hastily made an ice pack out of the ice bucket liner, tied up a knot, and swapped the book for the ice pack. I placed the book in the nightstand drawer.

"Maybe I was too harsh about the book."

"You mean when you told me Sayer missed the mark for a space romance?"

His face flushed. "Yeah, when I said that." He leaned his head back and rested the ice on his cheek. "This hurts like a mother. Got any pain medication?"

I dug through my toiletry bag and found the pill compact I used to store my ibuprofen, Tylenol, antacids, decongestants, and other medicines that come in handy when I'm traveling. I handed Luke two ibuprofen and he made a sour face. "You have anything stronger?"

"I have some pain medicine I take for menstrual cramps." My tone came out a bit challenging, like the pain meds might be too much for him.

"That'll do."

I handed him one pain pill along with a bottle of water. He washed all the pills down in one gulp. "Thanks, Red."

"No problem." I slumped down on the bed next to him. "I didn't mean to cause a fight. Sometimes my mouth runs off without my brain. My mom always lectured me on how my hot temper got me in trouble at school." And if I could just be more like my obedient sister.

"The Wookiee had it coming. I wish I hadn't been holding the trophy, then maybe I could have blocked the punch."

And if he hadn't been turning to glance at me. He never saw it coming. Luke's eyes grew glassy. He looked uncomfortable in the chair. I stood and motioned toward the bed. "Maybe you should lie down."

A small, crooked smile wiggled across his face.

"Not going to happen, Skywalker."

I regretted refusing the offer as soon as he stretched his long legs the length of the bed and his head settled on my pillow. Heat crept up my neck and sped like a Japanese bullet train to parts lower in my hemisphere.

"Is it hot in here?" I glanced around for the thermostat.

He took my hand in his. His blue eyes locked on mine. "Thanks, again, Red."

"Not a problem." I released his hand, hoping he didn't feel the fire raging under my skin. "I'll be right back." I turned tail and headed to the bathroom, avoiding the urge to run. I removed my Princess Leia wig and splashed cold water on my face. Really Jade.

I gave myself a mental pep talk about all the reasons climbing in the bed with him would be a bad idea. When I came out, the fire had been doused to a burning ember.

I'd dressed in yoga pants and a pink vintage Mrs. Pac-Man for President tank top, comfy and not the least bit sexy. I tucked my leg under me and sat down in the chair next to the bed. His square jaw held a hint of a five-o'clock shadow, and he had a small scar at the edge of his right eyebrow that I hadn't noticed before. But it was his eyes that set me on fire. Thankfully, they were closed, and his chest moved in a steady rhythm that told me I was safe for a while.

I wished I could tell him my name and how I loved his store. I visited Neverland Comics & Games the last time I was in San Diego. It had this cool, vintage vibe with some old movie theater chairs to relax in and preview comics. There were bins and bins of new and used comics to prowl through, and shelves of books and collectible figurines for those who had more money to burn than sense. I recalled a small coffee bar and an entire badass room for gaming competitions.

I took Raylynn's book from the nightstand drawer and read another chapter. The hero loved the barista, but the barista was scared to leave her world for the hero. "Don't even think about it, girl." Do you want to give up everything you worked for to move to a new planet with this guy? Not in my lifetime. I'd been there, failed that. Serious boyfriend number one and the reason I'd moved from Texas to Sacramento. And it was never happening again.

I turned to the next chapter. Read a few pages until I reached the sex scene. I slammed the book shut. Luke's long, dark lashes fluttered open. Damn. He turned his head and squinted trying to focus.

"Your hair." He made a floppy motion toward my hair. "I like this color best. It's like molten copper dripping with honey."

I reached up and touched my hair. He hadn't seen it since the Iron Man costume. And now, let down and brushed, it fell in tousled waves. I hadn't thought of my hair as anything other than auburn with a few blond highlights and unmanageable frizz.

"Thanks. Keep the ice on your jaw."

"Aye-aye, Lieutenant Red." He fumbled for the ice pack.

"Right now, I'm the captain." I stood, tucked the book back into the drawer, walked to the opposite side of the bed and cat crawled up next to him. He'd let the ice pack drop to his shoulder. I moved it back to his jaw.

"Why won't you tell me your name?" His words came out thick and slurred, then he dozed off. The medicine had kicked in.

"Because I'm starting to really like you," I whispered, putting my head on the pillow next to him.

I woke with a cold sensation pressed against my chest. Luke's arms were wrapped around me, his face inches from mine. His eyes were closed, and a faint bruise highlighted his swollen jawline.

My fault.

The ice pack had slid between my breasts and I shifted to move it. Luke's eyes opened and those baby blues focused on me. A smile spread slowly across his face, seductive. And cunning.

"Umm, the ice pack fell." I held up the bag of the melted ice. He took it from me and tossed it over his shoulder on to the floor. He pulled me toward him.

"Luke."

"Tell me when to stop, Red." He pressed his lips to mine, sweet, gentle.

My mind wanted me to say stop, but my body, the traitor, kissed him back with a passion that must have been bottled up like a seven-hundred-year-old genie. Holy tortured tequila! I just met the guy yesterday.

Wouldn't be the first time you met a guy and hopped in the sack.

My subconscious reminded me of several meetups in dimly lit bars, and that handsy guy from Sweetie Swipe. But I'm older now, more mature, I don't do one-night stands anymore.

"Umm." My concerns were cut off by his lips parting mine. Our tongues tangled and the blood strummed beneath my skin. He skimmed my arm with his fingers trailing goose bumps in their wake.

My prior self-talk was lost in the smoke of the raging fire burning from naval to toes. I decided I'd chastise myself later. He was hard in all the right places and so freaking cute. I ran my hand across his firm abs.

Yep, those five a.m. workouts were paying off, and I intended to take full advantage.

I ran my hand lower, tucked it inside his pants, and wrapped my fingers around him. He slit his eyes open and moaned into my mouth, then dove in for another round of sensual kisses. He trailed them across my collarbone until he returned to that sweet spot behind my ear. With a few efficient moves, he discarded our clothes, all but my lacy VS bra and panties.

Yeah, I'll take full advantage, right after his long artistic fingers find their way to my internal storyboard and create an interactive media sequence that includes the ultimate climax.

Somewhere in the middle of his fingers doing just that, I splayed kisses on his eyebrow scar, across his strong angled jaw, pausing to cut through a haze of lust, I remembered he had been hit in the face and he was in pain. "Sorry, your jaw must be on fire."

"I have other things on fire that need extinguishing." He rolled me on top of him, kissed me hard. His hands began a quest and found the front closure of my bra, clicking it open with one experienced twist of his fingers. "That's better," he murmured into my mouth, nipping at my bottom lip.

His fingers found my nipple. Electricity shivered up my spine and I moaned. I couldn't help it. Luke was doing all my favorite things, in all my favorite ways. I reciprocated working my way down and taking all of him in my mouth. His breathing increased with gasping moans as I used my tongue for something other than testing new drink ideas.

"Jesus, Red." He halted my enthusiasm pulling me up next to him. "I want to be inside you."

I ran tender kisses across his injured jaw. He didn't flinch; instead, he slithered down my body, kissing several important parts along the way. He tucked his finger inside the string of my bikini panties and slid them off. With a soft muffled cry, desire swept through me and sent any plans to avoid this man up in flames.

Making love to Luke was worth the risk. My fingers slid across that part of him that was rock hard. He groaned and did something with his fingers that shot me to climax faster than a speeding bullet. I blamed my sabbatical from sex, but he moved on top of me and I lost myself in blue eyes smoked with passion.

Somewhere along the way he'd rolled on a condom. The anticipation of him inside me scorched my brain and left logical reasoning in a charred unrecognizable blob.

"Now. Now. Now." Was that me begging, out loud? I was not the kind of girl who begged for satisfaction.

He slid inside me and kissed me until I moaned again. He thrust slowly, anticipating my cries for speed, for heat, for more. I raised my hips to take him deeper. My fingers raked across his back and he granted my wishes. Again, and again. And again. I let the power of my orgasms sweep me into his galaxy far, far away.

Chapter Seventeen

Luke

I regretfully surfaced from the blissful, dreamlike state that followed making love to an extraordinary woman. An over-the-top, sex-filled afternoon that ranked among my all-time best left me lazily staring at the beautiful face next to me.

She lay on her stomach, face turned toward me and glorious copper hair feathered across the pillow. A small tattoo, the zodiac sign for Gemini, marked the palm side of her wrist, and another one, a dragon, rested on the back of her shoulder. I traced the dragon and memorized the smooth curve of her neck. I'd add it on my heroine in *Cronman*. I prayed this wasn't the last time I'd get to see it. To see her. Hold her. Make love to her.

Her eyes fluttered open and focused on me. I'd hoped to see her as happily satisfied, but instead, those emeralds held panic. She bolted upright, catching the duvet before her tanned breasts were exposed and had me begging for more sex. Oh yeah, this woman sunbathed topless.

"Fucking Frangelico!"

"Yeah, I sort of thought so too," I laughed, but my warning sirens were alerting me she wasn't feeling the same.

"I can't believe we had sex, and then I fell asleep." She rubbed her eyes and the dragon's wings spread, ready to take flight.

I expected a climax-induced coma. We had a passionate tango in the sheets, and it took some effort on my part, being on pain medication and trying to hold back long enough to locate a condom in my wallet. Multiple times. "It's no wonder you passed out afterward. Girl, you rocked my world."

"I did?" The look on her face shared she doubted that she was the best sex I'd had in a long, long time. Maybe ever.

"Yeah." I ran a hand up her arm and watched the goose bumps spring to life.

A slow, smug smile spread across her pretty face. "You're not so bad either."

"Not bad?" I placed my hand over my heart. "Ouch."

She lowered down to her forearm, brought her lips within inches of mine. "Not bad at all."

I met her mouth and kissed her, feeling things stir again.

She pushed away, her face twisted in worry. "What time is it?"

I propped up on my elbow, glanced at the clock behind her on the nightstand. "Almost seven."

"Oh crap. I've got plans to meet Jerry for dinner."

"No problem. I work the booth at eight." I treaded lightly. I didn't want her to regret the best day of my life so far. "Red." I reached over and pulled her close. Kissed her gently on the lips. "You're amazing, and I'd like to get to know you better."

"How much better can you get?" She laughed, but her eyes didn't dance the way they did when she was ribbing me.

I knew when to back off. I stood and slipped into my clothes. I had just enough time to drive home, grab a shower, and make it back for my shift at the booth.

She watched me like a caged rabbit from the bed. "How's your jaw?"

I worked it a few times. "It hurts, but I'll live. The pain medication and the sleep helped." And the sex. "Thanks."

"Again, I'm really sorry."

"Sorry for my jaw pain or the time we spent together?" Dammit, I just couldn't let it go.

"I don't know. Maybe both. Maybe only the jaw pain."

Now was not the time to ask her name, but it gnawed at me. There was a reason she was being secretive, and I hoped it wasn't because she was seeing some douchebag.

Oh, what the hell. "So, here's the classic line. If you give me your number, I'd like to call you."

"For another lunch date?" She smiled and, for a moment, the tense energy in the room evaporated like cloudy puffs from a Smoked Old Fashioned.

"Yeah, another lunch date. And if it's anything like this one, I'll book your calendar for the rest of your life." I balanced a knee on the bed and kissed the surprised look off her face.

She started to wrap her arm around my neck and pull me in for another kiss and then stopped. "Can you hand me my phone?" She pointed toward the nightstand. "It's there."

I picked up her phone. The black screen winked open and a photo of three senior citizens smiled up at me. The Barflies, I presumed. She really did care about these people.

I gave a mental fist pump there wasn't some dude on the screen and handed her the phone. "Are those your friends from the bar?"

She looked down at her screen. "Yeah, that's Ed, Stew, and Marjorie. They're the best."

I gave her my number and she typed it in her phone.

The call was in her court. Whatever her reasons for being mysterious, she had to make the first play. At the thought she might not call me, my heart burned like I had taken a lightsaber to the chest.

"Thanks again for the triage, Nurse Red." I leaned toward her and kissed her goodbye. A slow, gentle kiss. A forget-me-not that begged for a permanent place in her heart.

"May the Force be with you, Jedi Knight."

I moved toward the door. She sat frozen in the center of a tangled mess of covers staring at me with her satisfied but crazy-eyed grin.

"Bye, Red." I reached for the door handle.

"Tomorrow!" She shouted loud enough to hail a New York cab driver.

My heart thumped with elated anticipation. I smiled and turned back toward her, then saw the conflicted expression on her beautiful face.

"Can we do lunch tomorrow?" A wide smile replaced whatever she'd been at odds with a moment before.

I held in a huge sigh of relief. I tried to look calm, manly, rather than the brooding romantic ready to drop at her feet and scream like a crazed Marlon Brando that tomorrow was like forever. "I'm working the booth tomorrow. Come by around noon, and I'll take a lunch break."

"OK." A slow half smile curved the corners of her mouth, but her eyes held an unexplainable apprehension. "I'll stop by tomorrow. For lunch."

"Lunch." I gave her a cocky smile and let the door shut behind me.

Chapter Eighteen

Jade

As soon as the door shut, I collapsed back on the bed. "What am I doing? I had sex with him. Amazing sex. And then I set up another date." I slung an arm across my eyes, blocking out the setting sun streaming through my windows. My previous sexual encounters didn't hold a candle, no, they couldn't light the match to light the candle to Luke. And he was injured. I couldn't imagine what he could do full throttle and without the pain meds fogging his mind.

Get real, Jade. Luke's not in the plan. Look at your history with men. If it was a book, it would be titled *Bad Choices and the Lesson I Haven't Learned from Them*.

Was Luke another lesson? He seems so different from the other guys I've dated. A nice guy, for one, and two, he had a great sense of humor, and three, well, three left me hot between my thighs.

I reminded myself I had the same thoughts about Big Mike, a.k.a. Girlie Cocktail. We both liked rock music. We both liked horror movies. We both had experience running a bar. Big difference. Big Mike, whose name didn't live up to anything about him, except he was a big liar, liked to control me. Control the bar. Control my life. Luke didn't give off that conceited, I'm-in-it-for-me-and-only-me vibe.

Besides, Luke liked gaming and comics. No way would Big Mike ever attend a Con. The only con he'd ever experienced was the one where he conned me out of my life savings. Mike tried to talk Theo into selling the arcade games and expanding the dance floor. Adding techno lights and a big-ass sound system. Thankfully, Theo didn't have the money or desire to make the changes.

My foot hit something soft. I lifted the duvet and pulled out Luke's T-shirt. He wore it under his costume, and I vaguely remembered yanking it off him. I pressed the shirt to my nose and inhaled the scent of the freshly laundered shirt along with a trace of citrus and cedar. The scent I can only describe as a warm summer hug.

I dropped the shirt over my head and let the smell wrap around me. I had to be honest with myself. I wanted to spend more time with Luke. I wanted to know him better, too. I wanted to fall in love with him. And I wanted to strangle my silent, self-centered sister. If she didn't show up soon, I'd have no choice but to tell Luke my fake name and kiss the promise of the possibility goodbye. The same way he kissed me goodbye only minutes ago.

I snatched my phone off the nightstand and thumbed to her number.

"Dammit, Raylynn, answer me." It went straight to voice mail. She never checked her VMs. Jerry did that for her. I climbed out of bed and changed to text.

Ray, you've been silent for too long. I need you to show up. For once in your life, I need you to show up for me. I can't do this alone. Please don't make me lie to all these people.

Especially not Luke.

I waited. Nothing. I threw my phone on the bed with such force it should have torn through the thousand-thread count sheets. An image of Luke and me tangled in them had me stomping toward the shower.

I scrubbed myself with the complimentary body scrub, allowing the hot water to wash away my anger at my sister, or at least calm me down to this is absolutely-the-last-time level. I used the shampoo and conditioner and shaved my legs with the complimentary razor and shaving cream. This place really was top-notch. I toweled off with the extra-fluffy towel big enough to dry an automobile and slathered on the eau de toilette body lotion with aromatic waters.

My meeting with Jerry demanded a new costume. I didn't want Luke to see me with him. It was common knowledge Jerry was one of the few people who knew R.D. Sayer. He practically shouted the fact that he represented the reclusive author. And, it was on his business cards.

After checking my phone for any missed texts or messages—there were none—I moved to the closet to decide on tonight's disguise. I was no longer hiding myself in order to be Raylynn, I was hiding from Luke. Only until Raylynn arrived. If I could keep from telling him my name for one more day, I was sure Raylynn wouldn't leave me stranded.

Princess Leia wouldn't do. I needed more makeup, a new face. A face Luke wouldn't recognize. I yanked open the bifold doors and perused the costumes hanging like body bags in a morgue, each labeled with the character's name.

Wigs, each mounted on its own Styrofoam head, sat on the shelf above the costumes. The first time I opened the closet to the line of white, eyeless faces I almost lost my shit.

Jerry organized the costumes by the date Raylynn wanted to wear them, but I had already destroyed her schedule and that gave me some satisfaction. I passed over the blond Zelda wig, and the one I knew matched the costume for Link. I stopped on the black wig with ox horns wrapped in silk brocades and ribbons. Chun Li. One of my favorite characters from *Street Fighter*, and one of the first females in a fighting game.

"Yes, definitely the Chun Li." I plucked the wig off the fake head. Maybe by wearing the Chun Li, I could channel some of her gumption. "After the original creators gave her fewer life bars than the men in her game, she had to prove herself." I explained to the empty faces.

"It wasn't my fault. I didn't plan on meeting a man here. I planned on making contacts, building my business." The faces didn't judge me, they waited patiently for the story. "He's fantastic, and we had such a good time battling our way out of the escape room." Not to mention what went on in my hotel room.

And the way he kissed me. Just when I was focused on my own story, Luke stormed in to rewrite the plot. I laughed at my little anecdote as I stepped in front of the mirror and pinned up my red curls. "I just want to be me for a change. Not R.D. Sayer, Raylynn, Red, or Jaylynn the bar manager. Just me, Jade." I pulled on the black wig, examined myself in the mirror, and blew out a sigh. "Not gonna happen. At least not yet."

After adding the brown contacts and layers of makeup that morphed me into the perfect Asian Interpol officer, I felt better, braver. With the busty padded costume and heeled boots, Luke wouldn't recognize me. I'm working on my...what did he call it? Character arc? Yeah, I think that was it. I can't let feelings for him interrupt my plan.

I slipped into the brown tights and white combat boots, then pulled the blue qipao, an early-twentieth-century Chinese dress with golden accents and puffy sleeves that reminded me of a princess, over my head. I snapped the chunky, spiked bracelets on my wrists, grabbed my handbag, and headed for the door. If I happened to run into Luke, he'd never recognize me. At least, I hoped he wouldn't.

Chapter Nineteen

Luke

After a quick shower, I drove back to the hotel and headed for my exhibitor booth. Tonight, my confidence brimmed over like I alone could conquer a galaxy. Red did that for me. Jean-Claude's mission to identify R.D. Sayer was like finding a diamond in a vat of crystals, but I'd find R.D. Sayer, get my name and my royalties from the next book, and put Jean-Claude in his place and out of my store forever. And who knew? Maybe I'd take this thing with Red to the next level.

Who was I kidding? She lives in Sacramento. An eight-hour car ride away. It wasn't New York City like my ex, but it would still be a long-distance relationship and those never work out. At least not for me.

"Just enjoy the weekend, Walker," I told myself as I turned the corner and entered the vendors area. "Quit overthinking this for more than what it is." Red hasn't told me her name, or why she's keeping it a secret. The reason is probably a deal-breaker. She didn't come off as a liar, or a cheat, or a married woman having a whirlwind affair at a Comic-Con. And she'd told me about her bonehead ex-boyfriend. So, what, then?

"Hey, Marty," I said, entering my booth. The college student was in the middle of a transaction with a group of teenagers. He gave me a chin lift followed by, "S'up." He side-eyed toward the back of the booth, and I followed his head tilt.

Jean-Claude, his lips pulled thin, his brows furrowed so deep it looked like a capital V had been etched in black ink on his forehead, stood in the back of my booth.

Marty shrugged at me.

"What's up?" I asked Jean-Claude, knowing this was probably about my book review.

At first glance, I thought he was in costume, but then again, I knew him. The Ichabod Crane duster combined with his all-black attire shouted he was in a broody Mr. Darcy mood.

"Your review was merciful. I wanted something to make R.D. Sayer march down to our booth and declare war. I wanted to out the recluse, but you said the heroine was gutsy."

"She was gutsy. Deciding to leave her world for a man she just met to go into space. It's scary and gutsy." Of course, the heroine gave up the hero, decided to stay and build her future, but I didn't mention that she became a strong, independent woman and risked losing her hero to do so. I thought this was gutsier, but Jean-Claude would have been more pissed off if I had posted my true opinion. Would Red leave her bar for me?

"It's slutty and immoral, and I wanted the author to suffer. I wanted that book to drop so far down the ranks that R.D. Sayer would need a drilling rig to find it." Jean-Claude smacked his leg with a rolled up Con schedule. "I should have written it myself, but I was tied up having dinner with my agent."

"Agent?" I swallowed hard. "I thought we were having dinner with your agent tomorrow?"

"Change of plans. I tried calling you all afternoon, but you didn't answer. Then after I read the blog, I changed my mind."

I did a mental head slap. I was with Red, and I'd muted my phone during the trivia game. After I left Red's room, I didn't bother returning Jean-Claude's *one* phone call. I figured he wanted to yell at me about the review.

"I have people commenting that they will read Sayer's book and make up their own minds." He pointed the schedule at me. "It's all your fault."

"Is that a crime? The book's not that bad, and shouldn't people make up their own minds anyway?"

"No!" He screeched like a vulture who just had its prey scooped up by waste management. "You find Sayer. I need that author's identity. I need dirt. I need to redeem this mediocre review and come out of this panel looking righteous, experienced, a reviewer who knows his shit so that readers flock to buy my next book."

My next book, I thought.

"What's your problem with Sayer anyway?" I stared down at him. "You don't normally get this worked up over a review."

"Sayer's been a pain in my blog since day one. Every time I released a book, that author's fan club would inundate my blog with their opinions, as if they mattered. Sayer refutes my work in every literary journal known to mankind. I had to change my pen name three times to get rid of the nuisance. It's the reason I became a critic. My books wouldn't sell because of Sayer."

"I didn't know that," I said.

"It was early on in my career. I changed my appearance, stopped writing books, and switched my platform to literary critic. I became ruthless, arrogant, beyond contempt—and the public took notice of my reviews. Then I had to hire you to write my books." Jean-Claude's shoulders sagged only briefly, before he straightened like a man with a new cause, one fueled by deep-rooted hatred.

"How am I going to find her? There are thousands of people here, and they're in costumes. Even if I knew what she looked like—"

"She?" Jean-Claude stopped fuming and looked at me. And then I remembered, yesterday at lunch, the couple at the table.

I nodded and told him about my conversation with Sayer's fan. "R.D. Sayer is a woman."

"I knew it." He slapped his program on his leg again, but this time it was more of a Good Golly, Miss Molly slap. "I should have known Sayer was a woman by the romantic undertones. No woman can write a good space opera."

"What about Bujold, and Ann Leckie? Or Becky Chambers?"

"The exceptions," he huffed.

I turned away from him, set my helmet down on the folding table. He caught sight of my bruise. "What happened to your face?"

"I had a go with a guy in the bar over a trivia game." I rubbed my cheek and wished I'd grabbed a few ibuprofens.

"You need to focus on finding Sayer instead of playing trivia and chasing women. Yesterday, I saw you get on an elevator with a scantily clad woman."

"She was dressed like Harley Quinn, and you have no say in my personal life."

"I do if it affects your writing, and based on that review, she's making you soft." He turned to leave, then stopped and turned toward me. "Find Sayer or find another job, ghostwriter."

I watched him leave. I almost felt empathy for the guy. The pain in my jaw throbbed, working its way up the back of my neck. I rubbed it absentmindedly.

"What's wrong with that dude?" Marty asked.

"He's pretentious."

"He looks like he stepped out of the pages of *Cronman*." Marty snorted at Jean-Claude's retreating back, then turned to help a customer.

"Indeed, he does."

The booth saw a lot of action for the next few hours. I joked with a few fans about my comic and sold, much to my dissatisfaction, several of Jean-Claude's graphic novels. I reminded myself he'd paid me to ghost-write. A woman stopped at the booth to finger a baseball hat with Jean-Claude's superhero on the front panel. The guy was all muscle and no brains. What woman would want a guy like that?

And then I realized that was R.D. Sayer's problem. Her hero was daft. All "let me save you from a dying Earth and take you away to my planet where I will have sex with you all day and you do nothing." She wanted to write an ultramasculine hero. A man who would remove all the heroine's problems. But he wasn't realistic. He didn't have a single fault, and the readers picked up on it. Even Jean-Claude's brawny super-hero was afraid of heights. I gave myself a mental pat on the back for having a superhero who couldn't fly until the psychiatrist heroine helped him overcome his fear.

I pulled my phone out of my zippered pocket and did an internet search for R.D. Sayer. I'd done one before, but I needed to go deeper. Use the drilling rig.

As expected, lots of unicorn emojis surfaced next to her name. I scrolled until I found information on R.D. Sayer dated around the time of her first release. More unicorns. Finally, I found a photo taken by paparazzi.

Actually, the photo was of Nora Roberts, a famous romance writer, at a luncheon, but in the background, sitting at a table with a man that looked familiar to me was a woman in profile. She wore a fedora that shadowed half her face, and the photo was grainy. I couldn't make out the details. She had brown hair that hung in long waves down her back. A red arrow pointed at the woman and the caption read, "Is this R.D. Sayer?"

I studied the profile. It resembled Red. I could see why the woman at the trivia game asked if she were Sayer. But the nose turned up a tiny bit on the end. I thought I had memorized every curve of Red's face but couldn't recall if her nose turned up like the woman in the photo. I'd do some recon tonight. With any luck, I'd find Red, rule out her cute nose, and secure our plans for the lunch date.

Chapter Twenty

Jade

Jerry asked me to meet him for dinner at the bar next to the Italian restaurant. Both were connected to the hotel. He had potential client meetings, good for him, but my stomach wanted Chianti and pasta smothered in sauce, not beer nuts and Jack Daniels. Once he finished with his last meeting, he promised to satisfy my craving for carbs.

The elevator took its time arriving at my floor. Figures. There were lots of people at this Con. My chance of running into Luke again was slim right? The kiss. My mind kept replaying that first kiss. Actually, it replayed our afternoon together. Absentmindedly, my index finger touched my bottom lip and was greeted with a gooey glop of lip gloss.

The ding of the elevator bounced me back from my mental breakdown of every second Luke's lips pressed against mine.

I nodded casually at the costumed people who crowded aside for me to enter. While digging in my purse for a Kleenex, I entered the elevator and wiped my finger with a slightly used tissue. Returning it to my bag,

I looked at my reflection in the mirrored walls and startled at the man behind me.

The critic, Jean-what's-his-name. Jerry had pointed him out to me earlier in the Con. He stared back at me, dark beady eyes focused at the level of my chest. He wore a black, floor-length duster that reminded me of the headless horseman.

The elevator stopped. Everyone except the critic got off at the mezzanine level. I, unfortunately, had to ride down to street level with creepy critic guy to meet Jerry for dinner.

"Excuse me." I moved to my left giving him more than his share of the small space.

"You look familiar. Have we met?" He studied my face like it was an objet d'art.

"Chun Li." I motioned at my costume and added a dah lift of my eyebrow.

"Ha, of course. Sorry, I don't think I've had the pleasure, Jean-Claude Cabaliér." He extended a hand.

"Nope, you haven't." Being raised in the South where manners were considered far more important than animosity, I shook hands and moved as far away as the elevator allowed, hoping it would stop at the next floor and pick up some of those thousands of people that normally made the elevator run at turtle speed.

"What brings you to the Con?" Jean-Claude stared at me like he was dissecting my innards.

Be nice, Jade. You fell asleep reading Raylynn's book, so maybe the guy had a point of view.

"You mean other than possibly running into my favorite hero?" I sent him a nervous laugh. Why did this guy make me feel nervous? He didn't chuckle at my joke, but waited with a tell-me-the-real-reason cocked eyebrow and half scowl. "I run a vintage arcade bar, and I'm hoping to make a few connections."

His face fell slightly, like my job disappointed him somehow. "What a coincidence, I'm an investor in such types of establishments. Maybe I could introduce you to a few of my friends." He flipped a card at me. "Why don't you stop by my booth tomorrow. I'll be signing my latest novel."

I took the card and read his name. My sister's voice echoed in my head, a saying we said together with linked pinkies. Born together, best friends forever. My twin alliance took over. I couldn't help myself.

"Aren't you the critic who flambéed R.D. Sayer's book?" I squinted my eyes at him. Take that, bad man. "I uhm can't recall the name of it." I threw in just to make myself nondescript.

He gave a lengthy sigh as if everyone he met in the elevator asked him dumb questions. "Why yes. Everyone has an opinion. I just publish mine."

"I thought you were mean. The book wasn't that bad." I hoped.

He huffed and rolled his eyes so far upward I thought he might lose his balance. "The author needs to get out in the world. It's obvious R.D. Sayer is Googling the facts from a La-Z-Boy recliner instead of experiencing them."

Couldn't disagree with him there.

"What did you say your name was?" His question sounded more like a pop quiz.

"I didn't." I rammed his card in my purse and pulled out my phone pretending to be involved in a text.

"For goodness' sake, I'm not trying to pick you up. I like to help struggling business owners who have a finger in the arts."

I lowered my phone and cocked an eyebrow. "How can you help me?"

"For starters, how's your social media?"

"Fine. I'm on all the channels, but my clientele doesn't really scroll through Facebook. They're mostly bikers and eighties headbangers."

"You need to change that."

"No kidding." Sarcasm dripped from my words like honey from Pooh Bear's canines.

"Most millennials, generation X, Y, Z, or whatever they're calling it nowadays, love watching reels and short clips. You need to target them."

"And you can help me with that?"

The elevator pinged open. "Drop by my booth tomorrow. The signing starts at ten a.m. Just follow the long line of fans."

He held the door, then stepped from the elevator behind me. His duster ruffled as he walked away.

Maybe he wasn't so bad. I couldn't see what Jerry was all upset about. Wasn't freedom of speech a constitutional right?

"She's your sister," the little voice inside my head reminded me.

"Yeah? Well, where is she if this book is so important?" I muttered as I walked toward the fancy Italian restaurant, praying Jerry had been in touch with the blood of my blood.

Raylynn was important, and her anxiety disorder was a huge problem for her. I tried to recall when it all began. In college, I thought. She was attending USC and dating some creep. I was busy flunking out of community college, but Raylynn told me how he humiliated her. She was always the shy one. I stood up for her most of our adolescent lives, but I wasn't there for her then.

I walked through the hotel lobby and into the atrium with its high ceilings and flashy artwork, finally found the bar, and wound my way through the high-top tables, noisy people, and splashy pink and orange art-covered walls.

The bar was too brightly lit and much too big for my taste. A bar should be dimly lit, playing jazz on the speakers, have candles on the tables and a sexy bartender with rolled up sleeves wiping down the scraped mahogany counter from too many broken hearts. A place where secrets were shared, life's mysteries debated and even sometimes solved.

Jerry waved me over. A frown creased his brows as I drew close. "You're wearing the Chun Li."

"So?"

"You were supposed to save that for the book presentation. Ray's main character was adopted by a wealthy Asian family and it's a tribute to them."

"Sorry. The Princess Leia buns were giving me a headache." I shrugged onto the high stool.

"You want a drink?" Jerry asked.

The smell of nachos and hot wings made my stomach growl. "No, I want pasta covered with red sauce. This bar is all state fair food. Finish your drink so we can eat the real stuff."

"Jade, your bar serves hot dogs."

"Yeah, but mine is an arcade. The theme is in the moment. Besides, my bar area is separated from the games, and it's clandestine."

Jerry snickered at my last word, as if I'd described the Hemingway Bar in Paris. "So, how were your meetings?" I asked him, unsure how he held a meeting with the all the racket.

"They went well. I met with an author who writes horror and another romance author, but honestly, after that recent review of R.D.'s book, she was skeptical." Jerry blew out a long breath. "Doesn't matter. Raylynn takes up all my time. She's needy."

"I guess you haven't heard from her?" I couldn't hide the eagerness from my voice.

Jerry raised his eyes at me over the fancy blue cocktail he sipped. A coy grin pulled his mouth sideways. "I know that look. You've spent some quality time with the Jedi."

I smiled wide. "I did, and let me say, the Force has nothing on this guy."

Jerry eyed me like a benevolent traffic cop and casually sat down his drink. "Careful. You've only known him a few days."

"This one feels different."

Jerry rolled his eyes. "They all do in the beginning, honey."

"It might turn out fine." What happens to me if I never take a chance on love? I stopped myself. I'd taken too many chances, and they'd all turned out bad. Call it what it is, Jade. "No worries. He lives eight hours away from me, so it's only a Con-fling." A fling I swore not to have, and now one I'm right in the middle of.

"Please tell me you didn't give him your real name?" Jerry threw back the rest of his drink.

"No. He calls me Red."

"Thank heaven." His face showed relief, then his eyes narrowed. "So, this guy took you on the ride of your life and he doesn't know your name?"

"Yeah, and I can't keep sleeping with him and not tell him my name. It feels wrong, cheap."

"People do it all the time." Jerry signaled the server for his check. "Jade, honey, you can't tell him your real name."

"It feels wrong lying to him."

"Raylynn is on silence, and if anyone finds out you're not her, well, you know..."

I did know. It wasn't good. On the other hand, Luke would think I was a big liar.

We were interrupted by a weary server handing Jerry an electronic device to input his credit card. It should be a leather-bound check presenter with the company name embossed in gold, I thought.

"Why can't I tell him? He can keep a secret."

Jerry huffed. "If you must, at least wait until tomorrow night."

"What's tomorrow night?"

"Don't you ever look at the schedule I prepared? It's the awards ceremony."

"There's an awards ceremony?"

"Yes."

I shot upright. "Raylynn won't win an award, will she? I mean, I don't need to prepare an Oscar speech, right?"

"Calm down. It's not the Oscars, it's the Eisner Awards. No chance R.D. Sayer will win. Not with that bad review and her book teetering on the bestseller list. Besides, the book didn't release in time to submit it for an award this year. And you're not going."

I thanked my lucky stars. "Isn't getting on that list the big deal anyhow?"

"Wrong." Jerry stood and I slipped off my stool. "Raylynn is a top ten producer."

"Well, like my favorite movie quote, 'If you're not first, you're last.'"

"Will Ferrell, *Talladega Nights*." Jerry smirked. "I remember watching it with you and Ray every weekend one summer. Y'all were mad for it."

"I loved the dad in that movie. Raylynn kept rewriting the script so he would stay and become the father the main character dreamed of. I wanted him to be my boyfriend."

"He was the worst," Jerry said.

"I thought he was cool. Away in a foreign country, racing fast cars, having love affairs, wearing cool sunglasses, and getting kicked out of Applebee's." I followed Jerry out of the bar.

Jerry huffed at me. "The guy was a turd, and you should set your sights higher."

"Like?"

"Look for a guy who will give your future offspring stability."

"Do you think that he'll be a good lover with all that stability?"

Jerry stopped short and I almost bumped into him. "You've got your priorities messed up."

"No. I'm here for the bar, not for a man." Then I thought of Luke, and somehow, I knew he was the kind of guy a girl could count on. He rocked my world. Maybe there was more to my Jedi than a fling at a Comic-Con.

Jerry left me standing in the foyer of the Italian restaurant while he checked on our reservation. The aroma of garlicky sauces, heavy candle wax, oaky wine, and cigars filled my airspace while I contemplated my foolish fling with Luke.

Even if Luke was a nice guy, I couldn't pursue this relationship. He lived in San Diego. I lived in Sacramento. He was right. Long-distance relationships never worked. There was no need for me to tell Luke my real name. No need to spoil Raylynn's deception. I'd attend the panel. Do my due diligence for my sister.

But I'd agreed to another lunch date. What was the matter with me? It was the great sex. My hormones caused me to shout out the request before my brain could stop me. I could cancel. I had his number. So rude to cancel in text. I'd stop by his booth tomorrow and tell him lunch was off.

I pushed back from my almost empty plate of penne all'arrabbiata and studied Jerry. We'd been friends so long he was more like a brother than a friend.

"Do you remember when Raylynn became afraid to go out in public?" I asked.

He dabbed his mouth with the linen napkin and settled it on his lap.

"Ray was always shy and never liked being the center of attention. Unlike someone else I know." Jerry tilted his chin my direction then leaned back in his chair recollecting past events. "During her last year of college, she dated some loser who embarrassed her."

"I remember. Did you ever meet him?"

"Once. He was doughy around the middle, had blond hair that reminded me of Bo Duke from that Dukes of Hazzard show—and he dressed like him too. Giant belt buckle, black felt hat, and boots. On a personality scale I'd give him a two."

"Ray always liked Bo Duke." I smiled. "Raylynn loved anything eighties. Especially the movie stars. My mom told her she had an old soul."

"I only met him the once. Wouldn't know him if I ran into him on the street unless, of course, he still sports the same fashion choices. That might give him away."

"All I know is he criticized her thesis in front of her colleagues." I sipped my sangria and paused for a moment deciding it had too much brandy. "She'd poured her heart and soul into that paper."

"The bastard. I remember she ditched school, moved into your mom's house, and refused to leave except for food and occasional trips to TJ Maxx."

"It was when Mom's MS had a bad flare. Ray quit school to help take care of her." I took a big sip of sangria and decided to confide in Jerry. "The Bo Duke asshat showed up at the house a few months later demanding to see Ray."

Jerry's eyes widened. "I didn't know the guy gave a fig about her."

I looked down into my drink and admitted my worst sin to Jerry. "I told him she died in a car accident."

"Jade. You didn't?" Jerry made a horrified face. "You're such a bad girl."

"I never told Raylynn he came to the house, but it served him right, the jerk. He was totally wrong for her. He didn't show any emotion when I told him my lie. You were right about the Bo Duke hair. I thought I was helping her, but her phobias have only gotten worse over the years."

"I know. She's seeing a therapist."

My head shot up and my breath caught. "She didn't tell me she was getting help."

"She doesn't want you to know how bad it's become, but since you're here, and a tad angry at her, I felt it was all right to tell you. She can be mad at me later."

I set my empty glass on the table. "What are we going to do if she doesn't show for the panel?"

"You're going to use those bullshit skills that have served you so well all these years. And if that doesn't work, I'm submitting my résumé to Nordstroms."

"Oh, jeez, Jerry."

"And Jade, for heaven's sake, read the book." Jerry placed his napkin on the table and pushed back his chair.

"Promise, right after a quick gaming session."

We stood to leave. "I know you, Jade. You'll get sucked into whatever game, stumble back to your room at one in the morning, and fall asleep before you finish a page."

"I won't. Cross my heart. I want another crack at the Python. After an hour of gaming, I'll head back straightaway and read."

We walked past the bar and I heard my favorite rumbly voice asking for a to-go order. I stopped short, looked up, and made eye contact with Luke. He leaned against the bar. The female bartender offered up a nice view of her cleavage.

His face broke into a wide grin. Damn. He recognized me.

Jerry looked at me, then at Luke. "Is this your Jedi?"

I nodded, unable to begin a sentence.

"Hello, Red." Luke's voice held a hint of amusement. I imagined the Big Bad Wolf used the same cocky tone when he greeted Little Red Riding Hood. Luke pushed away from the bar. "Looks like I found you, again."

"You d-d-did." I stuttered like a scratched vinyl record. Jerry gave my forearm a gentle squeeze, nudging my stuck needle forward. "This is my friend, Jerry."

Luke extended a hand. "You have a gift with the costumes." Luke's gaze drifted up my body, taking in the Chun Li. A slow burn from deep inside my core followed his eyes until they stopped on mine. "It's always a challenge to find Red."

Sizzle.

"Thanks." Jerry shook his hand, then paused. "Have we met? You look familiar."

"Luke writes the comic *Cronman*," I answered.

"Ah, yes. Very clever superhero. I'm sure I've seen your photo. I'm a publicist."

"Hey, hot stuff, your order's ready," the bartender called out to Luke. She frowned at me, obviously annoyed we'd interrupted her scoring an after-hours hookup with Luke.

"I'm working tonight." Luke hiked a thumb at the bar. "Just picking up dinner. Can I catch up with you later?"

"Sorry. I'm checking out the gaming rooms, then turning in early." I gave Jerry a defiant half grin.

"Tomorrow then. For lunch."

"Yes, tomorrow. For lunch. Meet at your booth?" I heard myself say. So much for canceling the lunch date.

"Yeah, you can't miss it. Keep an eye out for your favorite super-hero." He nodded at Jerry. "Nice to meet you."

"Likewise," I heard Jerry say but couldn't take my eyes off the long look that Luke sent me, turning my sizzle into a full-on flambé.

Luke turned toward the bar, and I yanked Jerry out into the hotel's concourse before he could make any remarks Luke might overhear.

Jerry purred. "Meee-ow, he's worth getting to know. At least for one night."

"Jeez, Jerry."

"What can I say? He's hot. Be careful. Don't let Jedi hottie use the Force and cause you to tell him all your dirty little secrets."

"Not for all the wupiupi on Tatooine."

Jerry looked at me with an open mouth.

"It's the money of the Hutts in Star Wars."

"You really are a nerd."

"Later." I laughed and walked away from Jerry toward the escalator that connected the hotel with the conference center.

"Read the book," he shouted after me.

Chapter Twenty-One

Jade

After dinner with Jerry, I took the escalator to the mezzanine level and returned to the Dragontoon gaming room in 15AB. I'd been 100 points from achieving the high score last night, and the near victory ate at me almost as badly as my infatuation with Luke.

A gangly, college-aged guy who spent too much time in front of video games and too little time washing his face sat at a hosting table. He looked up as I approached.

"Hi. I'd like to play Dragontoon."

"You're in time for the next session. Starts in five." He handed me a set of headphones and assigned me a gaming station.

"Thanks." I put on the headphones and slid into a cushiony chair next to another player.

"Cool costume, but I prefer the Harley Quinn." It was Rez from the mobile gaming room booth. "Your bottom showed in that one."

"Jeez, how very sexist of you. And it wasn't my entire bottom, only a bit of cheek."

"I can appreciate the female anatomy, can't I? Besides, we're fellow gamers."

"How did you know it was me?" I asked, halting any further discussion about my bottom.

"Your voice. It is unique." He tapped on his controller, pulling up the avatar screen. "I heard you at the check-in table."

"Really?" Next time I saw Luke, I'd keep my big mouth shut unless I needed to use it to kiss him.

"Where are you from?" Rez asked.

"Sacramento."

"I'm from Fresno. We're practically neighbors." Rez connected his headset and I did the same. "Have you played Dragontoon?"

"Yes. It's one of my favorites."

"I'm on the creative team. I'll work the check-in table tomorrow." Rez chose his avatar. "Good luck to you, woman of many faces."

I chuckled and chose my avatar, a green dragon, and played the game. During breaks, Rez got me up to speed on how to install multiple-player stations so teams could game together and online with other groups. I'd have to step up the internet speed at the bar, but I could see it working. Maybe in that old storeroom. It wasn't huge, but it was a start, and the washateria next door was one crapped-out dryer short of closing.

I tried to sound enthusiastic as Rez explained his setup, but even if I convinced Theo to sell Shadycade to me, I didn't have the money or the collateral for a loan. The storeroom wouldn't be big enough to make the money I'd need to buy gaming chairs, computers, flat-screens, not to mention an advertising budget to get the word out.

Currently, Rez worked his avatar, a cute blue hedgehog who wore a purple mask, to help me find a secret door. The furry guy was my ally right now, but as we closed in on the castle, it would be a battle between us for the win.

Luckily, there was no sign of the Python. We took down a pink dragon. That cotton candy avatar never had a chance. A player at the end of the table cursed and vacated his seat. I gave Hedgehog a high five. Three more levels, and I'd win this game. After killing Rez, of course.

Another avatar added at the bottom of the screen—a brilliant gold dragon.

"Ha. Little late for Gold Dragon to join the game." I threw a poisoned dart at another player and missed by inches. He'd never catch up with me and Hedgehog.

"The Gold Dragon, it's Python." Rez's voice escalated beside me.

"Don't let him get behind you." We took out another player with a ball of fire and a karate kick from Hedgehog. The kid had skills, I'd give him that, but he wasn't catching all the power bars. I found a triple-pointer in the last level.

"Python just leveled up. He's gaining on us." Rez stammered and missed another power bar.

"Don't worry. We're still way ahead of that snake." We fought devil rabbits around a volcano, Hedgehog taking out two at a time and using his last power boost.

"Big mistake, kid. You still need a power boost to defeat me." The high-pitched, synthesized voice echoed in my headset. Python sounded like Little Bo Peep in a rock band, which startled me, causing a fireball to singe my wing.

Gold Dragon leveled up quickly. Python appeared on my screen, wiping out the competition with fire and finesse. He came after Hedge-hog. Took him out with a bolt of lightning, poor little guy.

"How did he get to our level so quickly?" I drew an arrow and loaded my bow.

"He's found a shortcut." Rez leaned in, watching my screen. "Stay on the path." Gold Dragon blocked my way. He breathed fire at me, and I jumped sideways. Ha! Python! "You missed me."

"Watch out," Rez screeched, but it was too late. I'd stepped off the path right into quicksand. My dragon died a slow, humiliating death.

The gold dragon took a victory lap doing a flyby over my humiliated dragon.

"Dammit!" I glanced around the room, looking for a player with a smug look on their face. I wanted to see the Python.

Rez noticed me scouting the room. "He's not here. He hacks into the game."

"That's cowardly of him."

"He played in DOTA 2 last year and scooped up a ten-thousand-dollar prize from team OG. Then he donated it to charity. That's what he does. Squeezes out the competition right before they win the game."

Dang. Defense of the Ages 2 was a high-level game. The most famous gamers in the world played that game and won beaucoups of cash.

"You're real good. You would make many people very happy if you could beat him."

Before I could pay attention to a video game hacking Python, I had other mountains to climb. "Maybe one day, but right now, I need sleep."

I said goodbye to Rez and turned in my headset. The truth was, I wasn't tired. In fact, my postcoital nap left me with oodles of energy. I had to read Raylynn's book. I promised Jerry. I trudged toward the elevator and wished the gold dragon would swoop down and carry me away to a land without worries, without stress, and without unreliable, dishonest men.

I thought about Luke. He wasn't dishonest, not with those innocent blue eyes and that charming dimple in his chin.

Nope. I'm not going down that road.

Call it what it is, a Con-fling. A one-night stand. OK, I hoped it turned into two or even three sex-filled nights, but it had no future. Besides, Luke didn't do long-distance relationships. He told me straight up.

I doubled up the armor protecting my heart. Luke Sky Walker would not pierce it with that husky, sunrise-over-a-mountain morning voice or quick-witted banter. I was in control this time.

Chapter Twenty-Two

Luke

"Walker wins again." I pulled my headset down, resting it on my neck, and leaned against the pillow on my bed. Gaming came naturally to me. It was a release from my hectic world. A place where I had control instead of Jean-Claude.

I preferred gaming on my laptop instead of joining in the Con crowds. Red was out there somewhere. After work, I'd searched the gaming rooms for her in that sexy Chun Li costume, with no luck. Honestly, she'd gotten the best of me this afternoon. Yeah, I'd been on pain meds, but there wasn't a medication that could have kept my hands off her. I'd learned the hard way long-distance relationships never worked, but when I thought of Red, I wished they did.

My jaw ached along with my heart. I worked it absentmindedly and claimed the prize was worth the pain. I told my aching heart it was too soon. She was only a woman who would leave this Con and never look back. She'd return to Sacramento and run her gaming bar. I'd work at my store and write the graphic novel I'd been working on for three years.

In between running the store, Jean-Claude's books, blog, and demands, there wasn't much time for anything else.

I glanced at the clock. Shit. It was after midnight. I'd be dragging ass tomorrow. At least until lunch.

I woke the next morning from a dream that included Red, a bottle of champagne, and a tub of Jell-O. I couldn't get this girl off my mind. We hadn't selected a restaurant for our lunch date, but I didn't want to come off desperate, like I couldn't wait to see her, even though that's exactly how I felt.

After a cold shower followed by a long, hot shower, I checked my closet for today's cosplayer outfit. Thanks to my dads, I had all the Luke Skywalker costumes. His sandy-colored moisture farmer clothes, his X-wing pilot suit, Rebel Luke, Hoth outfit, Training outfits, Jedi Knight, and Jedi Master.

My chin still ached slightly, and I massaged the bruise shadowing my jawbone. I had forgone shaving in hopes a bit of scruff disguised my new battle trophy and chose the X-wing pilot costume with the helmet. I'd carry the helmet because the pressure against my jaw would increase the pain, but if I ran into my dads, I'd slip it on. If they saw my bruise, Steve would fret unnecessarily, and Paul would insist I get checked out at the ER.

Jean-Claude had a book signing this morning. I'd help out at the booth, do crowd control, then I'd text Red. Allow just enough time for her to be concerned I wasn't going to follow through. At least, I hoped she'd be concerned.

When I arrived at the booth, the book signing was well underway. A security guard stood at a distance, monitoring the crowd. Marty collected the money from those purchasing the newest Cabaliér sci-fi graphic novel. I'd worked hard on that novel and considered it my best work. Too bad I wouldn't get any credit.

Jean-Claude was deep in conversation with a cosplayer dressed as Gamora from Guardians of the Galaxy. The tight black leather pants fit like the skin on a grape over the tight ass leaning across the table to hear what stupidity Jean-Claude offered up this morning.

I moved into the booth behind the signing table, aiming to tell Jean-Claude about the line of waiting and slightly annoyed people behind the green-skinned Gamora double.

When she glanced up, those green lasers opened wide. "Luke."

My surprised smile turned into a concerned frown at her deep conversation with Jean-Claude. "Hey, Red. Looking for me?"

"Uhm...no. I mean, it's good to see you, but Jean-Claude asked me to stop by. He's interested in investing in my bar." She straightened and took in the booth. The giant Cronman blowup I'd had mounted on top of the booth, much to Jean-Claude's dissatisfaction.

"Wowzah, watermelon martini! Is this the booth for your store?"

I grinned at her choice of words.

"I see you've met my associate, Luke." Jean-Claude's mouth drew up into a wormy smile. "He can tell you what it's like working for me."

"With you," I added, even though it was true. I did ghostwrite for him, but his investment in my store was a partnership. Something he couldn't wrap that thick skull around.

Red paused. If she was surprised, she didn't show it. A small smile crept at the corner of her mouth. "That would be great. How about over lunch?"

I held back the goofy smile that threatened to ruin my macho Jedi Pilot image and went with a casual head nod.

"Sure, sure, take her to lunch." Jean-Claude tapped his watch. "Be back for the afternoon shift." As if the bastard knew the schedule or had anything to do with it.

We ate at a small coffee shop. Sandwiches and lattes. I barely touched my ham and Swiss on rye. The idea of her working with Jean-Claude made my stomach burn. I ran over scenarios on how to warn her about him.

"Where did you meet Jean-Claude?" I asked, hoping she hadn't already signed a contract with him.

"Yesterday, in the elevator. He told me he invests in small businesses and supports the arts. Does he support your store?"

"Yeah, he's an investor."

She looked at me over her Reuben. "Seems by the tone of your voice you don't care for him all that much."

"He's the famous critic that reviews books on his blog."

"I know. He reviewed the R.D. Sayer book. Ruthless, but somewhat correct. I had to agree with him. Sayer does need to get out of the house."

"He said that?" Those were my words. I'd written them in my review. Though he'd changed them to say that Sayer lacked drive, wrote unflattering characters, and lived in a glass bottle.

"Yep. I'm, um...rereading the book to check out his assessment." She fiddled with her coffee straw. Stirred the contents of her latte. A band of cosplayers dressed as Marvel characters caught her eye, and she turned slightly to watch them walk by the café.

I stared at her profile. Her straight nose had a cute, pointed tip and a small bump in the middle of the bridge. Not R.D. Sayer. I blew out a massive sigh of relief.

"Whoa. That was a balmy breath. Got something on your mind?"

"Even though Jean-Claude is my partner, I have to warn you about him. He's crass and annoying as hell to work with. I wouldn't consider anything he has to offer."

"Did your deal with him go south?"

"Not exactly. I own 50 percent of the store. I hope to buy him out next year. But he doesn't relinquish control easily. And he'll make your life a living inferno if he has any say in how you run the bar."

"Inferno, huh?" She poked playfully at my warning.

"You think the dungeons of Minecraft are a bottomless pit. Jean-Claude will spit fire and brimstone at you and then serve you dessert."

"OK, I'll be careful *if* I deal with him."

"Red." I raked a hand over my hair, wishing I could yank it out to get my point across to her. "Don't deal with him."

She stiffened. Her full seductive lips turned down into a how-dare-you pout. "I can handle my business deals."

I wasn't technically ordering her not to deal with Jean-Claude. Just giving her a heads-up. And why wouldn't she tell me her name? "I'm concerned about you. The last guy you partnered with ran off with your money, right?"

"He wasn't a partner, and I chalked it up to a lesson learned." She finished off her Reuben. Chewed her thoughts. "Once bitten, twice shy. Isn't that how the saying goes?" She placed her hand over mine. "I appreciate your concern."

I interlocked my finger in hers.

"Now that we've had three lunch dates and one afternoon of glorious sex, I'd say your secrets are safe with me." I sent her a smile that I hoped she interpreted as the third time's a charm.

"Three lunch dates don't warrant a confession of all my sins." She finessed her hand out of my grasp. Picked up her coffee cup.

"You know what I mean. Is there a reason you can't tell me your name? Like a married reason? I'm not a homewrecker."

She gathered her trash, making a move to leave. "I told you before. There's no one else in my life. I promise to tell you the last day of the Con. I can explain my reason then and you'll understand."

Or I won't. Wasn't that what she was afraid of?

I didn't want her to leave. I wanted to see her again. I wanted to have sex with her again. To be with her. To see those green eyes filled with lust and desire for me.

"You claim you're a decent gamer." My voice hinted at a challenge.

"Decent." She snorted. "I'm better than decent."

"Why don't you prove it? I'm pretty good. Meet me tonight at one of the gaming booths. If you beat me, I'll take you back to your room and do whatever your heart desires."

"Sounds like a win for you too." Another snort. The cuteness of it made me want to lean in and kiss her. Instead, I leaned back. Stared straight into those suspicious eyes. "If I beat you, you tell me your name."

"I get to pick the game?" Her tone sounded iffy she'd take the bet, but then she cocked a challenging dark green eyebrow an inch.

"Sure."

"Dragontoon. It's on the mezzanine level."

"You've been playing there?"

"Once or twice."

I narrowed my eyes at her. "Have you already won the game?"

"I've done well a few times, but a hacker called Python prevented me from reaching the castle. He's annoying. Almost as bad as Jean-Claude." She wrinkled her nose. Her cute, straight nose with a bump.

I chuckled at my unnecessary sleuthing. No way was this girl Sayer. "Sure, what time? I work the booth until nine."

"Nine will do. And let me know if you see Chris Pratt. He's your only competition for my affection."

"I can take on Star-Lord any day of the week."

"We'll see how good you are." She stood, flipped a strand of her Gamora wig over her shoulder. "Better rest those hands, Skywalker. I'll need at least an hour massage after I win the bet." She turned and strode toward the door.

I chewed my coffee straw as I watched her strut away. Win or lose. Either way, I was leveling up tonight.

Chapter Twenty-Three

Jade

I slid into the seat beside Jerry at the next panel. He turned toward me and nodded approvingly at my costume. "How's it going, my green-faced Gamora protégé?"

"It's going good." I held up my hands and wiggled my green fingers. "These are cool." I wore faux leather cuffs at the wrist of the see-through opera gloves that gave my skin the green Gamora appearance. They limited my use of body paint to my face and chest.

Jerry grabbed my hand and examined his workmanship. "I thought so. You look over-the-galaxy fabulous, by the way. I outdid myself."

"I do, and you did." My tight leather pants and matching jacket had made Luke's jaw drop to the floor. "I've had several people stop and take pictures with me, including two Star-Lord wannabes."

"Haven't found the real deal?"

"Nope. Raylynn's promise I'd meet Chris Pratt is running out of time."

"Keep your hopes up, doll." Jerry thumbed through the papers in front of him. "He's bound to be here. The entire Guardians cast is signing on Saturday. I don't know why you'd be interested in Pratt when you have that hot Jedi warming your sheets."

"Luke is a Con-fling. That's all." Maybe.

"Uh-huh," Jerry commented in the same tone he'd used in seventh-grade science class as he studied every detail of the frog we'd fileted. Time to change the subject before he began dissecting my love life.

I glanced around the room, taking in the crowd. There were more people dressed business casual than cosplayers in attendance. "So, what's this panel about?"

"Business." He stopped flipping pages and showed me an outline of the current session. "I wanted Raylynn to hear about all the things required to market her books, like book signings and personal appear-ances, making videos for TikTok, Facebook, and Instagram. She can't keep hiding away if she wants to be successful. That might have worked back in the day, but it's not working now."

"I agree. Even the bar needs a social media presence to be successful. I'm thinking about making some short videos interviewing the Barflies. Do a tour of the bar. Show clips of the gaming room I want to install. You know, those kinds of things. Create some interest." I was talking with my hands and, at the same time, admiring the way the fake green skin on my arms reflected the fluorescent lights overhead.

"That's a great idea. I hope you can get it all done before Theo decides to sell. The last time I was there, he was browsing brochures for Costa Rica."

"Double-scotch on the rocks damnation! Are you sure?"

"I'd bet money he'll sell before the year's end. He's got that wander-lust look in his eyes."

"How can I stifle that lust until I can raise enough money?" I slumped back in my chair. The confident vibe I had wearing the Gamora costume deflated like the Hindenburg.

"You'll come up with something."

"Who am I kidding? Since they put the highway through the south end of town, real estate has become a bidding war. And even though we're not on the highway, the property value is increasing daily. I'll never be able to match Theo's price. My days of running a local bar are numbered." And my dream of owning one? An illusion.

"Gamora wouldn't let a little money stand in the way of getting what she wants." Jerry patted my shoulder. "Pay attention to this panel and maybe you'll pick up a few good tips to help you with your social media."

Here was my segue to tell Jerry I might ask Jean-Claude for advice. He was going to be mad. I took a deep breath, called on my inner Gamora for courage, and went for it. "I, um, met someone here who invests in small businesses. He said he could help me with my social media presence. He's an investor in Luke's comic bookstore."

"Luke Skyyyyywalker," Jerry added a southern drawl to Luke's name and batted his lashes at me.

"Stop it. I'd never get gooey over a guy."

Jerry's eyebrow raised an inch.

"OK, maybe in the past, I've gotten a little too involved, a little too fast."

"Honey, you give Fast and Furious an entirely new meaning." He held up his hand, stalling my rebuttal. "The guy writes a good comic. I'll give him that. Did his investor cost the moon? Most of those guys charge high fees or high percentages. Read the fine print." He turned his attention to the class agenda.

"It's Jean-Claude Cabaliér." I mumbled the name, hoping Jerry had lost interest.

Jerry stilled, then shot me a look. The same look of disgust I'd seen on his face when Zayn Malik left One Direction for a solo career. "Jade, you can't be serious. That guy is a total fibber. Look at what he did to Raylynn, your sister. How could you consider hiring him to help you with the bar?"

"I'm not thinking about hiring him. I'm thinking about picking his brain. Maybe something will leak out that I can use."

"He excels at retrieving information. He's like the Barbara Walters of book critics. I think you're mental. The guy is bad news. He'll know all your secrets in five minutes, and it will be the end of me."

"Chill out, Jerry. I'll be careful. Don't you trust me?"

Jerry removed a handkerchief from his jacket pocket and dabbed it at his forehead. "Between you hanging out with Cabaliér's boy Friday and Raylynn's MIA stunt, I'm up to two gin and tonics before bed."

"What do you mean by Luke and Cabaliér?"

"They work together. I knew I'd seen Luke somewhere. He's always tagging along when Jean-Claude has a book signing or an appearance. I wouldn't be surprised if your boy wrote Cabaliér's books. They're way beyond that arrogant asshole's skillset."

"Luke is not Jean-Claude's errand boy. Jean-Claude's a partner in his store and doing a fine job of it. Luke's in prime retail space in San Diego. Their relationship couldn't be that bad."

"What did Luke say about Jean-Claude?"

"He compared him to Satan and warned me to stay away."

Jerry gave me the mark my words omniscient agent side-eye. "You should take his advice."

I scrunched down in my chair. "Jean-Claude wants to meet with me tomorrow."

"Did you tell Luke you were meeting with the devil?"

"It's not that I haven't told him. It's that it's none of Luke's business. And, besides, I haven't made up my mind if I'm going to talk to Jean-Claude or not."

"Do us both a favor. Skip the meeting with Cabaliér. Nothing good will come of it."

"Nothing good will come if I don't find a way to make enough money to buy the bar either. And by not good, I mean Shadycade will be turned into an Applebee's."

"Applebee's has a bar." Jerry turned toward the front as the moderator for the panel picked up the microphone to introduce the speaker. "They also have an excellent shrimp and spinach salad."

Traitor.

I took a break from the Con and returned to my room. I dropped my stash of freebies on the bed. Notepads, pens, stickers, gaming brochures, business cards, and a few free comic books from new writers hoping to break into the clique. How often had Luke had to give away his work for free before *Cronman* was published?

I thought *Cronman* was released last year. I remembered seeing it in the comic bookstore by my house. I couldn't recall ever seeing it before. Did Jean-Claude have enough clout to boost Luke's indie comic to a bestseller?

I turned away from the sack of loot and made Ray's book a priority. I sat in the chair and tried not to think about the way Luke made love to me in that chair. And on the bed. And on the floor.

"Oh, for stymied screwdriver! I've got to get out of here so I can concentrate." I took the book and a Coke from the small fridge in my room and headed toward the lounge area by the elevators on my floor.

After reading two more chapters, I realized the main character wasn't entirely me. There was a lot of Ray in here too. The heroine had a crooked nose that she hated and blamed on her sister. I chuckled, recalling the time in middle school when I coaxed Raylynn to ride on the handlebars of my bike. We hit a bump in the road. She went flying, landed on her face, and broke her nose in two places. Mom grounded me for a month.

"At least you had surgery to fix the hump on your bridge and added a cute little flip to the end of your nose." My mumbling over the dive into my past quickly faded away as I was pulled into the love story like a giant black hole sucking me into its vortex.

The elevator dinged in the outer rim of my mind, but I didn't want to quit reading to acknowledge any passing guests.

"Good book?"

My heart leaped into my throat and stuck there like an irritating piece of popcorn at the familiar voice. I swallowed hard and looked up into the beady eyes of Jean-Claude.

"Um... It's not bad." I closed the book and tried to cover the title with my hand.

Jean-Claude's eyes widened when he saw the front cover. "You're better off reading the tabloids. This book has no substance."

I bristled but reminded myself to control my temper. "I don't know. The characters seem to love each other."

Jean-Claude huffed. "When I met you in the elevator, you scolded me for leaving that bad review. I was under the assumption you'd read the book."

"I've read some of it." That was the truth. "I'm finishing the last few chapters."

"It's a ridiculous premise. You should be meeting with me about your failing business instead of wasting your time with that twaddle."

"About that—"

"Sunday at 1:00 p.m. I'll have time after the last panel. I'm scheduled to appear as the celebrity guest."

"Wow. Celebrity guest. You must be a good person to know." Had he been good for Luke?

"Of course, I am. Why else would they have me on the panel?" He squinted at me. "Are you sure we've never met before the Con? You seem familiar."

"Positive. Besides, you've never seen me out of costume. How do you know what I look like?" I leaned back, hugging the book to my chest.

"It's not your looks exactly. It's your mannerisms. And that quick wit. It reminds me of someone." A glint of recognition sparked in his eyes. Then he shook his head. "No. That's impossible."

Change the subject, Jade. Jerry's warning about Jean-Claude digging into my secrets made my heart start skipping rope.

"What are you doing up here?" I tried to keep my tone and my hands steady.

"I have a meeting on this floor." He glanced at his watch. "Excuse me, or I'll be late. I despise late. See you Sunday."

"Yeah. Sure. Sunday."

Speaking of late, Sunday after the panel would be too late. If Raylynn didn't show up, he'd meet the real me. I'd have to ditch my meeting and any help he might possibly be able to give me. Damn.

I watched him walk down the hall. He was heading toward my room. I gulped and shot to my feet. What if he'd found out where R.D. Sayer was staying? "Gossipy hotel staff. What happened to guest privacy?"

I peeked around the corner. He stopped two doors down from mine. Straightened his jacket and his spine. Knocked.

Jerry's voice greeted my sister's evil arch-enemy and invited him inside. My mouth flew open, and I jerked back around the corner, hiding from my best friend. How could Jerry meet with him? Was he ditching Raylynn for Jean-Claude? Was he taking on Jean-Claude as a client?

I ran down the hall to the sanctuary of my room. I slammed the door and sagged against it, my heartbeat going from simple jump rope to full-on Double Dutch. Clutching Raylynn's book, I drew a few deep breaths and tried to steady myself.

Jerry warned me not to meet with Jean-Claude, and here he was doing just that. Jerry had secrets too. It was time for Gamora to use a lifeline and call the one person who could make Raylynn come out of her cave and take responsibility for herself. I tossed the book on the bed and dug my cell phone out of my pocket.

"I'm calling the mothership."

Chapter Twenty-Four

Jade

When my mom was diagnosed with MS, Raylynn was working on her master's degree and I was getting my bartending certificate. Raylynn left New York and her degree behind and moved back to Sacramento. Mom was devastated Raylynn didn't finish her MFA, but Raylynn said she didn't need a master's degree to be a bestselling author. She was right.

I always thought there was more behind the sudden dismissal of the degree she'd worked so hard for, but when I asked, Raylynn was tight-lipped about her life in New York. I knew she'd had a crush on a guy there. I didn't think it ever went further than Raylynn fawning over him in class.

When it became difficult for Mom to walk, Raylynn paid for her therapy in a fancy care facility and a private nurse moved into my old room. I couldn't afford to help financially, so I took Mom on trips to the zoo, art exhibits, dinner at her favorite Italian restaurant, and occasional movies. She only wanted to see romantic movies where one of the main characters died. Totally depressing, but I struggled through them for her.

I hated asking Mom to call Raylynn, but I knew Ray would answer her call. I took a deep breath of courage, hit Mom's number, and added tattletale to my list of shameful qualities.

After a nice chat with Mom, learning she wasn't having a flare, I spilled my guts. I could almost hear Mom's mouth twist to the side. A thing she did when she was annoyed.

"I'll get in touch with Ray." The sound of Mom finger pecking on her computer followed.

"Mom, Raylynn's in writer mode. She won't answer an email."

"I'm scheduling a car. I'll go down tomorrow. This requires a personal appearance."

"Mom, no. I didn't mean you had to get out. I thought maybe you could call her."

"Ray will have her phone turned off. Remember the last time I fell? You had to break into her house to tell her I was in the hospital."

"She doesn't do that anymore. She has it silenced, but your number has breakthrough rights." My number used to be on Raylynn's emergency ring even if in silenced mode until I called too many times, interrupting Ray's writing with my soap opera–life problems.

"Nonetheless. Tomorrow's supposed to be a beautiful sunshiny day and I needed a reason to get some fresh air." Mom sounded determined. "Don't worry. Geneva will go with me."

Uh boy. Geneva, a feisty Black woman who pushed Mom to exercise and made the world's best chocolate chip cookies, became Mom's caretaker when Raylynn's career escalated. She was the grandmother I'd always wished for and could get things done with a look and a lifted eyebrow.

The image of Mom on her walker with Geneva's plus-sized body beside her pushing through Raylynn's door, both women demanding Ray stop writing and go to the Con, made my head hurt.

I twisted my bottom lip back and forth between my top teeth. A visit from Mom would force Raylynn to, at the very least, call me, but at the cost of ripping me a new one.

"Jade, quit chewing your lip. It'll be fine."

I stared at my phone, making sure I hadn't accidentally activated FaceTime. "Couldn't you just call her?"

"It's high time I paid her a visit. I'll figure out what has Raylynn on lockdown this time, after she showers, of course. You know how it is when she writes for days."

Ray would be holed up with her comfort foods, Cool Ranch Doritos, Raisinettes, and Moon Pies. After a few days of intense writing, she reeked of stale marshmallows and artificial seasonings.

I blew out a long, grateful breath of resignation. "Thanks, Mom. I owe you one."

"The new Nicholas Sparks movie is out next week. I'd love to go."

"Done deal." The agony of watching another damaged character die was worth it if Mom could roust Raylynn. This twin charade needed to end. I wanted to show Luke the real me.

"So, who's the new man in your life?" Mom's tone filled with the assurance a mom gets during an interrogation.

"How do you know there's a new man?"

"You had that lilt to your voice when you talked about the Con. It carries too much excitement to be a rekindling with Girlie Cocktail."

"You call Big Mike that too?"

"If the dress fits...."

"He never wore dresses, did he?"

Mom gave an *I wouldn't be surprised if he did* chuckle into the phone. "He wasn't the guy for you, Jade. Now, tell me about whoever has your heartstrings strumming and is worth calling me to intervene in one of the twin schemes."

I paused, deciding how much to tell. Luke was only a fling. I didn't want Mom to get excited and start buying baby clothes on Amazon. "His name is Luke. I barely know him. And get this, his middle name is Sky, and his last name is Walker."

"Sounds like the perfect guy for my sci-fi loving daughter. Just don't get sucked into his galaxy before he's vetted by the family."

"I doubt if I'll see him after the Con. It's just a fling."

"Uh-huh." Mom didn't sound convinced. "Have fun. You've always wanted to go to a Comic-Con. Make the most of it."

"Thanks."

She told me she loved me and blew smooches into the phone. I returned the *I love you* and thumbed off. I smacked the phone against my forehead a few times. Raylynn was going to kick my butt from here to the moon.

After touching up my green Gamora face, I left for the gaming room.

"Time to take on the Jedi." I intended to win and get that one-hour back massage followed by a night of passion and some cuddling. Maybe.

I arrived at the gaming booth but didn't see Luke. I'd start playing. Get in a bit of practice before he arrived.

Rez was working the desk. A bouncy blonde in front of me giggled at him. "I just love your Mexican accent."

"I am from India. There is a difference." Rez frowned and pushed the headset at her.

"Super cute." She took them and blew him a kiss as she stepped toward the gaming room.

He looked up at me, and it took a full minute before a hint of recognition crossed his face. He broke into a grin. "Namaste. Good to see you again. Dat is very nice costume."

"Thanks." I smiled back, also loving his accent. "But you recognized me, so the costume didn't do its job."

"Doubt I would recognize you out of costume. Are you a famous actor trying to be incognito?"

"No, I swear."

"No need to swear. Here's your headset." He handed me a disinfected one. "Station two is open."

"Can you save a seat for a guy I'm trying to annihilate?"

"Sure." Rez smiled wide, and his teeth showed bright white under the fluorescent lights. "Can't wait to see you demolish another avatar. Hopefully, the Python won't show up and squash your victory."

I held up crossed fingers. "This guy will be dressed as Luke Skywalker." I wrapped the headset around my neck and found station two.

I was into the game, focused on my level and throwing fireballs at a troll. Suddenly, a red dragon appeared behind the troll, scorching the troll's ass and eliminating him from the game.

"Hello, beautiful," rumbled into my headset. I glanced up and saw the controller of the new dragon at the station across from mine. Luke still wore the Jedi Knight X-wing fighter costume. His eyes locked on mine. A glimmer of challenge lurked behind them, followed by a cocky smirk.

My dragon yelped, and I jerked my eyes away from Luke and back to my screen. My dragon caught a lightning bolt in the wing. Dammit. Luke's not going to seduce me with those baby blues. I focused on the game and sent a blast of fire-filled breath at the troll who dared challenge me.

"My girl's badass," Luke purred into my headset. I fought off the almost orgasm induced by his silky, seductive voice.

A new level appeared, and Luke took the fortified manor, wiping out several armed Wolverines along the way. His timing and ability impressed me. "Wow, my guy's pretty badass, too."

Unfortunately, he claimed some powerful weapons with the raid. "Sorry, sexy, but I'm one step closer to having my way with you."

Damn.

"Oh. Jeez. Would you guys get a room and let me win the game?" The whiny voice interrupted my snarky reply to Luke's warning. A thin guy dressed as Harry Potter glared across the table at me. I pegged him as the Centaur.

An older woman to my right and not in costume sent a smug, wise-old-woman smile my way. She was the seer. And it could present a problem if she saw the way to the castle before I found it. We were the last four left in the game. I looked at my screen in time to see a fireball hit my tail.

Dark and Stormy darn dialogue distraction!

I eliminated Harry Potter first. I knew the Centaur didn't have much power. I turned my green dragon toward Luke. We were both going for the seer. I wanted her to find the castle and then wipe her out.

Luke cut me off, protecting the seer. He had the same idea I did, but he wasn't going to eliminate me first. My body shivered, recalling that thing he did between the sheets. I reminded myself that my name was on the line. This entire deceptive fuckery could blow up in my face for making this bet.

Stupid. Stupid. Stupid.

I threw a power grenade at him. He dodged and returned a stream of fire. The seer hit him with her staff from behind. He turned to defend.

"I'll get you now, my pretty." I pulled out my secret weapon. I'd been saving it for the castle conquest, but beating Luke was more important. I accessed my invisibility cloak, and my dragon vanished from the screen.

I heard a cheer behind me and caught a crowd forming, watching the game on the big screen. "What the fudge?" the seer squeaked into my headset. I felt Luke's eyes on me.

I drew my sword and sent it into the red dragon's heart, causing instant death. An inaudible noise sounded from Luke, and his dragon lay dead, eliminated. My dragon appeared back on the screen. The seer found a secret door. I threw a fireball at her and stopped her from the quest. I felt a twinge of guilt for killing the old lady as I flew through the door and placed my flag on the castle. The game showed my dragon receiving her crown of victory along with the keys to the castle.

"She kicked your ass." A pimply-faced boy standing behind me grinned at Luke.

Luke pulled off his headset. "That gives her a hat trick this week."

He was referring to our romp in the bedroom, not something I wanted a crowd of gamers to hear. I pulled off my headset and squinted my eyes at him.

"For real?" The boy looked down at me. "You got some sweet skills, lady. Are you on the circuit?"

"No. I just love to play."

We turned in our headsets, thanked Rez, and I told him I'd be in touch.

Luke walked with me out of the convention hall. "Normally, I hate to admit defeat, but this time, I'm looking forward to the spoils of war."

I sent him a cheeky grin. I was thankful I could keep my identity one more night. "How did you level up so quickly? I was playing before you got there and planned on starting over, to be fair."

"I've been playing the beta version for a while. There's a back door that skips a few levels. You have to beat a nasty troll to access it, but it got me to your level pretty quick."

I glanced at my phone. It was half past eleven. "I didn't realize it was so late. Maybe we should postpone my intense one-hour, deep tissue, aromatherapeutic massage for another night."

"Not for all the gold in the castle." Luke interlocked his fingers in mine and increased his stride toward the elevator.

Oh boy!

Chapter Twenty-Five

Luke

I pulled Red close in the empty elevator. Her Gamora costume transformed her into a mystical creature stealing my thoughts, my soul, my heart.

"Don't get too worked up, Skywalker. I intend to collect on every second of our bet." Her green eyes stared up at mine with a hint of mischief.

I ran my fingers up her arm, tipped her chin upward, and kissed her. Our lips fit perfectly together. The perfect kiss. I could taste the free peppermint candy she'd swiped off Rez's table after the game.

Her fingers carded through my hair. The moan that escaped from my throat sounded feral. I couldn't help myself. She ignited parts of me I didn't know existed. Her body pressed into mine, pinning me against the wall. My breath came heavy, and my palms sweated as if I were back in middle school and this was my first kiss.

Jeez, Walker. Slow down. Take a minute. You don't even know her name.

My body didn't listen to reason. My hand searched for the emergency stop. I wanted her here, right now, against the mirrored walls.

The elevator binged to a stop. Our lips separated, but she remained snuggled against me. I glanced in the mirrored wall and caught her green paint smeared on my left cheek. "You're rubbing off on me."

A man, an executive type who smelled of whiskey and cigar smoke, stepped inside. From the looks of him, he'd been at the complimentary happy hour at the bar and stayed. Now, probably on his way to one of the many Con parties. He looked at our costumes and the way I held Red. He shook his head.

"Aren't you two from different universes? Not sure a crossover would work. Star-Lord's going to be angry his main girl's smooching in the elevator with the competition." He gut chuckled as he tapped a card against the reader and pushed the button for the penthouse. Great. An alcohol-induced comedian. This dude thought he was hilarious.

Red released me and angled her chin up at the man. "Gamora chooses who she wants to kiss."

"Is that so." The guy ran his eyes down Red's body.

I pushed away from my irritated slouch against the mirrors and stood to my full height, ignoring the reflection of a jealous tirade brewing on my face.

The flash of a sober thought appeared in his eyes, and he changed tactics.

"You two going to the Dark Horse party in the executive suite?"

"No." My tone shouted *back off, dude, or we'll see if these mirrors are shatterproof.*

He took a step back. I leaned against the elevator's crash rail. When did I get so possessive? I'd never reacted like that when my ex got hit on, and that was all the time. I folded my arms across my chest.

The guy dug into his suit jacket pocket and handed Red a card. "Mention my name, and it'll get you in. I work for the company."

Damn. If he weren't such a douche, he'd be a good contact for me. That party would be an excellent place to mingle with the industry people. Get my name out there.

"Thanks." Red smiled at the guy. The elevator stopped on her floor, and I led her off. The guy gave me an apologetic head nod. So maybe not a douche, after all, just a bit buzzed. He looked on in envious silence.

She stopped me outside her door and turned toward me. "Do you want to go to the party? It could be good for your career." Red palmed her key card and looked up at me. Her lips, swollen from my kisses, parted slightly. My manhood signaled going to the party was a big, hard no.

It meant something that she was willing to give up an hour massage followed by what I hoped was a night of intense sex to help my career. "Nope. I lost the game. I don't want to prevent you from collecting the spoils of victory." I removed the key card from her hand and tapped the door lock.

The smile I received had me scooping her up, long legs wrapping around me as I walked us into her hotel room. Our mouths pressed together in a repeat performance of the elevator. I was never going to ride an elevator again without thinking of her. I saw lots of stairs in my future.

I didn't mind lowering my standards and throwing the game. Red played good, almost too good. She challenged me in more ways than the game, but I could have beaten her with my pouch of magic sand. Throwing it would have revealed her invisibility cloak. I would have won the game, the bet, her name. But if that had happened, I doubt we would be walking into her room, pulling our clothes off as we went.

I balanced against the desk, kissing her into a senseless stupor. Fire burned in my core, threatening to explode like the Death Star in *Return of the Jedi*. I wanted her, every inch of her. I willed my knees to hold steady and not buckle, taking us both to the floor. She did that to me. She made me weak. I worked the buttons on her vest. She fumbled with the chest box that made the X-wing costume look like the real deal.

She laughed when we both stood topless, working the knot on my costume's drawstring. "You're half-Hulk, half-Jedi."

I looked down at the green paint on my abdomen and guessed my face held more too. "Beware. If my Hulk side comes out, you'll see the savage side of me."

"Promise?" She ran her teeth across my jaw, nipped at my ear.

Damn, this girl.

I cupped her breasts with my hands, caressed with my mouth. I kissed up the curve of her neck to her ear and whispered naughty things I wanted to do to her.

She dropped my pants to the floor with a victory yelp and stroked my length, matching my dirty talk. Red had me begging, begging, begging for her to do those things. She was the Hulk and I a helpless Padawan waiting for my master to give orders.

She gasped as I sucked her earlobe and dipped into her panties. I groaned, anxious and disappointed, when her hand had me almost to climax. I stilled her hand and fumbled for the string of plastic packages I'd left, with high hopes, on the dresser the day before. Tore one off with my teeth, and she did the rest.

I moved her legs up, around me, entering her dampness. I balanced her ass on the desk, praying the thing wouldn't break in half. The heat surged between us, again and again, and again, as she led me into a wild-fire of passion.

"Good thing I lost," I said, lying sweaty and breathless on the bed after round two of our vigorous intimacy. "It was life-changing."

"Really?" She propped up on her elbow, the sheet falling away from her full breasts. My dick twitched, and I couldn't believe my body wanted another go. This girl did things to me I couldn't control.

"You bet." I held those green eyes for longer than I intended, and she looked away.

I rolled to my side and matched her angle. "So, how about you tell me your name?"

"That would be cheating. You lost the game. And now"—she rolled onto her stomach, her head turned away from me, and her arms angled next to her head—"I want my promised prize. An hour back massage, buddy, that was the deal."

I moved next to her.

"My favorite lotion is just there, on the nightstand." She pointed without turning her head. After our last round, where she sat on top of me and made me work my abs better than a personal trainer, I was happy to take a break.

I straddled her, poured the scented lotion into my palm and rubbed it between my hands to warm it up. Clean citrus flooded my nostrils, like a beach on an early summer morning. The smell of her. I smoothed my hands across her back, and she purred, not like a kitten, but like a panther satisfied with its most recent kill.

"You're good at this." She hummed out the words.

"I'm good at a lot of things."

"I know." She giggle-snorted, then we both laughed.

I wanted to know her. I wanted this to be more than a weekend of sex. More than a Con-fling. Just more. I took a deep breath and went for it. "Maybe I can guess your name." She stiffened but didn't respond.

"Is it...Amy?"

She lifted her head and glanced at me over her shoulder. "Do I look like an Amy?"

I laughed at her green face. We'd smudged her makeup, and she looked like a wicked warrior queen. It went well with the load of smutty words she'd yelled during sex.

"Nah, too pure." I tried again. "How about Haley?"

"No."

"Loretta?"

"Am I sixty?"

"Right, a little old-fashioned." I worked a tight spot on her shoulder, and she moaned.

"Give it up, Luke. You'll never guess my name, and I don't want to tell even if you did."

"Why not? If you're famous, I can keep a secret." My stomach tightened. Unless she's R.D. Sayer. But I was confident. Red was not Sayer. Sayer was a recluse. A mean-spirited hag who couldn't write a hero to save her life. If Sayer had written half the words Red had shouted out in passion last night, she'd have another bestseller. Anyway, I had ruled her out by the cute nose.

"Luke?"

I missed a question. "Sorry, I was focused on the giant knot you have in your trap. It's like a stone."

"Yeah, carrying the weight of life leaves its mark."

"You can share with me. I'm a good listener."

"And a cuddler." She giggled and squirmed her way until she was face up under me. "Ready for round three?"

Oh, this girl. "Easy." I prayed for self-control. "I haven't finished the massage, and I'm not sure I can keep up with another round of Rodeo Red."

"Are you sure?" Her bottom lip puffed into a pout. "I'll save the second half of my winnings for tomorrow night if you'll do that thing I like."

I gathered her in my arms and nipped at her bottom lip. She teased with her tongue, then deepened an already endless kiss. A rush of lust poured into me, and I groaned.

"Feels like you're ready, cowboy." She lifted her pelvis, coaxing me inside her. With her spine arched, her inner muscles spasmed around me. I drove into her again, deeper with every thrust. Finally, when I couldn't wait another moment, she screamed my name.

I wanted to follow her. Call out to her in the blinding abysm where nothing mattered. But I had nothing.

Not even her name.

Chapter Twenty-Six

Jade

I woke the next morning in a tangle of sheets. My Gamora costume pooled on the floor. Luke's arm draped over me, spooning me tight. I grinned a big, cheeky grin. I knew he was a cuddler.

I'd done it again.

Twice.

A lot more than twice, my sore legs reminded me. I had a flash of sitting astride Luke, tormenting him with the results of my daily Kegels.

Twice, I'd invited Luke into my bed. I couldn't help myself. He was like a drug dealer, causing massive doses of lust hormones to dump into my system. I was the addict. Hopelessly addicted to those warm fuzzy feelings. These addictions never ended well for the addict.

He kissed my neck. "Good morning." His gravel-filled morning voice reverberated against my back.

I squirmed away from his spooning and turned toward him. "You stayed. All night." My voice went all squeaky on the words *all night*. In my experience, guys snuck out in the wee hours of the morning, avoiding that awkward after-sex conversation. Only Girlie Cocktail stayed the night, and that's what sold me on his commitment to me.

I couldn't have been more wrong.

"I did. And I must say. Round three of Rodeo Red did me in." He chuckled a husky, warm-hearted chuckle that sprang a picture in my mind. Us, sitting on a fur rug in front of a crackling fire, drinking wine, and playing Yahtzee. Was I ready to Yahtzee with this guy?

He rolled off the bed and padded toward the bathroom. "If I didn't have to work the booth this morning, I'd sleep until dinner."

The muscles carved around his ass like Michelangelo's *David*. Oh yeah, I'd Yahtzee.

"I'll order room service, OK?" I liked watching his back muscles ripple as he stopped and scooped up his clothes.

"Sounds great." His face split into a wide, mischievous-boy grin. He returned to the bed, holding his crumpled clothes in a heap in front of him, blocking what I considered his best asset. He leaned down and kissed me silly again. "Then you'll join me in the shower?"

"You betcha."

Joining him in the shower was, in my opinion, the next step in a relationship. Did I want to encourage a relationship that wouldn't last beyond this week?

I sat on the side of the bed and called for room service. What did Luke eat? I ordered eggs, fruit, bacon, pastries, and a large pot of coffee. I usually skipped breakfast, but I definitely needed a cup of coffee, and maybe I'd indulge with a pastry. I was about to hang up when the chipper voice on the line cut through my mental breakfast selection. "Your order will be up in about fifteen minutes, Ms. Sayer."

I stared at the phone long after the person had disconnected, thanking my lucky stars I'd ordered room service instead of Luke. What was Raylynn thinking? Why didn't she register under an assumed name like they did in the movies?

I'd have to be more careful until I told Luke the truth. The awards ceremony was tonight. After that, I'd demand to tell Luke the truth. I'd stand up to Jerry and tell him Luke was more than just a Con-fling. I needed to tell him my name. Not R.D. Sayer, but me, Jade. I needed to know he liked me, not the mystery girl. Not Red.

I cracked the bathroom door and peeked inside. His muscular body silhouetted against the shower curtain. Lord have mercy. He was unlike anything my wildest imagination could conjure up, and I had a very active imagination.

"Sorry, we don't have time for kinky sex in the shower. Breakfast is on its way up," I called out, averting my eyes from the shower.

He grumbled something about eating it cold.

I shut the door before his naked body with water sluicing—yes, I learned that word from Raylynn's space romance—sluicing over his muscles sucked me into his tractor beam.

I sat down on the bed. What was I doing? "You're having a Con-fling," I said to the table lamp. "Let's not forget what's happening here. There's no point in taking the shower step." I might Yahtzee, but taking a shower together was, in my opinion, more intimate and violated some kind of relationship boundary.

"Good decision, Jade. He doesn't do long-distance relationships. You don't need another bad romance notch on your bedpost." The lamp didn't disagree with me.

A few minutes later, Luke exited the bathroom. A smile stretched across his face. He'd pulled on gray boxer briefs that hugged his body like it was chiseled from marble. I stood, and he, still smiling, kissed the tip of my nose. "You have a cute nose." He wrapped me into his bare chest. "A cute, straight nose."

Oh, my heart melted, and I caved into his hug. I mentally sheathed the carving knife I used for the bedpost and hoped he wouldn't require me to get it out again.

"Can you listen for the door? I'm going to grab a quick shower." I squeezed out from beneath his arm and scurried into the bathroom. "Oh," I hollered back out at him. "Do you mind getting some ice?"

"Sure," he chuckled, "but Red—"

I stopped his question by shutting the bathroom door quickly behind me. He would certainly want to know my name. How could I put him off another day?

Luke's steamy shower fogged the mirror. I swiped my frustrations angrily across the mirror and almost screamed when I saw myself. My Gamora makeup had smeared like a Salvador Dali painting across my face, giving me black eyes and a ghoulish pallor. My hair, resembling an eighties rock star on a bender, fell in angry tangles down my back.

"I bet that was real attractive last night while I was working my magic and riding him like my little pony."

I took a shower and washed my face until it stung. Luke's T-shirt from our previous day's rendezvous was on the bathroom counter. I pulled it over my head, inhaling Luke's scent, and decided I was keeping it. A souvenir from our time together. I added panties and a pair of shorts.

A knock sounded at the bathroom door. "I'm going down the hall to get ice."

"All right. I'll be out in five." I called and thought it odd we were shouting through the door. We'd just seen all there was to see of each other.

After drying my hair, moisturizing, applying a swipe of mascara and lip gloss, I pronounced myself 100 percent better than before.

Luke knocked, shouting something through the wood again. I opened the bathroom door to Luke, dressed in his orange X-wing fighter pilot costume, left open in the front, giving me a glimpse of his muscular chest. He stood in the center of the room. A full breakfast tray waited on the dresser behind him.

Holy piña coladas! Yum!

Chapter Twenty-Seven

Luke

I pulled on my X-wing costume but left the vest and chest box on the chair. Last night's escapades left a toll on the room. The duvet in a heap on the floor, a pilsner glass sideways on the nightstand, and a green thong straddling the table lamp. I chuckled as I extracted it.

"This girl makes me thirsty."

In more ways than one. The hotel had placed two complimentary bottles of water on the desk. I chugged half a bottle and caught the glint of the silver ice bucket behind the leather welcome portfolio. Red wanted ice. I removed the leather-bound room service menu and picked up the metal ice bucket. I enabled the security latch to hold the door ajar and walked down the hall, searching for a vending area.

The carpet cushioned my bare feet. Finally, I found the vending nook, which held three machines with gourmet snacks and drinks. "Nice." I'd been to many Comic-Cons here but never stayed in the guest rooms. My apartment above the comic bookstore was a short drive to the Con and easier on my wallet than an overpriced room.

I wouldn't mind having a repeat performance of last night's sex-filled post-gaming show, but the awards ceremony was tonight. The image of Red in a clingy evening gown brought on a smile. I doubted she would attend. It was only the entertainment crowd, not the Con fans. I'd ask her to go with me, but I'd already invited my dad as my plus one. He was stoked about going.

At least if Red wasn't there, she wouldn't witness my disappointment at not winning the Best New Comic series award. Maybe I could meet up with her after the awards dinner, a sure distraction from my sour mood over losing the recognition that comes with winning an Eisner.

"What are you doing, man?" I studied my reflection in the vending machine's glass while the ice plunked into the bucket. My hair was still damp from the shower. I liked her. Yet it was more than like.

The smart side of my brain, which didn't do long-distance relationships or fall for a weekend fling, reminded me I hadn't known Red long enough to have these intense feelings for her.

The other side of my brain, the side that held back while playing Dragontoon, didn't storm the castle, and allowed Red to beat me so I could spend the night with her, had a direct connection to my dick. It wanted to spend more time with her. Wanted to wake up with her again. Wanted to smell her clean, citrusy scent. And wanted to know her name.

"Jeez, man, get a grip." I picked up the ice bucket and walked back toward Red's room.

A brunette in a hotel uniform exited the service elevator with a tray of food, overly excited eyes, and a nervous grin. Her name tag read Brenda.

I inhaled the scent of dark roasted coffee and smiled down at Brenda. "Is that for the room at the end?" I motioned toward the tray set with a metal warmer covering what I hoped by the smell were eggs, bacon, and toast. A colorful bowl piled high with perfectly arranged strawberries balanced on one end. On the other end sat a pot of coffee flanked by two glasses of orange juice.

"Yes, sir," Brenda squeaked and tilted the tray. A few pieces of fruit slid off onto the floor.

"Ohmigosh!" Her face flushed the color of the strawberries scattered on the carpet.

I bent down, balancing the ice bucket in the crook of my elbow, and scooped up the spilled fruit.

"I've messed up her breakfast. She'll never give me an autograph now." Her wide, hopeful smile disappeared into a mix of fret and anticipation.

"An autograph?"

"I know we're not supposed to know, but my friend Amanda works in reservations, and she told me in strict confidence that R.D. Sayer was a woman, and she's staying in that room." She gave a head nod toward Red's door.

"R.D. Sayer?" A small cramp started in my lower gut.

"The famous romance author." She looked at me like I was daft.

"Right." I took a beat to catch up, and then every neuron in my body fired at once. The cramp escalated to a full-on kick in the balls. Shit. Red was Sayer. If she found out I left that review our whatever-this-was ended. I couldn't go back. I couldn't look her in those sultry green eyes.

"Are you all right?" Brenda's big brown eyes stared at me.

I straightened. "Sorry, I know her by her real name." As if.

"Oh. My. Gosh. You know her." She looked at me like I was her new best friend.

I paused a beat, trying to figure out what to say.

"I'm...um...a friend." If Red knows that I know who she is, and I don't tell her I'm the guy who ruined her career, I might as well kiss our thing goodbye.

"I can't wait to meet her. I'm a huge fan." Brenda grinned and continued down the hall. I trailed behind her, toward my impending elimination from Red's life. Game over.

"Should I ask for her autograph?" Brenda bubbled.

I looked down at the ruined strawberries in my hand. "You know, she's really particular about her privacy. Probably you should play it cool. If she found out someone gave out her room number, well...you don't want you or your friend to lose your jobs over an autograph. Right?"

"I didn't think of that." Brenda's smile faded.

"Maybe you should give me the tray, and I'll take it in."

Brenda's grip tightened on the handles. "My boss wouldn't like that. It'll be a thrill just to see what she looks like in person. I bet she's beautiful."

"You have no idea."

She grinned wide, and the tray wobbled again. Not her normal job, I suspected.

"Don't forget, not a word that you know her real name." I put a finger to my lips, then pointed to the fruit. She nodded, eyes wide with the fear of one about to lose her job.

I put a hand on the door and pushed it open while Brenda walked inside. I let out a breath I didn't realize I was holding. The gentle splash of the shower still running had me developing a new getaway plan. "Sorry. Looks like your favorite author is still in the shower."

Brenda sighed, lingering as she placed the tray on the desk.

I set the ice bucket down, tossed the ruined strawberries in the trash, and wiped my hands on a napkin I snagged from the tray. "I'll be sure and tell her she has a huge fan in room service."

The shower cut off. Brenda perked up a bit. I needed to get her out of here. Fast. I scooped up my wallet and pulled out a twenty. "I'll let you in on a little secret. Ms. Sayer is making a rare personal appearance at one of the panel discussions on Sunday. Stop by, and I'll make sure she gives you some special signed swag."

"Really?"

"Absolutely." I pressed the bill into her palm and my hand into the small of her back, then led her toward the door.

After Brenda left, I pulled on my socks and shoes. Fuck me. I needed to get the hell out of here. Red told me last night she had something she wanted to tell me. If that something was her real name, I was toast. I put on my vest and snapped the chest box gadget into it.

"Luke Skywalker, you are a coward," I told my reflection in the huge plate glass window that looked out across San Diego Bay. At least, I was until I figured out what I wanted to say to Red.

I scooped up my helmet from the chair and knocked on the bathroom door. "Red, something's come up. I've gotta bounce." Please don't open the door.

The door flung open. Her green eyes filled with concern. Her hair wet from the shower. She wore my T-shirt and a pair of shorts. Even in simple clothes, she was a stunner. I stumbled over my words. "I...I...I have to go."

"That's too bad. I ordered breakfast." She glanced at the tray of food. "Oh, it's here."

"Yeah, it came, but I can't stay. Jean-Claude wants me at the booth ASAP." I didn't look at her. Instead, I bounced a palm off my forehead. "Totally forgot I had a meeting with the douche...um, dude."

"Sorry you can't stay." She paused and inhaled. "It smells delicious."

"I'll grab something later."

She bit into a strawberry, chewed it slowly. Torture by seductive chewing. She tilted her head, watching me stuff my wallet into my pants pocket. "Will I see you later?"

I wanted to throw myself at her knees and beg forgiveness. "I've got an awards thing tonight. Probably won't be done until late." I fidgeted with my helmet. "Jean-Claude likes to flaunt his awards at the party afterward."

Silence filled the air. Was she waiting for me to invite her to the awards dinner, the party, or both? Fuck, R.D. Sayer would already have a ticket. Play it cool, Luke. "I'd ask you to go, but I sort of promised my dad he could go with me."

"Of course. I'll be in the gaming room if you want to sneak out of the party and try to beat me again." She gave me a coy give-it-your-best-shot smile.

Wasn't she going to the awards? I hid my curiosity under a stuttering dumbass. "Um...I don't know. It might be late. Probably the gaming room will be closed." I sounded like an idiot. Shut up, idiot.

She dropped her hands to her side, and her face grew somber. "Luke, I need to tell—"

I held up my hand. "No time. Gotta run." I gave her a quick kiss on the cheek, ignoring her suspicious green slits eyeing me like an injured kitten. I yanked on my helmet and hurried out the door, throwing a, "Later, babe," over my shoulder as I let the door bang closed behind me.

And I had called Jean-Claude a douche. I'd become the hypocritical hemorrhoid in my own love story. What a douche.

Chapter Twenty-Eight

Jade

Later, babe? Seriously did not sound like Luke at all. The breakfast tray looked delicious. Plump strawberries, eggs done just the way I liked them, and the way I'd hoped Luke liked them too. My montage of us sitting cross-legged on the bed, the breakfast tray between us, feeding each other strawberries came to a screeching halt after Luke was summoned by that devil Jean-Claude.

My appetite left out the door with Luke, but coffee and three slices of crispy bacon filled me up. Bacon was comfort food, right?

Luke had acted all kinds of strange. And then it dawned on me. This was it. He was ending our Con-fling. After last night, he had probably had enough sex. Was that even a thing with men? He told me it had been a while since he'd slept with a woman. Not as long ago as my last relationship with Big Mike, but it had been a minute. Maybe he'd just had enough of me.

This awards ceremony had me curious. I picked up the phone and called Jerry.

"Good morning, sunshine." He greeted me with the half-awake

tone of someone whose alarm had gone off, but they hit snooze and rolled over for an extra ten minutes.

"Um. Good morning. I want to go to the awards ceremony." I blurted out before Jerry could rub the sleep from his eyes.

"Absolutely not." His voice changed from Sleepy Dwarf to Grumpy Dwarf. "I can't be seen with you at the ceremony. It's black tie. No costume."

"Luke's nominated for an award. Can't you get me a ticket?"

A long silence followed by one of Jerry's signature sighs. "Did you tell him your real name?"

"Not yet. But I'm going to tell him right after the awards ceremony. I won't lie anymore." If he was ending things, I wanted him to know my name. A little voice whispered it was because I wanted him to miss me. To go the distance and find me. To want me again the way he wanted me last night. I couldn't believe he would let me walk away without so much as a goodbye.

"I haven't heard from Raylynn." Suddenly alert and awake, Jerry's tone sounded like he might throw a kink in my big reveal.

"I sent Mom."

A long pause. "You did what?"

"I've had enough of Raylynn's silent treatment. Mom hired a car to take her and Geneva to Raylynn's cave." My sister lived about an hour outside of Sacramento. Her Napa Valley home had a view of a neighboring winery. The idea of her sitting in her second-floor office, pecking away at her keyboard, shades drawn, and totally ignoring the beautiful view and my texts made me huffy all over again.

I heard Jerry swallow the fear through the phone. "If your mom can't get Raylynn out here, we're doomed."

"Don't lose the faith, Eeyore. Raylynn won't let us down. And if she doesn't show, I'll put on a good one. After I tell Luke all about my sister and my real identity."

"For the love of Pete, I'm begging you, please don't say anything until we know Raylynn will be here."

"Jerry. I can't—"

"No, I take that back," Jerry said.

I grinned. He was coming around to my point of view.

"Don't say anything until Raylynn is on the premises."

I scowled at my phone, wishing I'd FaceTimed Jerry, slave driver extraordinaire, so that he could see my misery firsthand. "I hate lying to him."

"You're not lying. You're just not telling him everything. There's a difference."

"That's still lying." I paused, considered telling Jerry I saw Jean-Claude at his room.

"Look, go do your gaming thing. Give me twenty-four hours. Stay away from the awards ceremony, and I'll do six months of free marketing for the bar."

"Six months?" That was worth a lot of money. It could help me save the bar. "Facebook ads, mailers, and social media posts?"

"Yes, the works."

"Deal." What's one more day, right?

"And Jade, your Jedi hangs with Jean-Claude. They're a team. If you tell him who you are, he'll blab it to Jean-Claude. The headline on his blog will read, Scared Sayer sends twin sister to pose as R.D. Sayer on Comic-Con panel. Is that what you want?"

"You're being overly dramatic. Luke wouldn't do that. He's not that kind of guy."

"He will. Mark my words. Jean-Claude has some dirt on him, forcing him to be that kind of guy. So, think twice, young Padawan, before you get into bed with those two."

He disconnected.

Eesh. "Too late. At least with one of them." I tossed the phone on my bed and followed it down, rolling onto my back and staring at the white ceiling.

Since "the" review, I've read Jean-Claude's blog every day. Sometimes there's compassion in his words. Other times, he's Satan himself writing the reviews in the virgin blood he stole during his sacrifice.

I pulled up Jean-Claude's blog. Jerry was right. The post from last night, where he re-reviewed Raylynn's book, was a little more forgiving about her meatball-brained hero. The word choices were more interesting. The post from the day before had sliced some sci-fi dude's book to smithereens. The no blood, no foul attitude bled from the pages. Was

Luke writing for Jean-Claude? And if so, which one of them left the nasty review tarnishing my sister? Surely Luke had no part in that. I refused to believe that Luke covered for Jean-Claude like that.

I'd like to be a fly on the wall at that awards ceremony.

I shot straight up on the bed. All the authors received complimentary tickets to the awards ceremony. I remembered reading that in the flyer and seeing an envelope in the Comic-Con tote bag I'd left on the desk. Raylynn wasn't up for the Eisner award, but she would have a ticket.

I found the bag and opened the envelope. Pulling out the ticket, I danced the room.

Move over, Eisner, here comes Red.

I slithered into the little black dress Raylynn had chosen for the award ceremony. There was a short blond wig that went with the dress, but I looked like Marilyn Monroe and felt stupid. I chose the brown wig. When I put it on, I looked like Raylynn. At least back in her college days. Except for the freshman fifty she'd packed on that first year. Although now, she'd lost the weight and had her hair highlighted and cut short in a pixie à la Tinker Bell.

I grabbed the high heels designed to go with the dress and sighed. The boots I'd worn with the Gamora costume had rubbed a blister on my right pinky toe.

"No FMPs for me. I'll waddle like a duck." I chose a pair of black strappy sandals with kitten heels. Based on how Luke held me last night, I didn't need sexy heels to get him hot in the bedroom. The dress would hang longer than intended, but it would pass. I sprayed my favorite perfume, Guilty by Gucci, and paused. Did I feel guilty for keeping the truth from Luke? It's not like I wasn't going to tell him my name. I just needed to know I could trust him to keep it a secret until Raylynn showed up.

"Not Guilty." I tucked my phone into the cute velvet evening bag—Jerry really did think of everything—and headed out the door.

The awards ceremony was in the two-story ballroom. Crystal chandeliers added the fancy and my heels clicked as I walked across the marble floor. A stage ran the room's length, and linen-covered round tables dotted the area from doors to stage.

I kept to the wall, head down, and took the stairs to the unassigned tables on the upper balcony. The table closest to the railing had a great view of the lower level. I spotted Luke immediately. Yum. That guy could rock a tux. He walked with his dad to a table near the stage. Much to my disappointment, Jean-Claude strolled in and sat at the same table. Luke's dad's body language told me he wasn't happy about it, but Luke greeted Jean-Claude with a smile.

After an hour of watching Luke like a love-scorned stalker, my ass hurt. The awards part of the evening had begun. I recognized some of the winners. Jean-Claude won his category. His acceptance speech was dull, brief, and in my opinion, didn't show any signs of the charismatic critic who cut writer's innards out and strung them like party garland across the internet. Maybe he needed to criticize himself to sound legit.

I snort-chuckled at my joke and got the evil eye of annoyance from the older woman sitting at my table. She was an obvious fan by the collection of Cabaliér pins she wore on the breast of her sequined evening jacket.

After a brief break, the ceremony continued. I passed on the dessert of chocolate mousse with raspberry cream sauce and chose a second glass of wine instead. Finally, last year's winner announced the nominations for Best New Comic series. When he said Luke's name, my heart swelled like an overjoyed Princess Peach watching Mario beat his competitors to the finish line in Mario Kart. I balanced on the edge of my seat, holding my breath.

"The winner is our local Jedi, Luke Sky Walker." The presenter chuckled out Luke's name.

I leaped to my feet, released my breath along with a loud whoop, whoop complete with fist-pumping gestures. The guests at my table and a few surrounding tables looked on in awe.

"Sorry, I'm a huge *Cronman* fan." Even evil-eye lady was clapping with enthusiasm.

After Luke received a hug from his dad and fist bumps from everyone at his table, he made his way to the stage.

Luke held the award close to his chest. He didn't read from a prepared speech printed on paper or hastily scribbled on a napkin. He spoke from the heart. "I'd like to thank my dads for their support, my friends at SCREAM! Independent Publishing, and Jean-Claude Cabaliér for giving me the criticism I needed to be a better writer." A few guffaws followed from the crowd. Luke paused, and his chin dimple deepened, making my insides turn all ooey gooey.

I was still standing, grasping my hands over my heart. Proud tears streamed down my face. I wiped them away, knowing my mascara ran while I listened as Luke continued his speech.

Evil-eye gawked at me. "Gosh, you must really love *Cronman*."

"A hero is only as strong as the writer's imagination," Luke said. Applause boomed throughout the room.

I slammed down into my chair. I knew those words. I'd read them in Jean-Claude's horrible review of Raylynn's book. Was Jerry right? Was Luke writing the blog? Maybe he even wrote that graphic novel Jean-Claude just won an award for.

Shock, then reality, hit as hard as my ass on the straight-back chair. I must be losing my mind. I didn't act like this. I didn't get all touchy-feely over a fling. At least, that had been my new year's resolution. Was evil-eye right? Did I love Luke? Did Luke love me? I had to find out the truth.

Was Luke the Padawan, or was he the master? It remained to be seen. I followed the crowd down the stairs and into the foyer trying not to run to the escalator to find Luke. *Cronman* was a great comic. Luke deserved to win. I couldn't wait to tell him congratulations and tell him my name. A truth for a truth. He might be Jean-Claude's ghostwriter, but no way did he write all those mean things in Jean-Claude's blog. It just wasn't in Luke's nature to be mean. He was the hero. He was the good guy. He was the guy I loved.

Luke had some explaining to do, and he needed to do it to Jade. I'd find him and tell him the truth. Sorry, Jerry. This couldn't wait.

I turned the corner and then jerked behind a potted plant. Jerry stood inches in front of me. If not for the camera flash, I would have bumped into him. Jerry had his back to me, watching a perky journalist interview Luke. Luke's dad beamed at him from the front row of the crowd that had gathered. Jean-Claude stood next to Luke. Both men were holding their awards. Perfect. Jerry told me not to attend the awards ceremony, and here I am with all three of them. Jean-Claude would see me without my armor. Stupid, Jade. Stupid.

Wait a minute, Jean-Claude didn't know me. He didn't know Raylynn. I could just motion to Luke to meet me after the interview and be on my way. Maybe I could get Luke's attention without Jerry turning around and busting me. I stepped out from the plant and tried to catch Luke's eye.

I waved my hands at Luke, but he was focused on the journalist. My phone dinged with the tone of a recent text. I glanced down and saw Raylynn's name on my screen. First relief, she'd finally answered, then distress at standing two feet behind Jerry, waving my hands like I was singing show tunes. "Shit, Ray. Bad timing."

I glanced up at Jerry. He seemed involved in the interview. I stepped back behind the potted palm and read the text.

Sorry, sissy. I didn't know about the panel. I'm so mad at Jerry for signing me up that I could just spit.

Wow, Ray never spit. That was more my thing.

I typed *When can you get here?* Followed by a little sweating emoji.

Little bubbles, then they disappeared. I glanced at Luke. He high-fived Jean-Claude, who looked distraught at the gesture but eventually gave in and high-fived him.

Little bubbles began again, and I blew out a sigh.

Jade, I'm up to my eyeballs in my next book. Can't get away right now. My characters need me. Try to be there before the panel.

Can't you come sooner? If anyone asks my name, I'll have to lie.

Little bubbles. Stop. More bubbles.

Promise I'll be there before the panel on Sunday with lots of valium so I can participate. Please stay with the plan. You're a super-duper sister for doing this. I owe you. Thanks for subbing, sissy. Hug emoji followed by five hearts.

Jeez. Texting from Raylynn was like receiving an old-fashioned telegram. I'm not coming (stop). You deceive people you care about (stop). I'll show up at the end for the big stick it to them (stop). All my love (stop). And, she was being as sweet as sugar. No doubt, Mom was leaning over her shoulder while she typed.

I pocketed the phone. Red, Harley, Chun Le, Leia, Gamora. How long would Luke wait before demanding to know my real name? At least Raylynn was coming—good news to tell Jerry. I stepped away from my artificial cover and moved behind Jerry again.

Luke and Jean-Claude posed with their awards. Jean-Claude's hand clapped Luke on the shoulder like they were best friends.

I had to know. I had to know tonight if Luke wrote the review.

The journalist asked Luke another question, and the cute dimple my tongue had explored only hours earlier deepened with the smile he sent her.

I waved spirit fingers at Luke like a clumsy cheerleader hoping to catch his eye.

Jean-Claude removed his hand from Luke's shoulder and angled toward me. He froze when he saw me and my magic fingers. His face drained of what little color it had, making a perfect match with his white tuxedo. An undeniable look of recognition displayed across his face.

Jerry turned, and he went bug-eyed, which I thought was pretty impressive for his deep-set eyes. His lips squished into an angry scowl. Through clenched teeth, he growled, "Jade."

"Uh-oh." I glanced back at Luke. He stopped his interview mid-sentence, turning to see what had caught Jean-Claude's attention. I ducked back into the ceremony hall and made a fast dash toward another exit.

"Bumbling Bushwhacker." Jerry had caught me, and what was up with Jean-Claude? Did he know my sister? Now I was screwed. If Jean-Claude knew Raylynn, I couldn't tell Luke the truth. He'd be prepared for the panel. He'd screw me in more ways than one.

Chapter Twenty-Nine

Luke

I held my Eisner award close to my chest. It was still surreal that I'd won an award for *Cronman*. Jean-Claude babbled away at a journalist interviewing us like *Cronman* was his idea.

After a quick photo, the journalist asked me who inspired the villain in *Cronman*. I cut my eyes at Jean-Claude. She smirked with recognition. I placed a finger to my lips. She sent me a smile of allegiance, then asked Jean-Claude if he liked the villain.

When Jean-Claude didn't spout off a quick retort, I turned and looked at him. Something on my right had drawn Jean-Claude's attention. His face, pastier than his normal vampire pale pallor, wore a shocked expression.

"Mr. Cabaliér?" the journalist held her recorder closer to Jean-Claude.

I turned to my right to see what had spooked the devil himself and didn't see anyone I knew. Jean-Claude shook his head and smiled at the journalist. "Sorry, I thought I saw an old flame."

"Maybe you did. There are a ton of people at this ceremony. It's the biggest in Comic-Con history." The journalist's glossed lips quirked to the side. "I'd love the scoop on the woman who captured the heart of Jean-Claude Cabaliér. Some people think you don't have one."

"A girlfriend?" Jean-Claude's eyebrows shot upward like he was surprised people would think the unscrupulous book reviewer couldn't get a girlfriend.

"No. A heart." She pushed the recorder toward Jean-Claude's mouth.

Even I thought the question was out of line.

Jean-Claude shook his head. "It wasn't her. It would be impossible." His eyes darted toward mine, and I saw a sadness I'd never seen before. Seeing a raw emotion, or any emotion other than anger or bitterness, coming from Jean-Claude was creepy.

The journalist finished up the interview. Jean-Claude, unusually quiet, allowed me to answer all her questions without adding his two cents. Once the interview ended, the guy looked like he'd lost his favorite dog.

"Should we take our awards to the party?" I held mine up and grinned.

"I'm not going. Those are for drunks and the underserving writers who wiggled a win." He frowned down at his award as if he might chunk it off the balcony. "You go. Take your pretty new friend."

Jeez. I couldn't tell him I found Sayer, not until I figured out a plan in my head. And, I couldn't let him go back to his hotel room alone, not like this.

My dad joined us, taking my award and admiring the plaque at the bottom. The place where my name would be engraved.

"How about we celebrate our victory by stopping at the bar?" I asked them. "I heard their Smoked Old Fashioneds are pretty stout." I needed the time. Time to figure out what I wanted to tell Red. No. Not Red. R.D. Sayer. Jeez. I still didn't know her first name. I had to work out how to tell her I had written the review. I was the bastard who'd dragged her name through the mud. If I'd only known her first. I still had trouble imagining my feisty, flirty, Red writing a boring-as-hell hero. There was nothing boring about her.

"No. No can do," my dad said, bringing me back into the conversation and handing my award back to me. "Paul's working the late shift, and I'm going to finish binge-watching *Yellowstone*. You know how he hates anything with horses in the cast."

Before Jean-Claude could resist, I said my goodbyes to my dad and steered Jean-Claude into the nearest bar.

J ean-Claude nursed his drink. Whoever he thought he saw affected him deeply. He'd had many women on his arm over the years. None I would call a girlfriend. No one he even saw more than a few times. My ex tried to set him up with one of her friends, and he declined, telling her he didn't need help in that area of his life.

He had never shared any details about his life before I met him, and honestly, I'd never asked. I spent most of my time dodging personal questions, and he did the same. I assumed he'd never been married. Maybe I assumed wrong. We'd never shared a drink unless it was a business meeting. Never expressed our thoughts, dreams, or future goals to each other.

"What a surprise I won, right?" I gave a humble laugh, still amazed myself. I had an Eisner sitting on the table alongside Jean-Claude's second win.

He paused and looked up at me. "You accepted it like a gentleman." He swirled the large square ice cube around in his glass. "You're a great writer, Luke, and a talented artist. Don't think I don't know why my books are hitting the bestseller lists."

"I think that's the nicest thing you've ever said to me." I added a cheeky tone, but my words spoke the truth.

"I can be quite theatrical and crass at times." His sigh challenged Darth Vader's as he lay dying and admitting to a lifetime of regrets. "Maybe I am, as the journalist put it, heartless."

"C'mon. I never thought you were heartless." Maybe an asshole, overly critical, somewhat belittling, and let's not forget, totally twisted.

He noticed me glance at my watch. "Do you have a date with the woman of mystery?"

"No." It wasn't a lie. "I'm trying not to get too involved. She lives about an eight-hour drive from here, and you know I don't do long distance."

"If she's the woman who puts that dopey smile on your face, you shouldn't let a few miles keep you from having it all." He lifted the glass to his lips and let the amber liquid slide down.

"You're giving me relationship advice?"

"I know you think I'm a cold-hearted clout, but there was a woman once."

"Was that who you saw after the awards ceremony tonight?" I cocked an inconceivable eyebrow at him. "The one that got away." More like ran away screaming with glee that she was free of him.

He gave a weak nod followed by a hard shake of the head. "It wasn't her."

"How can you be sure?" I took a swig of my drink and let the burn cool my guilty conscience. I should be in Red's room telling her I wrote the review instead of nursing Jean-Claude's mood over a long-lost love.

"She's been dead for ten years."

I sputtered the liquid I'd brought to my lips. "Shit, man, I'm sorry."

"I loved her from afar—an unrequited love, if you will. When we accidentally bumped into each other at the coffee house, she asked me to have a caramel mocha latte, extra whip with her. My favorite. That led to helping her with her thesis. And that led to..."

"I think I get it." I smiled at him. "She didn't love you back?"

"I never got the chance to tell her my feelings. I was quite shy, you see."

"You? Shy? I don't believe it."

"I was a fat, greasy-haired writer. A pathetic nobody in love with the Princess Peach of Princeton."

"What happened?"

"I was up for a mentorship. It was a huge deal. Two years working under one of the biggies in the publishing industry. We were both up for it, actually."

"Is that when you worked under Stan Lee?"

He smiled, a slight pull at the corner of his mouth. A miserable smile. Then he nodded, looking down at his drink like he wanted to drown in the golden liquid.

"I stopped by the dean's office to drop off some paperwork, and she was there. I heard her voice coming from the other side of his door. He was talking all sweet to her. I heard her thank him for the opportunity. He was giving her my mentorship. It was mine. I had the better grades. I'd helped her write her thesis for God's sake. I burst in like a bull running toward the matador's red cape."

He paused and polished off the whiskey.

"I was hurt and stupid. I accused her of sleeping with him and insisted he give me the mentorship, or I'd expose the affair. We all know how good I am at spreading rumors."

"You're one of the best." I raised my glass in a toast of agreement. He frowned at me.

"The dean had six kids and apparently didn't have such a great track record with his wife. He caved immediately. My embarrassed princess called me a selfish moron and left in tears. What I didn't bother to realize was that the tears were there before my false accusations."

"Dude." I didn't know what else to say.

"The next day, she wasn't in class. She wouldn't take my calls. I knew I'd been selfish. I later learned she'd left school and gone home. A few weeks later, the dean handed me the mentorship. He told me she wasn't in his office to accept the mentorship. She was there to tell him her mother was sick, and she was dropping out and going home. The mentorship was always mine.

"I got on a plane the next day and flew to her home. Her sister told me she had died in a car wreck on the way home from college. Then she slammed the door in my face."

"Sorry. Tough break, man." I swallowed the grapefruit-sized knot in my throat. Jean-Claude had bottled up his self-loathing anger and was squirting it all over his reviews like Sriracha sauce.

He smacked his fist on the table, making the ice cube in his glass jump an inch. "What I'm telling you is if this woman's the one for you, don't let petty things like she lives a train ride away to keep you from discovering if she's your Princess Peach."

I stared openmouthed at him. I didn't expect the guy to have feelings.

He coughed a nervous little huff into his fist like maybe he had shared too much of his loss with me. A clock somewhere in the bar chimed the hour. "It's late. I think I'll turn in for the night."

It was my turn to stop being a callous dickhead. "Jean-Claude." I touched the sleeve of his jacket as he moved by me. "Thanks. Your story helped me in more ways than you know."

"Yes, well...Luke Skywalker always had a big heart."

I checked my watch. A quarter past midnight. The gaming room shut down at midnight and Red was probably fast asleep. My time spent with Jean-Claude had me searching my soul to figure out how to tell Red I wanted to continue our relationship. What if she didn't want to see me anymore? She told me she wasn't ready to jump headfirst into another relationship.

I'll finish my drink and bang on her door until she wakes up. I'll beg, on my knees if I have to. No. That's not very hero-like at all.

I finished off my second, or was it my third, whiskey. My head spun slightly.

"Too much whiskey," I said out loud, catching the attention of a well-endowed blonde at the bar. "I sound like such a dick when I've had too much to drink." Tomorrow would be better. I had to work the booth, but I could catch her before she left for the panel, explain things. This way she wouldn't be blindsided by Jean-Claude.

"Hey lover, how about you and me go upstairs and get naked?" I looked up in the direction of the voice. The blonde stood next to me holding a martini glass filled with a pink liquid. Her sparkly silver dress clung to her assets.

"Are you talking to me?" I asked.

"Yes, sugar. You're all alone, and guess what?" She moved around and plopped down on my lap. "So am I."

"Um..." I swallowed hard. "Sorry, I'm not interested."

"Are you sure?" She leaned forward giving me an up close and personal view of her tits. My eyes trailed to the perfect mounds of artificially enhanced cleavage barely concealed by the fabric hung on her nipples. She smelled like sweet sticky liquor. I knew she'd had too much to drink and was looking for a good time. Unfortunately, even buzzed I knew that wasn't me. I mean it should have been me, but my urges had been ruined. They could only be satisfied by one red-headed hellcat.

I unwound her arm from my neck and assisted her off my lap.

"Too bad. You don't know what you're missing." Her words slurred and she stomped away.

"Confounding Kamikaze!" The words escaped from my lips and I gut laughed out loud. "What has Red done to me?"

Chapter Thirty

Jade

"That was badass." A girl with purple hair and a nose ring looked over at me. "You totally sneaked in a back door and got the dragon."

"Thanks. A friend told me about the shortcut."

Luke hadn't shown up at the gaming room and he hadn't texted. That familiar creepy feeling snuck up my spine. He's ending things.

"One more game?" Her eyes were bright, and hopeful.

"You're on." I stretched out my jean clad leg. I'd gone back to my room after fleeing the awards banquet and changed out of the skintight dress into my comfy jeans, an Avengers T-shirt, and sneakers. I'd kept on the brunette wig but couldn't do a costume tonight. If Jerry found me, I'd tell him, "Game Over." I didn't want to lie anymore. I'd promised Raylynn I'd keep pretending to be her until she arrived. Hopefully before the panel. But I wanted to tell Luke the truth. I struggled with myself. He'd told me he'd have to attend the awards party, but it didn't sound like it was his thing. I could drop by and see if he was still there. And what? Tell him my real name, or my fake one?

The girl beat me, but my heart wasn't in the game and it made her night to take second place. Right below Python. The jerk. He wasn't on tonight, but I couldn't beat his high score. I turned in my headset and thanked the guy at the table. Rez had the night off.

"You had it coming." I reminded myself and walked across the mezzanine toward the hotel towers. The fancy hotel was huge and my room in the south tower was farthest from the gaming room. I passed Con attendees straggling out of gaming rooms and heading for the bar scene.

I checked my phone for the hundredth time. No message from Luke. Should I check the awards party and if he's not there, call for a car to take me to his place? He told me it was over the comic bookstore. Too forward, Jade.

He was probably already at home and didn't want to be bothered by the girl with no name.

I took the escalator down to the hotel lobby and walked toward the elevators, passing a closed coffee shop, a restaurant, and stopping to browse the windows of the gift shop.

I caught a white tuxedo out of the corner of my eye. Jean-Claude. He left the hotel bar and headed for the elevator. I backtracked and lingered a minute by the closed coffee kiosk. I didn't want another elevator ride with the jerk. When Raylynn arrived, I'd ask her if she remembered meeting the critic because he certainly seemed like he knew me, or rather her.

After I was sure Jean-Claude had taken the elevator, I continued to my room. I passed the bar and stopped dead. My mouth dropped open to shriek, but I quickly closed it and hurried past, head down, heart ripped in a thousand pieces.

Luke hadn't texted me because his arms were full of a busty blonde bimbo. He was sitting at a cocktail table with her on his lap. His eyes focused somewhere between perky nipples and Grand Canyon cleavage.

I slammed my hotel room door, probably waking the dead and the guests on my floor. Tossing the wig, I slunk down in the chair next to my bed and tried not to cry. "He made it clear he didn't do long-distance relationships, and he was keeping his end of the bargain."

Stupid, stupid, stupid. "What is wrong with me?" I pounded my temples with my fists. "Why do I always fall for these guys?" Somewhere a little voice squeaked, *Luke's not like the other guys.*

I huffed at the voice. "Screw you, Luke Sky Walker." And before the tears could fall, I yanked open the mini-fridge and chugged a pint-sized bottle of vodka.

After I had a thirty-minute hot as fuck shower, my fury calmed and I had reevaluated the man mess I'd created. Why? Why? Why couldn't I have a normal fling? Other women do it. That floozy in the bar probably did it every weekend. And then, I pictured the floozy cuddled in bed with Luke and lost my shit, again.

I wore my own pajamas. No more wearing his T-shirt and inhaling the scent of him. I sat in the chair and finished reading Raylynn's book to take my mind off Luke. The hero was dull, but he was real. He was offering her a place to live with him. He loved her for her. And yeah, he was a little dim-witted but there was no big mistake. No *uh-oh I slept with another woman but I really want you*. No lies. No cheating. No bad moment the characters must suffer through in order to be together.

I tossed the book on the bed and paced the room, considering another twelve-dollar single serving bottle of liquor. Sanity took over and I decided getting drunk by minibar wasn't in my budget.

"I can do this," I told the table lamp. "I've pretended to be Raylynn my entire life. I can fool a room full of fans, an obnoxious book critic, and one loser Luke Sky Walker."

Was that fair? Luke was a nice guy. He didn't have any commitment to me. Hell, we hardly knew each other. I was acting like a jealous, jilted lover. I was having a Con crush, and it stopped now. Luke was free to sleep with whomever he wanted and so was I. But my heart squeezed, causing an ache in my chest as if a dragon scale had been thrown like a ninja star and pierced my heart. The thought of never feeling his lips on mine again, or his arms around me, made my eyes swim.

I dropped onto the bed, fighting the urge to curl up and cry. Raylynn's book slid toward me. The hero all muscles and smiles on the cover. The heroine happy and content wrapped in his arms.

Her hero reminded me of Superman. Superman loved Lois Lane. Superman was a one-woman man. And even though he lied to Lois

Lane about his true identity, she still loved him. I dreaded tomorrow. I dreaded the look on Luke's face when I walked out on that stage pretending to be Raylynn. I dreaded that Luke was not Superman. And like the character in Raylynn's book, my happily ever after wouldn't include the man of my dreams.

Chapter Thirty-One

Luke

I hummed the *Star Wars* theme song, trying to ignore my nerves as I walked toward Red's room. Last night, Jean-Claude reminded me how stupid I was. I reminded myself I shouldn't jump headfirst into the feels, but man, she sure made me feel something. I inhaled a deep breath, recalling the shivers that made their way up my spine when she looked at me with those wide jade eyes. And the way she held me close. It had been a long time since I'd felt that way.

Correction, no one had ever made me feel that way.

I spent the morning and most of last night going over what to say to Red. I had to work the booth until noon and then my dads were going to help Marty close it down while I attended the panel. It had been a successful Con. After news of my award circulated through the Con, I sold out of the *Cronman* comics. And a few agents stopped by the booth and handed me their cards.

Yep, good work Luke, except with Red. And I was about to change that. No way was R.D. Sayer going on that panel without knowing the truth.

I stopped at one of those expensive shops that wound around the lobby floor of the hotel and bought a mixed bouquet of flowers. Daisies and daffodils. She didn't seem like the roses sort of girl. Wildflowers matched her moods more than a delicate rose. More hardy, like her, I'd bet.

I glanced at the time on my phone, then slid it in my back pocket. I had just enough time before the panel to explain the review I wrote to Red. Just enough time to hope she'd forgive me.

I hummed another tune, but it was no use. My nerves had my stomach upside down. I turned the corner and stopped short. Red was standing by the elevator with a valise slung over one arm. The long blond wig of her Zelda costume hung down her back. OK, I could get into Zelda. I'd recognize that face, that body, in any costume. She turned toward the elevator and fussed with the strap on her shoulder bag.

The hallway was empty, and I knew the elevators were slow. Now was my opportunity to get the girl. My moment to rescue myself from a lifetime without her.

I snuck up behind her. Wrapped my arms around her waist. My left hand encircling her breast. My right showing her the flowers. I rumbled low in her ear. "Zelda make me your love slave."

She startled, dropped her valise on my foot.

"Yowch!" I released her to rub my foot. A moment later, I stared up at the ceiling fresco.

"What the hell, Red?"

"How dare you, you...you perve." She turned to walk away.

"I...wait...what?" I grabbed her ankle.

She bent down. Then, I saw nothing but black.

When I came to, something wet lay across my forehead.

"There he is." Zad's voice hovered close above me.

I blinked a few times until Zad's face came into focus. He leaned over me. His brows pulled tight and his eyes held the same look I'd seen a dozen times over the years. A fall from the monkey bars, a late hit in football, a minor fender bender. My dad knelt on the opposite side, mirroring Zad's face.

"Is he going to be OK?" Dad asked Zad. His hands held to his chest, fingers interlocked the way he did in church during the Lord's Prayer.

"What the hell happened?" I asked, trying to sit up. My stomach rolled and I was pretty sure I had spit sliding down my chin. I wiped it away with my shirt sleeve.

"Easy. Take a minute for your head to clear." Zad removed a wet cloth from my forehead, clamped a hand on my shoulder, and helped me sit. "I was coming back from the hospital to help with the booth and saw you laid out on the floor. I was two seconds away from calling the paramedics."

"You don't know what happened?" Dad asked.

"I saw Red, and then she flipped me like a wrestler, and then nothing. Everything went black."

"Based on the mark on your neck, I'd say you were tased." Zad pointed at my neck, and my hand massaged a tender area just above my collarbone.

"Why would she do that?" Dad asked.

I thought for a second, and then like the proverbial light bulb, recalled grabbing her boob. I blew out a long you-dumbass breath. "I snuck up on her. Maybe did something not so gentleman like. I was playing, but maybe it didn't come off the way I intended."

"Show's over, people. Go back to the Con." my dad announced, and I glanced up at the small group of people crowded behind my dads. "He's fine."

"Just a case of low blood sugar," Zad explained and winked at me. The gawkers faded away.

"Can you stand?" Zad stood and extended his hand toward me.

"Yeah." I gripped his outstretched hand and he pulled me upright.

"I don't understand why she'd taser you. The two of you seemed to be getting along so well." Dad placed his hands on his hips. A sign he suspected there was more to my story.

I replayed the encounter in my head and cringed at the reminder I did in fact grab her boob, but when she turned and we stared at each other for a moment, for that brief second, her eyes wore the brown contacts, and did I imagine she showed no recognition of me whatsoever?

My dads waited. Their inquisitive eyes on me.

"I was going to her room, but I saw her standing by the elevator and decided to surprise her instead."

"Some surprise," Zad said.

"She acted like I was a total freak. She called me a perve."

"Why would she do that?" my dad asked, his voice escalating like I might just have fucked up the best relationship I would ever have.

"I might have grabbed her...uhm, breast."

Both my dads' eyebrows shot up and they shook their heads in tennis competition synchronicity.

"OK, I guess that was pervy, but the last time we were together..." My words trailed off, indicating there might be a reason I thought the playful gesture was acceptable.

Dad frowned. His I-raised-you-better frown. "Did you say or do something before you left?"

"No. Not that I remember." *Yeah, you coward. You bolted because you found out she's R.D. Sayer.* I couldn't tell my dads, not yet. Not until I sorted this out.

I scratched my chin. "She said she had something to tell me." Yeah, her real identity.

"Looks like she told you all right," Dad said, not hiding the disappointment in his voice.

I gave Zad a one-sided hug. "Thanks for helping me. She'll be at the panel. I'll sort this out afterward." *If she gives me the opportunity.*

"Next time, son, choose the roses." Zad patted me on the shoulder.

"Geesh, women." I scooped up the remnants of my bouquet and dropped them into a nearby trash receptacle. "What time is it?"

Dad checked his watch. "Ten after one."

"Damn, I'm late for the panel."

I hustled toward the panel, scratching my head, and then it dawned on me. She must know I wrote the review. It was totally uncalled for her to taser me. She could have just talked it out like two normal people. I mean, yeah, she had a right to be mad, but maybe she had more secrets than her name, I thought. "See Walker, this is what happens when you fall for a woman you barely know." But I did fall. Hard. I fell like a drifting asteroid crashing into the warm earth.

I'd go to the panel and watch Jean-Claude squash her with the heel of his proverbial designer loafer. Then afterward, I'd explain, from a distance, and hope she'd understand why I manwhored myself out to the sharp-tongued devil.

Chapter Thirty-Two

Jade

I peeked through the slit in the curtains that divided my sanctuary from the audience. Dang, a packed ballroom. There were even a few stragglers standing. For cripes sake. Who knew the outing of R.D. Sayer would attract this kind of crowd?

I searched for Luke. He wasn't in the front row reserved for publicity peeps and annoying reporters. I was surprised Jean-Claude didn't demand his little Padawan be here in person.

Luke wasn't the only one who was MIA. Raylynn hadn't shown up yet, either. She promised she'd be here. And she had never ever broken a promise to me. She wouldn't make me lie to all these people. "She'll definitely be here."

"She's not here." I jumped a foot at Jerry's voice behind me.

"Holy Tequila Sunrise! Don't sneak up on me. I almost peed my pants." I sucked in big gulping breaths of air.

"Sorry." Jerry caught a glimpse through the curtain. "It's a full house. I hope you brought your A game."

"I'm not going out there. Ray will rescue me." My words sounded weak and wavering. A wishy-washy version of my normal self.

"Oh, crap." Jerry put his hands on my shoulders and turned me toward him. "I know that look and that weepy wisp to your voice. You had a fight with the Jedi."

"No." I shook my head as if I could somehow shake away the cobwebs of hurt collected in the corners of my brain. "It was a Confling. After the panel, Con's over. And so is conning people to believe I'm R.D. Sayer."

"You'll get over Luke, just like you always do." Jerry gave me his optimistic, pursed lips, men-are-shit face, and took his hands off my shoulders. "You'll be great."

Time to woman up, Jade. I could be Princess-Leia brave, it's just that I hate lying. And I had to pull this off. Jerry and Ray were counting on me. I couldn't let this end with Jerry looking like a bumbling publicist. Or Raylynn looking like an inept female in the male-dominated sci-fi genre.

"Girl, you got this." Jerry squeezed my arm a little too hard. "I'll be in the front row. If you get in trouble, look at me, and I'll try to help."

"Thanks."

The emcee, Lauren something or other, was a television journalist and broadcaster on a local news channel. She was tall, slim as a cocktail skewer, and dressed sharp, like a prosecutor on a murder trial.

Lauren, a microphone pinned to her lapel, sat center stage, in a row of chairs facing the audience. One empty chair on her right. Two authors were already seated on her left. Exhibit one for the audience was Scott Simons, a mid-list sci-fi author. I'd read one of his books. I'd liked the story and recommended it to one of the Barflies.

Exhibit two, a pudgy female author I didn't know. She wore a tacky floral dress from the Little House on the Prairie collection and a nervous beauty contestant smile.

The third chair on the left waited for exhibit three, R.D. Sayer. If she didn't show, it would be my exclusive electric chair.

Jean-Claude had used his blog to rip all three of us a new one. Technically, he had ripped those two and my sister a new one.

Where the friggin-fudge are you, Ray? Instead of wearing a

costume, or hiding under a wig, I'd worn the only other dress Raylynn had in her arsenal. A super-short green tunic dress with flouncy ruffled sleeves. If I was careful, I wouldn't show the audience my girlie parts. My mood wanted to wear black head-to-toe combat gear, but the crowd wanted to see the real Raylynn. I couldn't give them that, but I could give them a smidge taller, red-headed, green-eyed, smart-mouthed version of her.

Raylynn had lost all her chub after her big ordeal at college. We looked more identical these days than we had in the past several years. Dark circles under the eyes, frown lines forking the forehead, and broken heart included.

I pulled out my compact mirror and checked my hair as well as my makeup one last time. I had to make sure my dark circles were hidden behind enough concealer to lay tile. I slid the compact back into my purse before an assistant took it and handed me a bottle of water.

"Don't drink this now, it will mess up your lipstick." She gave me a quirky-cool smile. "I loved your book. And I'm shocked, by the way."

"Shocked?"

"Yeah, I thought you'd be a creepy old lady who never left her house, but you're really pretty."

"Thanks." I guess.

"You've got about fifteen minutes until Lauren introduces you. The sound guy will turn on your microphone when you enter the stage." She smiled again. "I'll stay with you until you go on."

Come on, Ray. It's almost time. I scanned the crowd while the emcee made introductions. No Raylynn. No Luke. A large guy wearing a Hulk costume entered the room. He was more bulk than brawn. I'd give him a B for effort.

The Hulk turned down an aisle to find a seat and my heart stupidly stopped. Luke stood behind him. My halted heart revved like the engine on the *Millennium Falcon* preparing for a jump into light speed.

Luke hustled down the side aisle and took the last remaining reserved seat in the front row.

Anger and resentment boiled my blood and sent my blood pressure teakettling to the point I thought my ears would whistle.

Calm down, Jade. He never said this wasn't anything more than a Con-fling. He never said he wasn't dating other women.

Did I imagine he was that into me? Had I fallen headfirst into Raylynn's romance novel?

Jean-Claude was introduced. A few boos erupted from the crowd. He sauntered out from the opposite side of the stage and waved to everyone. He wore a dark suit, his hair mussed like he'd just woken up and climbed out of his coffin. He took the chair on the end. Sat across from the authors with a macabre smile on his smug face.

I wanted to punch that pasty-faced, sour-mouthed excuse for a book critic.

Lauren cleared her throat loudly into the microphone. "Welcome, everyone. There will be a Q and A session after all our authors have had time to speak. Now let's get started." She began by reading an excerpt from the sci-fi author's book, then she read the review from Jean-Claude.

I leaned closer to the assistant. "What an asshole."

"Yes, he is. He really bashed Scott. Poor guy."

Lauren turned to Jean-Claude. "Mr. Cabaliér, why do you consider Mr. Simon's book irrelevant?"

"I found it boring, the pace was unsettling, and he writes like a third grader." Jean-Claude explained a few more things about the author's writing that sounded legit, but I really had no idea. Whatever his issues with the guy's writing, the way he spoke was mean-spirited, and it slid under my skin like a sinister sandbur.

"That's your opinion." Scott Simons sounded like he'd sucked a pebble up his nose.

"My opinion sells books. How are your book sales this year?" Jean-Claude did a thumbs-up and then slowly turned it down, drawing giggles from the audience.

Simons gave Jean-Claude a double-bird salute and stomped off stage right.

Lauren paused, gave the church whispers rambling through the crowd time to settle. She read the pudgy female author's bio and a short synopsis of her book. Then she read Jean-Claude's scathing book review. The purr in her voice said she enjoyed the takedown. Maybe not the actual kill, but demeaning and demoralizing the author suited Lauren just fine.

Jean-Claude tore apart the writing, the characters, and the plot, pointing out the faults and gaining the crowd's support.

The author began to bawl. Not just tiny tears she wiped away with her fingers, but big racking sobs.

"Ouch. That's gotta hurt." Lauren handed her a Kleenex and she blew her nose. It trumpeted into the microphone, causing her to blush big-time. She waved off Lauren's question, refused to respond.

"Eesh." I glanced at the assistant then back to the stage. "Jean-Claude really is the devil."

"And that brings me to our surprise guest." Lauren glanced back at the curtain.

I jerked my head around, no Raylynn.

Fuck me. Fuck you, Raylynn.

"She's the bestselling author of at least a dozen romance books and recently tried to cut her teeth on the sci-fi genre. After Mr. Cabaliér's snarky review, her latest novel nosedived off the bestseller list. This reclusive author has agreed to come out of hiding today for the first time. And she's ready to tell Jean-Claude exactly what she thinks about his cutting review. Please welcome New York Times bestselling author R.D. Sayer."

"OK, you're up." The assistant nudged me forward.

Come on Princess Leia. We're really doing this.

Chapter Thirty-Three

Luke

D amn, I was in deep poodoo. Jean-Claude hated when I was late. But I'd made it to my front row seat in time to see the panel moderator introduce the first author.

Jean-Claude had reserved seats for his staff. People were standing against the walls, for Christ's sake. But he insisted on the front row. Me, up front, watching Red reveal her identity to the packed ballroom of rabid Jean-Claude fans. My gut clenched at the much bigger problem than being late, and the hot dog I'd scarfed down for lunch threatened mutiny. At least Red wasn't onstage yet.

The emcee, Lauren, a friend of my ex's, didn't like Jean-Claude. But she didn't mind playing both sides to get panelists' tempers flaring and a rise out of the crowd. I'd bet my Luke Skywalker landspeeder she was keeping R.D. Sayer for the finale.

"Hey, man. You just made it." The guy sitting next to me offered a knuckle bump. I recognized him as one of Jean-Claude's millennial minions. He worked as the go-between for the publisher.

I knuckle-bumped the guy. "Yeah, lucky me."

My tone was just short of rude, and the guy looked puzzled. Red had tasered me, which ticked me off, but I secretly hoped she'd pulverize Jean-Claude, blast him into another galaxy. She had the balls to do it. And even though I'd written the review, I understood now why the hero didn't win the woman and get his HEA.

The first author stomped off the stage. I liked his work, but he rushed through his latest release and ruined the character arc. I wanted to encourage him to work harder, give the follow-up novel more time, better editing. But Jean-Claude added his bullshit rhetoric to my review, twisting it totally toxic.

The guy next to me leaned in. "Whoa, that was nasty, man."

"Yeah, Jean-Claude can ruin a year's work in three paragraphs."

"Nah. He's brill." The guy squinched his face at me and shook his head. "Everyone at the publisher thinks his reviews are spot on."

Lauren introduced the second author. Jean-Claude made her cry. Her novel was all fluff. I tried to be constructive, but some people needed blunt words. Words meant to help, not hurt. Jean-Claude hadn't added much to my harsh but balls-on review. I felt sick over the way I had shamed her work.

This feeling of guilt cut so deep that my bones ached from the pain I had caused these authors, and I didn't like it. In the past, I'd done whatever it took to keep my comic store in the black. But now, since meeting Red, I wanted to help other writers, not blacklist them. After the panel, I would quit. I'd never write another revolting review again. Screw Jean-Claude.

"Who am I kidding?" I murmured. Jean-Claude had my nuts tied to a contract.

"Shh." The librarianish-looking woman to my left gave me a shut-the-fudge-up look. She didn't seem like the cursing sort. "I think she's about to introduce my favorite author."

"Sorry." Fuck. Maybe Jean-Claude and I could work things out with the contract. I'd finish his graphic novel series and quit writing for him.

No more bad reviews.

No more blogs.

No more.

I should have gone to Red last night. Woken her up and explained I had written those reviews. I was the one who tore the author's work apart, channeling Jean-Claude with a repulsive repertoire of adverse adjectives, overly dramatic digs, and unfair analysis.

I knew why I hadn't gone to her room. I was angry she hadn't told me her name, and I was a coward. The Sayer review was, by far, the worst of the three. I didn't know how to explain to Red that I was the callous asshole who wrote that scathing review of her work. A review that forced her to reveal the one thing she held sacred, her identity. "I deserved the tasing."

The guy next to me arched a concerned eyebrow at me.

"Sorry, just thinking out loud."

"I get it," he chuckled. "It's like these authors are getting tased by the overlord of critics."

If Red knew I wrote those reviews, her eyes would tell me the moment they met mine.

Finally, Lauren introduced R.D. Sayer. The audience went ballistic. Maybe Jean-Claude didn't have all the fans. I took a deep breath and prepared for the worst. If she hated me, I'd beg for forgiveness. If she didn't know, I'd tell her the moment the panel was over.

The curtain parted, and my heart balanced like a tightrope walker on a thread, waiting to see if it would fall and break or if I could counterbalance until I reached the safety of the panel's end.

Red wore a dress the color of her eyes. Long, copper curls fell around her face and down her back. She was gorgeous. How could I have been so stupid? She waved at the crowd, and then our eyes met. She looked fierce. A woman ready to defend herself.

I looked away. Unsure if she knew. Unsure if I could sit here and watch Jean-Claude discredit her work. Unsure if she still had feelings for me. But damn sure I had feelings for her.

She sat down, and her short dress rode up, exposing long, graceful thighs. Thighs my mouth had been between only yesterday.

Lauren commented on Red's appearance.

Red smiled politely, but it was short and her lips pressed tight as she stared at Jean-Claude.

"Daaamn." Millennial dude nodded approvingly. His eyes stared at the peek of black lace before she adjusted her dress. My hand fisted, and I thought about removing that leer off his face.

"Shh." The librarian hissed at both of us, giving me the evil side-eye.

Lauren read Sayer's bio. Jean-Claude looked stupefied. That was a first. I rubbed my chin. Worried Jean-Claude might be having a stroke. The guy was whiter than a one-armed Wampa on the snow planet Hoth.

Lauren turned toward Red and asked her why she decided to write a sci-fi novel.

Red finished her response with a powerhouse punch. "I made the characters real. Real people with real problems and real emotions. The kind that makes you finish the book, hold it tight, and cry out, *You go, girl!*"

The crowd broke out in thunderous applause. Red sent Jean-Claude a smile that screamed, you're-a-gigantic-prick. Lauren pig-whistled, and the crowd quieted down for Jean-Claude's reply.

Whatever had him disengaged earlier had disappeared. His face regained its natural pasty color, and he spewed venom in the form of hateful words.

Red straightened, her eyes narrowed at him. "I disagree. The hero wasn't two-dimensional. He simply wanted to love a woman without having a long-distance relationship." She cut her eyes at me. "Because we all know long-distance relationships don't work."

I swallowed the hard knot of guilt stuck in my throat like the dry pinch of bread at communion and looked down at my hands. She'd used my words like a double-edged lightsaber.

Jean-Claude fired back with an incorrect comment about the book. I looked up and shook my head at his ignorance.

"Unbelievable." I didn't mean to say it out loud. I received an irked huff from the librarian. Then Red's gaze settled on me. As if she read my mind, she zeroed in on Jean-Claude, accusing him of not reading the book.

Red was standing up to Jean-Claude. She was giving him the old one-two jab in the kisser. A blaster pistol attack from all directions. I wanted to rush onstage and wrap my proud arms around her ballsy self.

Murmurs shuffled through the crowd. Smartphones appeared videoing the slam-bam-take-the-critic-down show.

Then it happened.

The shitstorm of all shitstorms.

Chapter Thirty-Four

Jade

I took a deep, lifesaving breath, threw my shoulders back, and pushed past the curtain. I waved to a faceless crowd keeping my eyes on the empty chair waiting for me and avoided looking at Luke.

At the last moment, I glanced his way. Our eyes met, then he looked away. He didn't seem shocked to see me. He didn't seem surprised the woman who shared his bed all week was the author his business partner had dragged through the literary mud. He didn't seem stunned, startled, or even stupefied.

Not. One. Bit.

I sat and crossed my legs. Catching Jean-Claude staring at me, I double-checked that my dress wasn't too high on my thighs, hadn't caught on the chair and accidentally exposed my private lady pixels.

Jean-Claude had a surprised look on his face. The same look I'd seen after the awards ceremony. Like he was confused. Like he'd seen me before but couldn't place my face. Like he knew me. The real me.

He never saw me out of costume, so he couldn't possibly know I'm Luke's—

What? What am I? After seeing Luke wrapped in the arms of that blonde last night, it was obvious. I was Luke's Con-fling. Nothing more.

Lauren finished reading Raylynn's bio. "Isn't she gorgeous? Beauty and a bestseller!"

A few whoops and whistles sounded from the crowd. Out of the corner of my eye, I saw Luke nod. He's got a lot of nerve.

Lauren settled her gaze on me. "After so many successful romance novels, why did you decide to dip your toe into the sci-fi world?"

I vomited out the speech Jerry had made me memorize. "I wanted to write a book where the hero lived in outer space, and the heroine had to make a choice to stay with her life on Earth or choose his more exciting one. The only way to write my story set in outer space was to change to the sci-fi genre."

"Um-hmm." Lauren posed a skeptical eyebrow at me, then at the crowd.

"And I fucking nailed it!" This bitch wasn't besting me. Game on.

The sound of applause echoed in the ballroom. Maybe Raylynn had some fans here after all.

"OK, OK." Lauren held up her hand stop-sign fashion, hushed the crowd.

I looked out among the sea of faces—some in costume, some not. "I made the characters real. Real people with real problems and real emotions. The kind that makes you finish the book, hold it tight and cry out, *You go, girl!*"

The crowd went crazy. I looked over my shoulder to see if the assistant was holding up an applause sign. No sign. I sent Jean-Claude a victorious smirk.

Lauren stood, mic in hand. "Hold on. Pipe down. Put a cork in your piehole, will you?"

Faces smiled back at me. People whooped and hollered for me. For my sister. OMG. This crowd loves Raylynn.

Lauren got so frustrated that she pig-whistled. Finally, the crowd got quiet. "Mr. Cabaliér has a different opinion." She read Jean-Claude's nasty review, then turned toward him. "Care to expand?"

Jean-Claude's pressed lips wormed into a confident, cats-got-the-canary smile. "You didn't write a science fiction novel. You wrote a ridiculous romance set in outer space. The hero was two-dimensional and boring. You should have stuck with your regular romance genre instead of trying to step into my domain."

A few claps and "yeahs" shouted from the audience. I fought the urge to scrunch down in my chair. I refused to let him scour the floor with Raylynn's good name in front of hundreds of fans.

"I disagree. The hero wasn't two-dimensional. He simply wanted to love a woman without having a long-distance relationship because we all know long-distance relationships don't work." I cut my eyes at Luke. I couldn't help it. Our eyes locked and held for what felt like a parsec until he looked down and studied his hands like he'd never seen them before.

I didn't miss the glimpse of guilt on his face. Was he feeling guilty for lying to me? For working with the scum review critic? Or for cuddling with the blonde bombshell?

Suddenly, his head snapped up, and he stared at Jean-Claude. I tuned back in and realized Jean-Claude was yammering on about how Sayer stepped over the line by labeling the book science fiction. "The heroine was obviously going to choose the hero. It was obvious from the beginning."

"All the lovey-dovey feels of a romance novel." Lauren smirked at me like a professional dart thrower one ring away from the bullseye.

"That's correct." Jean-Claude leaned back in his chair, a confident and cocky tone to his voice. "The plot was pedestrian. The heroine flies away with her muscle-bound boy-toy. The ending was as boring as the hero."

Wait a sec. Jean-Claude was wrong. Raylynn had written the book based on my life. She'd shown me I could choose myself. That I don't need a hero for my happily ever after. There was no feel-good, happy ending for the characters. Only the satisfaction and security the heroine had about the choice she made.

Clearly, Jean-Claude hadn't read the book. I stole a glance at Luke. His face held a horrified expression.

"Jean-Claude, did you even read the book?" I loaded my tone and my face with all the venom he'd injected into hundreds of authors. It was time for this snake to shed his scaly skin and expose his ugly self.

"Of course, I read the book." A glimpse of uncertainty settled in Jean-Claude's eyes.

The audience waited for his response with their silence. An uncomfortable shift in a seat, a dry cough, the rattle of the air vents. The silence spotlighted his blunder.

He waved me off. "It was so unmemorable. I can't remember if I finished it. I assumed that the hero and heroine would have their HEA, just like in every romance novel."

"How can you critique a book that you didn't even read?" I tried to keep my cool, but a molten lead rock skipped across the acid pool filling my stomach. Then sank deep. Right to the bottomless pit. There was only one explanation for the in-depth, hostile but well-written bashing of Raylynn's book.

Luke wrote the review.

"I don't have time to read every pathetic love story. I have people for that." Jean-Claude scowled at Luke, like maybe Luke had come up short in the synopsis department. And the contrite look on Luke's face confirmed my suspicions.

"And did your people tell you the plot of the book? Or did they describe the..." What was that thing Luke harped on? Character arc. "The character arc for the heroine and the hero?"

A smile spread across Luke's face. He must like that I'm attacking Jean-Claude. And winning. God, I loved that smile, but this was no time to drop my guard.

Jean-Claude's pasty-white face turned a blotchy pink. "Thousands of people read my review and agreed in the comments on my blog."

"Actually," Lauren broke in, "several readers have reported they left comments on your blog in support of Sayer's novel. Comments that were never posted." She aimed her darts in a new direction.

"Rubbish. I don't filter my blog. Besides, I'm surprised it took my bad review to lure you out of your cave. Writing isn't only about the author's talent. You need a social media presence. Maybe you should have come out of hiding a long time ago and earned the respect of the readers."

"Earn their respect? Is that what you do when you destroy an author on your blog?" I sent him an air shrug with wide open arms and wild eyes. I was a woman in the moment, a woman on a mission.

The crowd had settled into an uneasy silence. This was getting *Magic Mike* uncomfortably nasty.

"Destroy an author?" He clicked his tongue and looked at me like a vampire dad whose only child brought him a salad for dinner. "I make writers better by challenging readers to demand better books, not to settle for subpar novels."

"Oh yeah? Is that what you really do? Or do you hide behind a blog that you don't even write?"

Jean-Claude jumped to his feet, his face an explosion of red. "I'll sue you for slander."

I stood too, catching the shocked look on the female author's face. Her bleak expression turned bright-eyed and hopeful. My fury was a beacon of hope. Hope I'd destroy the mothership of critics. Hope I'd end the nightmare of Jean-Claude Cabaliér. Hope I could conquer the foul-mouthed beastie.

I glanced at Jerry in the front row. He was giving me the cut-it-out, slit-across-the-throat move.

A few chairs down, Luke's smile had changed into a full-on frown. Was he upset that I didn't tell him I was Sayer? But I wasn't Sayer. And I wanted him to know the truth. I wanted the entire room to know the truth.

"Mother of all Bloody Marys, isn't it true that you have a ghost-writer for all your award-winning novels?" I lifted my chin in a defiant only-the-British-get-away-with-it move.

A whoosh of murmurs swept over the crowd. Jean-Claude's eyes widened. His frog mouth dropped open. His face grew grim. Beaten. Then, a spark lit in his beady eyes, and he mouthed the name Gamora. He knew. He knew I was the girl in the costumes having lunch dates with Luke.

"You." He poked a long, accusatory finger at me. "You slept with my employee to extract details about my novels. Details that only the author would know. You wanted to embarrass me in front of my fans."

Another disbelieving whoosh from the crowd.

"I...I...I thought he was your partner." This was going to crap. Luke hadn't told me that he wrote Jean-Claude's books. I'd assumed.

Stupid. Stupid. Stupid.

And now I'd unleashed the truth into a room full of reporters and readers and fans. Jean-Claude had a ghostwriter. And I'd slammed Luke.

"I even went to your publicist, or so he calls himself, to meet you before this *shitdown*." Jean-Claude moved toward me. Lauren backed out of the way. "You're a shameless slut."

"That's enough, John." A woman in the third row stood and pulled back the hood of her cloak. It was Raylynn. She wore a Zelda costume and a rage that I hadn't seen since we were kids. "You're trying to get back at me for all those years ago. Just like you did at Princeton. Embarrass me in front of my peers. Well, it won't work this time. I'm not going to put up with this fuckery."

"Raylynn?" Jean-Claude stared at her. The red had drained from his face leaving it a chalky greenish-white, and he looked like he might faint.

"Yes, it's me, you arrogant asshat." Raylynn made her way to the center aisle and stood in front of the stage. "How dare you criticize my work and shame me for a phobia you created all those years ago."

Holy shit-zees. My sister was unleashing years of pent-up anger.

Wait. He created? Years ago?

And then I looked at Jean-Claude. Really looked at him, and I saw the chubby guy who broke Raylynn's heart in college. The guy who appeared on our doorstep after Raylynn refused to return to the world.

He'd begged to see Raylynn. I'd been drowning in grief over Mom's scary diagnosis. Raylynn wasn't helping. She was too busy nursing her broken heart. I'd—oh-fucking-hell—I'd told him Raylynn died.

Stupid. Stupid. Stupid.

"I didn't write that review." Jean-Claude whimpered like a Stormtrooper begging for mercy from Darth Vader. "She's right. I have a ghostwriter. He's sitting right here in the front row. He's the one who wrote that review. It was his opinion, not mine, that the book stunk. I don't have time to write all the reviews. Tell her, Luke."

The crowd shifted their attention to Luke.

Luke's eyes went guilty-wide, his mouth opened to speak, but no words came out.

"Pardon me." Lauren took control. "If you're R.D. Sayer, who is this?" She pointed at me like I was a wart on the Book of Life.

I stole a glance at Luke. He was staring at me, eyes still wide. The shock of being outed as Jean-Claude's ink slinger written all over his sexy face.

"This is my twin sister, Jade. She agreed to represent me here today because of my fear of crowds. But I decided to take the advice of my heroine. Face my fears and do what was right. So here I am to tell all of you"—Raylynn turned to the crowd—"my book is spot on. No woman should leave her live stream for someone else's dreams."

The crowd cheered.

It must have been so hard for Raylynn to come here, to face the crowd, and defend her work. Tears stung my eyes.

"You're here. Really here." Jean-Claude hopped down from the stage. He stood in front of Raylynn, eyes filled with awe. He opened his arms. Was the egghead going to hug her?

Raylynn slashed at the air like she drew a mighty sword halting Jean-Claude where he stood. "I loved you, but you were too busy accusing me of having an affair with the dean to notice."

There was a collaborative inhalation from the crowd. Like all the air had been sucked from the room in one grand *Oh my gosh*.

"I know. I came to tell you I was sorry. To apologize for my wrong-doings. I thought you were dead." Jean-Claude's voice cracked on the last word. The fragile tone of a man's misery spread like a broken yolk across the ballroom.

"Dead?" Raylynn looked confused, but her tone held doubt.

"When I found out you didn't sleep with the dean, that you weren't after my mentorship, I flew to visit you." Jean-Claude held his arms open wide.

"You did?"

"Yes. I was told you died in a car crash." Jean-Claude's face changed from pathetically pleading Raylynn's forgiveness to accusatory.

A giant-sized "Ohhhh" came from the audience. And an Ohhh-noooo, I'm screwed, echoed in my head.

Raylynn placed a hand over her heart. "Who in the world would have told you that?"

All eyes turned toward me. I gave a little finger wave. The blood that normally pulsed at an even pace through my veins gushed toward my face. Away from my legs. Legs I needed to run. I swallowed the peach-pit-sized lump stuck in my throat and found my voice.

"Um...sorry." Praying my anemic legs would carry me out of this room. I rushed through the curtain. I'd told a lie that made Jean-Claude's bogus reviews look like a love poem.

Chapter Thirty-Five

Luke

I felt angry and exposed. My life spiraled down the toilet when Red announced to the ballroom, make that the world, that a ghostwriter had written all Jean-Claude's books and, for fuck's sake, the reviews.

On top of that, Jean-Claude pointed at me, outing me as the ghostwriter faster than light speed. At the very least, the board would retract his awards.

All eyes, and smartphones, turned toward me. But the only ones I cared about were the wide, green, beautiful eyes that looked down at me from the stage.

Eyes shining with tears.

I slunk down in my seat, cringing at Jean-Claude's buffoon responses trying to defend himself and my humiliation at aiding him in the journey.

"Can you believe this Jerry Springer sideshow?" Millennial dude leaned over and slapped me on the back. "You wrote those graphic novels? They're great, man. You deserve all the credit."

I ignored the guy and tried to hear what Jean-Claude was saying to Sayer. He thought she was dead. What?

Red's mouth dropped open, and she paled. Tears slid down her cheeks.

It made sense now. Her lack of knowledge about the writing process. She was Raylynn's sister. And she knew. She knew I killed her sister's career. And to make matters worse, Jean-Claude and Raylynn had a fling.

The annoying guy kept talking to me. "And to think I almost ditched this panel for the interview with Stephen King. No way his panel could be this thrilling." He held up his phone and pointed it at Red. "Wow. Sayer's sister is hot!"

He snapped a picture, and I snapped. I grabbed the guy by the shirt and knocked his phone from his hand. Out of the corner of my eye, I saw Red run from the stage. I reared back to hit him and stopped.

This mess wasn't his fault. "Sorry, dude."

"You got issues, man." He picked up his phone, checked the screen, and took off.

A shocked R.D. Sayer was still standing in front of an even more shocked Jean-Claude.

I walked over to them. "I'm sorry about the bad review. Your book deserved better."

"You fucking little career-killing asshole. I wish I could send you into warp speed and drop you into a black hole." Raylynn's hands fisted beside her.

"I'm a better person than that. And I'm so sorry I let my greed overshadow my moral compass."

Jean-Claude put a hand on my shoulder. "It's my fault too. I paid him to write those reviews. I pushed him to be fault-finding and cynical. He's a great writer. The books he writes for me win the most awards."

"Why don't you write your own damn books?" Sayer's scornful tone spanked Jean-Claude with the slap of a wooden spoon, but her eyes softened.

Jean-Claude dropped his head and then looked up at her. "I couldn't write anymore after you...you know."

"Died?" Sayer's mouth twisted toward her cheek. And I caught the same snarky attitude that attracted me to Red.

"I invented a whole new me after that. Lost weight, dyed my hair, and became a book critic." Jean-Claude looked down at himself. "Jean-Claude Cabaliér, arrogant asshat at your service."

"Jean-Claude? You're pretending to be French? Eesh!" Sayer did a palms up at Jean-Claude. "The guy I loved in college was John Carver from Spokane."

Jean-Claude's face turned a blazing shade of crimson. "I thought it added flair." Then he blinked a few times. "You loved me?"

"Yes." Raylynn's mouth drew into a soft, secret smile.

I turned and looked at the stupefied audience, everyone waiting for the next chapter.

Shouts and sneers. Calling Jean-Claude names. Reporters throwing questions at us like, *Will Raylynn sue? Did they have sex in college?* Jeez, this crowd needed to take five.

Lauren stomped her stilettos and whistled. "Show's over people."

"Let's get out of here." I nudged Jean-Claude's shoulder.

"No. I'll stay and take my lumps." He offered his elbow to Sayer. She hesitated, then slid her arm into his with a sly smile.

"Any chance you can catch Red before she leaves?" Jean-Claude asked me.

She was probably upstairs in her room, packing her costumes. I shook my head. "Later."

I walked toward the exit. Red. She lied to me. She lied to Jean-Claude. She lied to her twin sister.

My heart begged me to run after Red. Find her and ask for forgiveness. But my head, the sensible one, reminded me I'd only known her for a week. Not even. Five days. No way could I fall in love in five days. Right?

Reporters swarmed me before I could decide what to do about Red.

"He's not answering any questions right now." A stern, pushy voice had heads turning away from me. The guy I'd seen with Red a few times, Jerry, I think, pushed through the crowd and grabbed my arm.

"Who are you?" someone shouted at Jerry. "I'm his publicist, and he has NO COMMENT."

Jerry escorted me through the crowd. He leaned in next to me, keeping his voice low enough for only me to hear. "You can fire me later."

We cleared the crowd, left the ballroom, and hurried toward the bank of elevators. I turned toward Jerry. "Thanks."

"Son." An arm wrapped around my shoulders. It was Steve. My dad had come to the panel. Neither of my dads knew I wrote the reviews. I was too embarrassed to tell them.

I turned toward him. "Did you hear?"

"Yeah." He didn't show disappointment on his face, only concern for me.

"I'm sorry I didn't tell you."

"I don't think I'm the one you should be apologizing to." Steve's head whipped around, searching for Red.

"Red's not here." I sighed a week's worth of regrets. "Dad, this is Jerry. My um..."

"Publicist." Jerry held his hand out to my dad.

"Steve." My dad shook hands with Jerry.

Jerry glanced at the herd of people heading our way. "I think you should save your atonement for another time."

"The van's loaded, son." Steve cut his eyes at the elevator. "We can leave anytime you're ready."

"Good luck." Jerry handed me his card. "If there's anything I can do for you. Media control, publishing advice, or possibly put you in contact with...someone important, give me a call."

"Thanks." I took the card. It felt like a red-hot poker against my palm. A pain that shot straight to my heart.

Jerry caught the next elevator. "Going up?" He looked hopeful.

My legs wouldn't move, paralyzed by the choices and possible outcomes buzzing in my head like angry hornets. I shook my head.

The doors closed. My dad put a hand on my shoulder.

"You may need his help. It'll be all over the media how the asshole revealed you wrote his blogs and his books. You'll get publicity from this, so it doesn't hurt to be ready."

"I know."

We made it to the van, and Dad beeped the locks open.

"I'll drive you out of this circus." Dad climbed into the driver's seat and clicked on his seatbelt. "I've been known to take first place in Mario Kart."

I got in on the passenger side. "I'm sure the media is busy with Jean-Claude. I'm just the woebegone ghostwriter."

"It's not too late to find her." Dad looked at me the way a dad does when he knows his child is hurting.

"She lives in Sacramento. I don't do long distance." And she wouldn't want to see me now.

"Sacramento is only a place in our dimension. Maybe you should take that jump to light speed and find out what it's like to travel to a new galaxy. One that might open a new chapter in your life."

I smiled at my dad's quirky analogy. "Maybe. I'll think about it. Let's go home. I have stuff to do at the store. If I even still have one."

Dad started the van. "If Luke Skywalker had stayed on Tatooine—"

"He would have died." I finished my dad's sentence. "I just can't see her right now."

"Han Solo wouldn't let Princess Leia walk away without a fight." Dad tried again.

"I'm not Han Solo, Dad. And I have things to make right before I can convince a Princess to settle for a ghost."

Dad shifted into gear. "Then let's get this van unpacked and get started."

Chapter Thirty-Six

Jade

My suitcase lay open on the bed. Tossing my clothes in at warp speed, I cursed myself for being a total idiot. How could I have told Jean-Claude that Raylynn died in an auto accident? What in the hell was I thinking? But it was Luke's look of disappointment that had sent me running for the hills.

"You're a big disappointment too, Luke Sky Walker," I said, stalking into the bathroom to pack my toiletries. The Con-fling was over. He'd return to his store, snuggle with the blonde, and burn sage to heal all the horrible memories of Red—the girl who destroyed his ghostwriting career in five minutes.

I slammed my toothbrush into the toiletries bag and zipped it with enough force to send it to the moon. Except the teeth didn't mesh and left a huge, misaligned gap.

Just. Like. My. Life.

A big, gaping black hole in my galaxy, sucking my dreams inside. An uncalibrated cog in my brain that didn't sync, that made everything I wanted, desired, worked for, gap like the misaligned zipper. A backfire of synapses that made my big mouth spill secrets, tell lies, and destroy people I loved.

I took the toiletries bag and marched out of the bathroom to toss it into my suitcase. I scooped my dirty clothes off the floor and threw them in too.

On top of the pile was Luke's T-shirt. I froze, then picked it up and brought it to my nose, inhaling his scent. Luke didn't do long distance, but before I screwed things up, a tiny sliver of my heart hoped he'd change his mind. That Red would make him want to go the distance.

I didn't think the pain of never seeing him again could hurt any worse, but a deep sting, as if the sliver of hope broke from my heart and shattered into shards, stabbed until tears pricked my eyes.

I couldn't face Luke. He'd never forgive me. Besides, he'd moved on. Like our time together was nothing more than a first draft of *Cronman*, easily wadded up and tossed in the trash.

I looked down at the shirt and pushed away the memories of making love to Luke—the soft cotton against my skin, slick with sweat. Luke's mouth turned up at one corner in that goofy, sexy smile. His long legs stretched out on my bed while he traced the dragon tattoo on my shoulder with the tip of his finger.

I could leave the shirt in the closet with the costumes. I'd ask Jerry to return it to him. The costumes. Raylynn. I pressed the shirt to my face blocking the tears that threatened.

I'd have to face Raylynn. Would she ever forgive me? The whole thing had been an accident. I didn't know she had loved the chubby guy all those years ago. And no way would I have known it was Jean-Claude. He'd certainly turned into a lanky jackass. It was hard for me to picture Raylynn with the soulless vampire.

The door lock beeped, and Raylynn pushed her way into the room.

"Can I come in?"

She was already "in" but I didn't point that out. "Sure, it's your room. You paid for it." Eesh! Why did I always lead with attitude? Why couldn't I just apologize?

"Yeah, I did, but I can see you're having a moment." She eyed the clothes piled in my suitcase. "You just going to stuff those clothes in the bag without folding them?" My packing screwed with her OCD.

I twisted Luke's shirt in my hands and squeezed the life out of it. "Raylynn, I'm so sorry. I didn't know how much Jean-Claude meant to you. I was so caught up with Mom's diagnosis and you bailing on school because I couldn't afford to care for Mom that I didn't think when he showed up at the door. I thought he was an asshat, a fling. You'd get over him. He'd get lost and never come back. I thought that's what you wanted."

Raylynn held up her hands to stop my worthless apology. "I wasn't very open with you back then. I didn't tell you about John. And to be honest, I wanted him to get lost. We needed time to grow up."

"You're not mad at me?"

"No. I'm just as much at fault. I shouldn't have asked you to pretend to be me. I need to take responsibility for myself, my job, my life."

A huge weight lifted off my chest, and for the first time since the panel, I felt like my lungs could get air.

"Do you think y'all will like..." And the thought totally grossed me out. "Get back together?"

After Jean-Claude recovered from seeing the love of his life return from the dead, he'd looked like Charlie, the boy who won the golden ticket to Willy Wonka's Chocolate Factory.

Raylynn took a deep breath and released it slowly as if she exhaled years of regret. "Once upon a time, he was a great guy. It's hard to see the future with everything he's become, but I caught a glimpse of that guy I loved. So...maybe. He wants to have dinner tonight."

"I ruined his career." And probably Luke's too.

"I doubt it. Sometimes a big scandal is just the thing to make a person do better." She took Luke's shirt from me and folded it like a five-star general. "This shirt smells so good. Like a man who gave me a hero-worthy apology today."

"It's...Luke's shirt."

"I ran into Jerry. He told me about you and Luke. It's not too late to make amends."

"Luke tried to ruin your career."

"Like I said before, even bad publicity can be good. The media circus around the mysterious author showing up to duke it out with her archnemesis had curious minds buying my book. My sales skyrocketed this week." She grinned that giddy grin from childhood, the one from after we'd had a victorious twin swap at school. "And on my way up here, Jerry texted me. I surged on social media. The video of Luke punching some guy went viral."

"Luke punched a guy?"

She plucked her phone off the belt of her Zelda costume, tapped on her screen, and handed it to me. The person recording the disaster was standing behind Luke. The video caption read, "*Cronman* creator fights for his heroine at Comic-Con." The guy next to Luke pointed his phone at me standing on the stage like a frightened green leprechaun caught in her own trap. Luke knocked the phone out of the guy's hand, then reared back to punch him. Unfortunately, the video followed me running off the stage, then cut back to the guy scooping up his phone from the floor.

"Luke was only a Con-fling." I tried to hide my hurt with an insignificant wave of my hand. "Just like all my other flings. And besides, Luke doesn't do long distance. He told me so, and his job is here. He has a comic bookstore in San Diego."

Raylynn moved closer and placed her hand on my shoulder. "Jade, it's just geography. If you really like the guy, you should give him a chance to storm your castle."

I gaped at her gaming metaphor, then we both giggled like teenage girls at a high school dance.

I handed her the phone and turned back to my suitcase. "I've got bigger problems. Theo called. He's got a buyer for the bar. He's given me a month to come up with the money, or he's selling to the corporate clown."

"I wish you would let me help."

"You're taking care of mom's expenses. I can't compete with that. I don't want to be on your support list too."

"You know I don't look at it like that."

I tried to shut my suitcase and failed. "I know, and I appreciate the offer, but I need to do this on my own. I have a few ideas. I'm going to focus on them. Maybe something amazing will happen, and I'll figure out my life's plan."

She nudged me aside, removed the toiletry bag and began folding my clothes. "I'm so proud of you and thankful you stood up for me. You always have."

I picked up her book from the nightstand and gave her a cynical arched eyebrow. "So proud you wrote about me in your book?"

She sent me a thoughtful smile. "It wasn't all you. It was sort of both of us. I took all your incredible qualities, some of your faults, and my seriously demented quirks and melded us into one character. And believe me, I wanted to give her that happily ever after with hunky captain amazing, but I couldn't. I wanted her to stand on her own two feet. Take charge of her life."

I flipped through the book's pages and thought about Raylynn's brave character. "Maybe I'll summon her strength, find a way to save my bar, and be the lead character in my own story."

Raylynn smiled, refolded my pajamas. "You will. I'm sure of it. And maybe in book two, they might just get their HEA."

"It was a great book." I placed the book on top of the clothes Raylynn neatly folded. "I don't care what Jean-Claude thinks or what Luke wrote in that review."

Raylynn wrapped her arms around me and hugged me tight. "Thanks, Sissy."

I hugged her back tighter.

"Jade, I can't breathe." She tapped out on my forearm.

I released her, and both of us had a shine in our eyes.

"Thanks for sending me to the Con." I blinked back tears. "I enjoyed wearing the costumes. They were fantastic. And the Con, well, let's just say it was almost worth the price."

"You're welcome. Now, let's talk about you siccing Mom on me."

Jinkies Gin Fizz!

Chapter Thirty-Seven

Luke

I swiveled in my office chair at Neverland Comics and stared out the window. Summer rain pattered against the sidewalk, reminding me not to water the flowering plants growing in large terracotta planters that flanked the door to my store. At least, I hoped it was still mine.

Last week was the best week of my life and the worst. Meeting Red had been life-changing. That first kiss in the escape room was epic. My dick twitched at the thought of her. I reminded my traitorous body part I had things to do that didn't involve driving eight hours to have Red chop my block off with her sassy attitude. Man, I loved that sass, and the ass that went with it.

I scraped a hand over my neglected stubble and groaned at the mental replay of what went down at the panel. After Jean-Claude outed me, telling the world that I wrote his repulsive reviews, Red looked at me with angry green eyes. Beautiful, even when they shot lasers that could vaporize a dude to dust. Now, I understood how she got her nickname, Jade, but she'd always be Red to me. I also understood why she didn't want to tell me her real name.

Twins. I groaned again, pressing the palms of my hands against my eyes as if that could take away the embarrassment.

"You're an idiot, Walker." I should have known that wasn't her at the elevator. When I wrapped my arms around her, she felt different, cold. I deserved everything I got, but I couldn't get past the fact she didn't trust me enough to tell me the truth.

Now she was back at her bar. I imagined her making drinks for her Barflies, telling them what a sketch she'd met and how I'd ruined her first Comic-Con. She probably had tons of men to pick from who spent time at her bar.

Was that jealousy?

Raindrops ticked against the glass window, sounding like *you, you, you*.

Who, me? I wasn't the jealous type. Never.

You, you, you.

Holy Heinekens! I was jealous. I raked a hand through the hair I'd forgotten to comb that morning, chuckling at the drink reference. I missed her quirky libation exclamations. I missed her soft skin. I missed...her.

"Hey, Luke, where do you want me to put this new batch of collectibles?" Marty hefted a cardboard box into my office from the storage room.

"Which ones?" I half-cocked my head his direction.

"The Marvel bobbleheads. Captain America is f-ing impressive. Might have to add that one to my collection."

"You can put them on the front display, third shelf. But only if you move the Star Wars action figures to the second shelf. It's better to keep all those together."

"OK." Marty turned to leave, struggling with the oversized load.

"And if you can't move the Star Wars collectibles to the second shelf, you should put the bobbleheads on the antique credenza, but only if you can move the Magic cards to the third shelf. And the Dungeons and Dragons game boards to the shelves against the opposite wall. Try the fourth shelf." I wasn't really paying attention to what I was saying. My conscious mind wanted to think about Red; my subconscious was organizing my store.

Marty gave a giant belly sigh. "That's an awful lot of caveats and addendums."

I glanced over at him. "Sorry, Marty. I'm scramble-brained today."

"Maybe it's that NPC you met at the Comic-Con. She's got all up in your cerebral cortex. Have you called her?"

"Not sure the term non-player character fits Red. She doesn't take orders from anyone, and she doesn't want to hear from me."

Marty cocked an eyebrow, and his glasses angled with it. "Are you sure about that? Because she looked pretty into you when I saw her at the booth."

"Yeah, I screwed that up at the panel." I gritted my teeth and felt my jaw tick.

"I heard about the panel. Jean-Claude's gettin' what's been coming to him, if you ask me." He balanced the box on his hip.

"Yeah. That's what the media is reporting." *Mine's coming too, buddy.*

"All I'm sayin' is she was looking at you the way Wonder Woman looks at Steve Trevor. The way Star-Lord looks at Gamora. The way Snoopy looks at Charlie—"

I held my hands up. "I get it, kid. I just don't think she'll look at me like that ever again."

"Like, try an apology, dude. It's a start, that is, you know, if you're into her."

The kid was right. "Padawan, you are wise beyond your years."

"It's been known in the realm that I carry a wise soul." He beamed at me and juggled the box. "I'll put these on the third shelf and leave everything else in their already stellar locations."

I chuckled at his back as he left my office.

After the panel, my dads had an intervention, and we agreed Jean-Claude needed a permanent reboot. He hadn't approached me or fired me yet. He was busy wooing his long-lost love, and I couldn't blame him for taking time.

I finished my morning invoices and found Marty checking out the only customer in the store. We were having the midafternoon slow time and the rain added to the lag in business. He waved goodbye to the customer and returned to counting the bobbleheads, comparing them to the purchase order.

"I'm going to take lunch," I told Marty. "Maybe game awhile." Try to get my mind back on my current graphic novel and craft the ultimate apology.

"All right." Marty shifted away from his inventory list to look at me. "If you decide to send Red an apologetic text, you should let me read it first."

I frowned at him. "Do you think I'm going to misspell a word?"

"No, but I can keep it vibing. You know, prevent you from using all those Star Wars references. Besides, I have to report back to your dads, and they'll want to know exactly what you said."

"My dads have you spying on me?"

"Not spying exactly." Marty gave me a sheepish smile. "They're worried about you. They want to make sure you don't do anything too nerdy that might drive her away."

"How do they know I'm going to contact her?" My dads were worse than a meddling mother-in-law.

Marty lifted his shoulders. "They're dads. They know these things."

"If I text her, you'll be the first to know. And no, you can't proofread it." I went to the back refrigerator, grabbed a sandwich and a Coke. I sat down at my laptop, logged in, and let my mind wander to a land of make-believe. One where the hero wins the game, gets the girl.

There were lots of players on Dragontoon. It made the game more interesting, but I couldn't concentrate. The other players were gaining on my avatar. One purple dragon, in particular, was kicking my ass to the curb. I blamed my poor skills on my lack of focus. The player characters had learned some of the backdoors, where the secret passages to level up hid.

I pushed a large rock away from one of the secret passages and stepped through the entrance. A blue flash of light shot across my screen. My avatar hit the stone floor and stared empty-eyed at the castle's ceiling. Twinkle stars circled my head, and my last lifeline vanished. Game over.

"Gotcha!" The purple dragon laughed its sinister, sarcastic computerized guffaw into my headset. More laughter echoed in my headset, and voices spouted unbelievable encouragement to the purple dragon for defeating me.

"You guys can kiss my gimlets!" I spewed the Red-flavored curse into my headset and closed my laptop. I'd gotten my ass handed to me, and I couldn't get the smile off my face. I finished my Coke, pondering all the ways to apologize to Red. I had to see her again.

"Fuck," I groaned, leaning back and staring out the window, raindrops stuck to the screen like tiny tears. Tears that welled in my eyes at the thought of never touching her again. Never feeling her soft skin under my hands. This woman had burrowed into my soul. Even if I looked into those Jade eyes and they rejected me, I wouldn't always wonder, *what if?*

Opening my computer, I searched for gaming bars in Sacramento. What did she call it? Shaddowcade? Then I saw it. Shadycade. I clicked on the link, found the address, and zoomed in on Google Earth. Bingo! She'd told me there was a coin-operated laundry next door, and this strip center had one. It wasn't so bad. The bar was on the corner. There was plenty of parking and a small, covered outdoor area. I had an idea. And maybe it was time I stopped being so hardheaded, accepted my situation, and figured out how to make it better.

I picked up my phone and sent a text. No need for Marty to read this one. I sent it from my heart.

A few minutes went by, and I received a text back.

I've been waiting for you to ask.

Chapter Thirty-Eight

Jade

I placed two fruity drinks in front of my Barflies. "Here you go."

"So let me get this straight." Marjorie shifted her cheetah print–clad full-figured buttocks on her barstool. Her graveled voice and excessive wrinkles were the only signs she'd been a chronic smoker. I was proud of her for quitting after a cancer scare.

She tapped a long, red fingernail against the Key lime martini glass. "You met a guy, a totally hot guy, who loves this gaming thing as much as you do, had mind-blowing sex, then left him without saying goodbye?"

"Yep, that's it in a peanut shell." I didn't mention he was Jean-Claude's ghostwriter.

Stewart tasted his strawberry margarita and smiled appreciatively. "Why's he not rushing up here to beg you to take him back?"

"We had an agreement. Con-fling only." I wiped my hands on the towel tucked into the waistband of my half bistro apron and filled a tall glass with ice.

Stewart adjusted his peace sign–adorned headband above his full, bushy gray eyebrows and then they lifted. "He's missing out. You're a wonderful person, Jade."

I filled the glass with sparkling water and added a twist of lime, then placed it in front of Ed. He was driving the bus today and couldn't indulge in an afternoon cocktail. The other two Barflies looked over at his drink of choice, then at him.

"Gotta pick up the little dudes." Ed's nickname for the group of elementary students he picked up after school. "They have a field trip, so they're getting back later than normal." He sipped his water and looked longingly at Marjorie's martini. "I agree, Jade. The guy's lost his marbles if he can't see what a great gal you are."

I released a long, depressing sigh followed by my lips motorboating frustration. I leaned against the counter behind me. My slumping shoulders hinted at the terrible burden they carried. A burden I needed to tell my Barflies.

Stewart looked up at me. "Don't worry about that teabagger."

"Stewart!" I shook a finger at his naughty gaming reference. "Luke wasn't a bad person. We had an agreement, that's all."

"You don't need that PC. You've got us." Ed wiggled his dark eyebrows at me.

"Ed's right." Marjorie fiddled with the string of yellow beads she wore around her neck. Part of the Wilma Flintstone collection. "Take it from me, another player character will come along, and you'll forget you ever met him." Marjorie's five divorces proved her the romantic professional of the group.

I wished she were right, but my heart felt broken. No, it felt shattered, with the pieces spreading from San Diego to Sacramento. I'd never be able to puzzle them back together again. When Luke didn't come to my hotel room or try to call me, I knew he never would. We made a deal. I'd played all my credits. Game over.

Now, I had to deal with the bar. I pushed up the sleeves of my white button-down. It was now or never. They deserved to know the truth.

"I hate to break the news to you, but Theo has a buyer for the bar."

A simultaneous gasp, followed by a long slurp from Stewart as they processed, and he finished off his drink.

"What do you mean Theo's sold the bar?" Marjorie's lips pressed into a tight, faded pink line. Her hot pink lipstick imprinted on the martini glass.

Another angry slurp from Stewart, but his glass was empty.

"I thought he was selling it to you?" Ed placed his elbows on the bar, steepling his fingers and leaning toward me.

I looked at the three people I loved. They supported me when I first moved to Sacramento, covered the bar during times when my mom was sick, and drug me out of the self-deprecating sewer I'd wallowed in after Big Mike took off with my life savings. "He's been talking about it for a while, but he received a good offer. They're buying the entire strip center. He can't wait much longer, but he gave me a month to match the offer he's received."

"Oh, honey." Marjorie batted her fake eyelashes and sent me a concerned look. "What can we do to help?"

"Yeah, what can we do?" Stewart pushed his empty glass to the side.

"We can help." Ed changed his steepled fingers into prayer hands, and I hated to tell him it would take more than prayers to raise the money.

"Thanks, you guys." I shook my head, holding back tears reserved only for the shower and my pillow at night. "I want to buy the bar, but I just can't afford it. After Mike ran off with all the money I was planning to use for a down payment, I couldn't recover. And then there's the whole issue of my credit. He ruined it by borrowing money and fixing up the bar, then not paying the bills. I'm having trouble getting a loan."

"Maybe you should quit being so pigheaded and let me cosign on the loan for you."

All heads whipped around except mine. I looked up at Raylynn standing in the alcove to the bar area. She looked as refreshing as a summer mojito and a lot like Mom in her blue cropped pants and flowing floral shirt. She walked toward the bar, greeting the Barflies.

"It's been too long since we've seen our favorite author." Marjorie gave Raylynn air kisses.

"You're right." Raylynn gave the two men side hugs. "I plan on making Shadycade my new brainstorming bar. I need a place with smart, sassy Barflies to help me invent smart, sassy characters for my next sci-fi adventures."

"I'm in." Stewart sent Raylynn his most romantic bedroom eyes.

"Jeez, Stewart." Ed elbowed his tie-dyed T-shirt-wearing, Grateful Dead–loving, granola friend.

"You attended the Comic-Con in my place. We agreed I'd cosign a loan for you." Raylynn slid onto the open barstool next to Marjorie.

"Thanks, Ray. But even if you cosigned, I'd still need the down payment." Raylynn opened her mouth to reply. I jerked my hands up to a full stop. "And I won't take your money."

"Let's raise the money." Ed motioned at the bar.

"Yeah, we can raise the money." Stewart did a finger drumroll on the counter. "We can do that gaming thing you talked about."

I picked up my bar towel and began drying a glass. "I ran the numbers. Even if we could turn the storage room into a gaming room, it could only hold about six people. Eight would be tight, ten impossible. And even if I did host a gaming tournament and fill all the slots, it wouldn't be enough. And even if we added a tournament and included all the vintage games, I couldn't make enough money for the down payment."

"But there has to be a way." Ed pounded his fist on the bar, making the nuts jump in their plastic bowl.

"The guy I met at the Comic-Con, Rez, would give me 80 percent of the intake in exchange for advertising his company. Theo offered to let me keep 100 percent of that minus overhead, but it still wouldn't be enough for the down payment. And then, there's the cost of advertising to get people to come for the tournament." I shook my head again. "Sorry, it's a no-go."

"What if people brought their computers?" Marjorie flapped her hand at the bar area. "Couldn't they log on? I mean, look at all these tables."

"And there's room on the patio." Stewart gestured toward the patio and for another strawberry margarita. "People could sit outside. Sign in from their own stations."

"A LAN party." Ed's face filled with excitement.

"That would add a lot of other PCs," I agreed. "The problem is getting the people to fill them up. We're not exactly in the mecca of the gaming world." And we only have a month.

"What would draw them here?" Raylynn stole a cherry from the garnish center, held it between her teeth, and plucked off the stem.

"I'd need a good advertising campaign. Jerry offered to market. Rez said he'd help, but I'd need something spectacular that people would want to see."

"Maybe you could invite that hacker. The one that always breaks into our game and kicks our avatar's ass-end." Stewart smiled when I slid another drink in his direction.

"The Python?" I raised a ballsy eyebrow at Stewart for his equally ballsy idea.

"Yeah, that guy." Stewart sucked in a mouthful of his drink and swallowed. "If he agreed to expose himself, you'd draw a crowd."

"You mean reveal himself." Marjorie corrected.

"Yeah, that too." Stewart grinned and followed it with a satisfied slurp.

"The Python would never reveal himself. He's a hacker. He'd never show up at my little bar." I dried another wine glass with my towel and slid the stem into the overhead rack behind me.

Raylynn plucked one of the tiny drink umbrellas from the tray beside her and twirled it between her fingers. "Revealing the Python would draw a crowd. And if we could get the Python, I know someone else who might advertise it on his blog."

I guess things were on the mend between Raylynn and Jean-Claude. I looked at the four hopeful faces. "I guess it doesn't hurt to ask."

Stewart held up his glass. "To the Python, may he squeeze his last victim right here at Shadycade." Three glasses, one tiny umbrella, and my bar towel came together in a Musketeers huzzah.

Chapter Thirty-Nine

Luke

The *Star Wars* "Imperial March" woke me early Saturday morning. I grappled for my phone and blinked to clear the sleep from my eyes—8:15 a.m. I wasn't due at the store until eleven. I hoped to catch up on my sleep and get in a late workout before heading to the store.

The sound played again from my custom doorbell, a Christmas gift from my dads, followed by an impatient knock.

"Jeez, I'm coming." I pulled on a pair of athletic shorts and drug a T-shirt over my head as I walked toward the door. Was Marty having problems at the store? It wasn't even open yet. Checking the peephole, I saw Jean-Claude staring back at me. Was he here to collect on my loan? Shut down the most important thing in my life?

A tiny voice in my head added Red to my list of most important things. I ignored the voice and studied the ceiling above me. I could pretend I wasn't home.

"Might as well get it over with." I yanked open the door like I was ripping duct tape off a hairy arm. I assumed my face reflected my unease.

"Good morning." Jean-Claude's gaze followed my bedhead and wrinkled tee down to my bare feet. His starched white button-down and pressed jeans meant he was here on business. If he were here to reprimand me, he'd wear one of his infamous designer tracksuits.

My gut twisted. Our partnership was doomed, a collision of opposite forces like an out-of-orbit asteroid colliding with a space shuttle.

I took a deep breath. "Morning. I...um...just woke up."

"I can see that." He glanced behind me. He was either checking to see if I had an overnight visitor or having an internal seizure at the state of my apartment. "Can I come in?"

"Sure." I stepped aside. "I haven't had time to pick up."

He paused in my living room, took in the comic books strewn across my couch, a week's worth of takeout boxes on the coffee table, empty beer bottles lined up like soldiers next to the takeout, then moved toward my small kitchen table. He removed the T-shirt I wore yesterday off the chair and sat, spine rigid, frowning at the dirty dishes in my kitchen.

"Do you want water or something?" I raked a hand through my disheveled hair, mentally recalling there was no *or something* in my fridge.

"No. I want to talk about our partnership."

My mouth went dry. Here it comes. The moment I find out if I'll have to engage in an endless lawsuit with the world's biggest jackass to keep my store. I grabbed a bottle of water from the fridge, pushed a stack of dirty laundry off the chair and onto the floor, and sat across from him.

"OK. What's up?" I took a long drink of get-my-shit-together, twisted the cap back on the bottle, and met Jean-Claude eye to eye.

"I wanted to let you know I've had an epiphany." He straightened the cuff of his sleeve even though it didn't need it.

"An epiphany?"

"Yes, I don't believe I've been fair to you." His gaze stayed on mine as if he probed my thoughts for any doubt that I didn't believe he was an unfair, irritating asshole.

It was all I could do to keep my mouth from dropping open. But I held firm. I didn't want Jean-Claude to know I worried about my future at the store.

"Telling a room full of reporters that I was your ghostwriter wasn't the best way to secure the income from your future books." I set the bottle down on the table and looked at him. What game was he playing this time? He'd practically blackmailed me to finish his series. And now he apologized before dropping the guillotine and ending my career?

"You're a good writer, Luke, and I've been a fool not to credit you for the work you do." He breathed a long sigh, and I could almost see the years of disdain releasing with it.

"Why did you do it?" I tore at the wrapper on my water bottle. "Why did you single me out, destroy all the work I did for you?"

"I didn't want Raylynn to hate me. Blaming you seemed easier at the time. You're a better writer than me. If I released you from your contract, you'd be my competition. My books would tank, and my blog would be a cutthroat, angry rant over my past misgivings."

I opened my mouth to reply, but he waved me off.

"You're the better person. You kept the blog alive and intriguing and spoke from the heart. You gave my 'words,'" he made air quotes with his fingers indicating he knew his words were my words and he wasn't taking credit for them any longer, "the perfect balance, letting authors know their weaknesses and urging them to work harder. I screwed up your words with my drive to hurt because I was hurting."

I was speechless. Maybe the guy'd had a stroke. He'd never spoken to me this way.

"Does this mean I get to keep the store?"

"Of course. I know my reputation has a black mark, but the store is doing well. Whenever you're ready, you can buy out my share of the contract."

"I've been working on that. I have a plan I'd like to discuss with you." I stood and walked over to my backpack, withdrawing a folder containing the buyout plan I'd been working on all week. I handed the folder to him. "I have investors who will help me buy you out."

He looked over the contract and nodded. A sad little nod, like he wasn't expecting to end our collaboration so soon.

"This is a fair price for the store. I've decided to add your name to all my previously published books. And I'd like you to cowrite the last books in this series."

"For real?" My ears heard his words, but my mind wasn't comprehending any of them. I'd expected him to fight the contract. Tell me the price was way too low. Tell me I'd never make it on my own. Tell me to go to hell.

"Yes. I'm backing out of fiction. I was only marginally good at it anyway. I'm much better at telling it like it is. Of course, I'll continue writing nonfiction, with a few significant attitude changes."

The guy was atoning for everything. I sat back in my chair, dumbfounded. "I know the panel screwed with your career, but you've recovered from worse. Why the sudden change of heart?"

"More like a heart-to-heart. With Raylynn. I decided I needed to make changes in my life. Especially if I'm going to win her back."

"So, you two were a thing, huh?"

"I had the biggest crush on her. It's no wonder Jade looked familiar to me. But I couldn't see beyond the costumes to realize I was looking at a mirror image of the girl from college."

My eyes dropped to my hands at the mention of Jade's name. I missed her but didn't know how to win her back. I'd wanted to get my life in order before I sought her out but couldn't wait. I tried calling, but it went straight to a computerized voice mail. I couldn't hear the snarky tone of her voice, or the smoky laugh I'd loved the first time I met her. She obviously never wanted to see me again.

Jean-Claude studied me for a moment.

"You know, Raylynn asked me for a favor." His lips did that quirky pull-to-the-side thing that happened when he had an idea for ridiculing an author on his blog.

"What favor?" I crossed my arms over my chest. Would I have to write another scathing review about one of his or her competitors?

"She asked me to promote a certain gaming competition on the blog. It's in Sacramento, at her sister's bar. Apparently, they're trying to out the Python." He wiggled his eyebrows at me.

"The Python?"

"Isn't that the hacker Marty complains about on a regular basis?" Jean-Claude's mischievous tone almost sounded like he was ribbing me.

"I didn't know you played Dragontoon."

"There's lots you don't know about me." He chuckled and waved his hand across the table, mimicking a particular avatar in the game. "I enjoy gaming late at night, just like you."

"You sneaky bastard." I smiled at Jean-Claude. "I would have never guessed that was you."

"You should go to the competition. She's trying to save her bar."

"Yeah, I know." The idea of seeing Red again had me slumping in my chair. "I can't drive up there. She won't speak to me. Besides, I need to get my life under control before I see her."

"Seems to me you're on your way." He tapped the contract in front of him. "Take it from me. Fight for what you want. Don't let life's hackers steal your dreams."

"Life's hackers?" I raised an eyebrow that I doubted he could see under my mop of hair.

"The things that stab your soul..." he paused, pressed his lips together. "Like abandonment."

I looked wide-eyed at him. This man I had hated for years knew my deepest, darkest secret.

He nodded. "I know all about your mother. I research my employees—" When I stiffened, he rephrased. "My partners, thoroughly before I go into business with them. I can say I chose you because of it. My mother also left me on the doorstep of a social worker. I assumed you would have the same warped view of the world. But I was wrong."

"My dads deserve the credit."

"I wasn't so lucky, but other things hack into your life and make you miss living it, like sickness, ego, selfishness, anger, jealousy. All are mere setbacks, boy, not jail cells. Don't wait until it's too late. Break free and run fast toward what makes you happy."

"Whoa." I wasn't expecting words of wisdom from Jean-Claude. He'd leveled up his avatar from evil sorcerer to soul-mending healer. "That's something to think about."

"I've removed the chains that shackled you these past years. What you do now is up to you." He stood and picked up the contract from the table. "I'll sign this and give it to my lawyer. You should hear back by the end of the week."

I held out my hand. "Thanks, Jean-Claude. I can honestly say this time, it's been a pleasure doing business with you."

He shook my hand, then walked to the door. Before he left, he turned toward me. "Get to outlining the next book in my series. I'd like to have a meeting next week to firm up the details. Make sure your plot points aren't subpar." He winked at me and shut the door behind him.

There he is. I chuckled at the absurd notion that I'd imagined Jean-Claude, the control freak, was gone forever.

Chapter Forty

Jade

The Barflies worked hard cleaning the storage room. Marjorie picked out a pretty shade of blue that she called Texas Bluebonnets, and Stewart painted the walls. Ed commissioned a few students from the high school art class to design a gaming-themed mural on the long wall across the back.

I had scrubbed every inch of the stained cement floors until they sparkled like china. Rez stopped by a few times to troubleshoot the setup. On the day of the event, he was staying in Stewart's guest room so he wouldn't have a three-hour drive back to Fresno.

Twenty gaming stations sat in what we'd christened the Zoom Room. We'd pushed together the square four-top tables in the bar area to create two long gaming tables with electric strips for personal laptops.

Theo increased the internet bandwidth to allow for more computers on the Wi-Fi without slowing the gaming to a tortoise pace. Raylynn helped make flyers and distribute them throughout the neighborhood as well as putting them on her social media site. As promised and although I had royally screwed up the twin swap, Jerry added his flair to the marketing campaign. Even Jean-Claude, who had become a permanent fixture on the weekends, promoted the competition on his blog.

Competition day came faster than I wanted. The bar looked amazing but tonight was the finale. If I didn't raise enough money, I was one whiskey sour away from finding a new career.

I poured brass cleaner on a cloth and began shining up the antique brass beer taps. The bar looked amazing. It was all coming together except for the giant hole in my heart. Luke had called a few times, but I didn't answer. I didn't want to hear his apology for lying to me. Or that he thought it was better to end things, and he'd be moving on with the blonde.

"Jade?"

I blinked at the sound of my name. Raylynn stood in front of me, hands on hips. "I swear you were light years away. I asked if you'd figured out the signature drink for the gaming night."

"Um, not yet. Maybe a Tom Collins?"

"Tom Collins? Are you eighty?" She looked at me with that disappointed lift to her left nostril. The look I'd never been able to copy. "Even Marjorie would turn her nose up at that one."

"Sorry." A strand of hair fell across my face. I brushed it away with the back of my hand. "I've been so focused on the gaming night I haven't put much thought into it."

Raylynn laid a hand on my shoulder. "Why don't you call him?"

"Call who?" I knew who she meant but didn't want to acknowledge my desperation to see him.

"Luke." She twisted her mouth into that annoyed expression that announced she had reached her limits with me. "You stare off into space more often than you should, and John—"

"I don't care what John, or Jean-Claude, or whatever he calls himself these days, told you. Luke lives eight hours away and doesn't believe in long-distance relationships. We had a Con-fling. We both agreed to it. He also lied to me. And I'm tired of being involved with lying, thieving jerks."

"Oh, honey, I don't think he compares to Big Mike."

"I'm not comparing. I'm stating facts. Besides, if the Python doesn't show, nothing will matter." I focused on the beer taps, polishing until I saw my reflection in the brass.

"John has good reason to believe he'll show."

I stopped polishing and stared at her. "How does he know?"

"He can't say, but he's been taunting the Python on his blog. Throwing down the gauntlet for your cause."

Raylynn had forgiven Jean-Claude, but I hadn't, not yet.

"For once, he's using his blog for a good cause." I discarded the polishing rag and turned toward the garnish station. I stabbed a few cherries with a pink plastic mini-sword, put it into my mouth, and pulled off the fruit.

"The fans love it." Raylynn bubbled, and I had to do a double-take to make sure she was my sister. The same sister who, only a few weeks ago, wore a pen behind her ear, an invisibility cape, and a permanent frown. "So many fans will be live streaming the gaming night. I hope the Python does some dramatic reveal."

"Live stream?" The cherries fell out of my mouth and dropped on the bar.

"Yeah? Didn't Rez tell you? He can live stream the gamers. When the Python shows up in person, we'll probably max out the internet."

I sat down hard on the barstool. "I didn't know that was happening."

"Not only that, Rez promised to give you half of the affiliate proceeds he receives tonight. He said it could be quite a bit of money."

"Holy Tom Collins!" I couldn't believe my ears.

"Please." Raylynn grabbed a cocktail napkin and scooped my wayward cherries into the garbage. "Come up with something better than a Tom Collins. And do it quickly. I'd like to make a sign advertising the drink and get it on social media."

Raylynn left me taking inventory of my stock. I'd forgotten about the signature drink. Rez suggested a drink that could be made virgin for gamers under twenty-one.

Maybe a strawberry daiquiri? Boring but tasty. My mind wandered back to sharing cocktails with Luke and how he grinned that Han Solo lopsided grin at my cocktail-flavored exclamations.

A small fire kindled deep, and my traitorous body craved Luke. I craved the scent of him. I craved to touch that deep dimple in his chin. I craved the way his stupid Star Wars analogies made me giggle. And I craved how his eyes danced at my ridiculously loud, throaty belly laughs.

I ran a finger across my liquor bottles, picked up the Fireball. Perfect.

"Look what came in on time." Rez placed a stuffed manila package on the bar.

"What is it?"

"Open it and see for yourself." He smiled wide.

I sat the bottle of Fireball down and tore open the top of the envelope. Vinyl stickers of Dragontoon avatars fell onto the counter. "Cool."

"They're clings for the glasses. You know, for the signature drink."

I picked one off the pile. A gold dragon with wings spread and breathing fire. The Python's favorite avatar. I attached it to a highball glass and poured in grenadine until red syrup coated the bottom, then filled the glass with ice.

"Are you making the drink?" Rez seemed fascinated by my shiny cocktail shaker.

"I'm experimenting. You can be my test subject." I grinned at him and grabbed the cocktail shaker measuring a two count of rum. Matching the rum with the same amount of cranberry juice, I then added a small scoop of ice and shook until the ice melted. I poured it carefully into the glass to avoid mixing it with the grenadine. Then I combined the Fireball, bourbon, and peach nectar, gave it a few shakes, and poured it into the glass. The drink lit the gold dragon like it was on fire.

"That's the coolest thing I've ever seen." Rez stared at the faux flaming glass, licked his lips. "You're dope with the drinks."

I skewered an orange slice, cherry, and a few Hot Tamale candies for the final garnish. I had to admit, the cocktail was a work of art, and I could charge a nice price for it. I pushed my masterpiece toward Rez.

He obliged without hesitation, taking a sip and giving me a "yum" followed by a chef's kiss.

"I can leave out the alcohol and add cinnamon syrup and some spritzer for the eighteen to twenty-year-olds." Anyone with a big Sharpie

X on their hand, compliments of Theo and one of his bouncers manning the door.

Rez took another long drink. "What's it called?"

"The Python Killer."

"That's perfect." He grinned ear to ear.

"Let's hope he shows, or we'll have a bunch of angry customers." I wiped down the bar and returned the alcohol to its place in the liquor line.

"Nah, they'll enjoy the experience. But I'll bet my He-Man collection the Python won't be able to resist this competition. He can't hack into it, so he'll have to show up in person." Rez snapped a pic of the drink. "This baby's going online right now, and I'll tag him in it."

"Can you send that to Raylynn? She wanted it for her social media."

"More like Jean-Claude's blog." Rez chuckled. "He's been poking the Python all week. The guy'd be a total wuss not to show."

I hadn't read Jean-Claude's blog since the panel. I hadn't even been on social media except to approve Raylynn's posts about the bar. I attached the clings to the highball glasses and made a mental note to check out the blog.

"I'm going to run home, grab a shower and change clothes." I inhaled a deep breath and let it out in a nervous *woosh*. "Get ready for the big night."

"I'll hold down the fort until you return." Rez lifted his glass in a toast.

Rez was right. Shadycade was my fort, and I was preparing for a battle to the death.

Chapter Forty-One

Luke

"Fucking idiot!" I swerved to avoid the imbecile who changed into my lane without a glance.

He wore a ponytail, tank top, and stack of gold chains. He stuck his tattooed arm out the open window, answering my curse with an offensive hand gesture. His red Dodge Charger cut off two more cars and exited the freeway.

"Dickhead."

A backup on the I-5 through LA put me way behind schedule. I punched a frustrated fist on my steering wheel. I should have listened to Jean-Claude and left early this morning, but I needed—no, I wanted—to take care of things at the store before heading out.

"Marty's perfectly capable of running the shop," Jean-Claude told me yesterday. I knew he was right.

I'd told Marty I needed a break from the store—a vacation. Now, my vacation was behind schedule. I'd never make the gaming competition on time. My plan to sweep into Red's bar and proclaim my love for her like the white knight in Dragontoon minus the dragon he rode, my white Jeep Wrangler would have to do, wasn't going to work. According to my GPS, the gaming would be well under way before I arrived.

My goal to help Red save her bar and win her back needed a plan B. I just wished I had one. A new notification pinged my phone. I glanced at it while stopped in bumper-to-bumper traffic.

R.D. Sayer's social media posted another blurb about Red's bar. Captioned under a photo of a radical drink, likely made by Red, was "Signature drink, the Python Killer." Farther down, "Looks like poison to me. Maybe the brave Python should see how invincible he really is." The location and time of the gaming competition followed the blurb.

I'd started following Red's sister after the panel and laughed at the irony. Who'd have thought I'd be following an author I'd almost destroyed?

I closed my phone as traffic started moving again. Would the Python reveal himself? He'd been an enigma for so long. An unknown entity that traveled behind a veil. A front for the autonomous release of pent-up anger, frustration, and resentment.

Was the Python brave? I didn't think so. I thought he was a coward. But tonight, I hoped he'd prove me wrong and save Jade's dream.

My cell buzzed, and the store's main number flashed on my screen. I answered on my car connect. "What's up, Marty?"

"Hey, Luke." Marty's voice sounded unsure. "Sorry to bother you on vacation, but did you see that Jean-Claude confirmed the Python is making an appearance at that bar in Sacramento?"

"No. I'm driving. What did the asshat do now?" Even though I'd made amends with Jean-Claude, he'd always be an asshat.

"He posted on his blog that the Python will definitely be at the bar." Marty huffed a breath of disgust. "Figures he'd know that slimeball."

"Takes one to know one. Right?"

"Yeah. Have a fun trip. Don't worry about the store. I've got it covered, but you don't mind if I watch the live streaming of the gaming competition tonight, do you?" Marty's voice was just shy of pleading. "It starts before I get off, and a few regulars asked if we were showing it on our big flat-screen. I don't want to miss the reveal."

"Sure." Shit. "See you next week." I hoped it would be next week and not tomorrow. It was all up to Red.

I disconnected, the traffic picked up, and I left Los Angeles behind me.

After a brief pee stop and a restock of caffeine, I returned to the road. The traffic was light on this stretch of highway, and I was thankful to be out of the LA congestion. I cranked up the radio and sang along with one of my favorite country singers for the next several miles.

As I drove through the San Joaquin Valley, a flash of red in my rearview mirror caught my attention. It was the dickhead who cut me off earlier. He pulled up alongside me, radio blasting some rap shit, and sent me another one-finger salute.

"Fuck. This guy's a dick."

I ignored him, turned down my radio, and concentrated on the road. He played gun-the-engine for a few miles. He'd speed up, then slow down until he was even with me, snake his car, and laugh when I hugged the shoulder.

Up ahead, I saw a mop of a dog start to cross the road. I glanced in my rearview mirror. Cars in the distance. I pointed ahead, but Dickhead flipped me off again. He didn't see the dog.

I pressed my horn. The dog stopped in the center of the road. "Shit!"

I slowed down, waving at Dickhead to stop. Dickhead paced me.

"You wanna piece of me?" he yelled, tapping his chest like King Fucking Kong.

"Stop, you idiot!" I motioned toward the road and stuck my tongue out pantomiming a panting dog. I must have looked like a frantic freak.

He stared at me, then glanced at the road. His face went all confused. Then his mouth opened in an oh-fuck-me moment. He veered in my direction, making me plow into the ditch. I saw the dog bounce off his right corner panel. Dickhead didn't stop. His tires squealed, and he sped off down the road.

I slumped back against my seat, glanced across the road at the mound of fur lying still on the shoulder, and knew I'd never reach Red in time.

Chapter Forty-Two

Jade

O ne final walk-through was needed before I opened the doors of Shadycade to gaming night.

"It's beyond my wildest imagination," I whispered with a breathlessness sparked by nerves and an adrenaline rush. I took a moment to soak it all in and my chest swelled with pride.

Two bartenders, who agreed the signature drink was the bomb, waited with anticipation behind the polished mahogany bar. A slew of extra wait staff prepped nachos, burgers, hot dogs, wings, and other offerings on our menu in the tiny kitchen.

I walked between cocktail tables situated toward the front of the bar. The Barflies had their laptops already stationed at the long table, choosing to let the paying gamers have the Zoom Room.

I took a deep breath and hoped I'd recoup the money I'd borrowed from Raylynn and the small amount I'd saved since the Big Mike debacle, plus earn enough for a down payment on the bar.

"Looks good." Theo stood by the door. He rubbed his little goatee and nodded approvingly. "I like what you've done with that old back room I used for storage. It's cool."

Around the edges of the main room, vintage games lit up like Christmas lights. The pinball machines hummed, their melodic sirens beckoning gamers to try their luck. But the new Zoom Room outshone them all. It glowed sapphire, reminding me of a crystal cave I'd seen in a travel brochure.

"Thanks to the uplighting installed by Stewart and all the hard work from Marjorie, Ed, and the staff." I moved next to Theo. "I appreciate you letting me do this."

"I've always wanted you to have the bar." He wrapped an arm around my shoulders and squeezed. "I'd have given it to you if I could have, but retirement doesn't come cheap."

"I know." I leaned into the hug. If I could have chosen a dad, it would have been Theo. He kissed the top of my head and left me to check in with his muscle manning the door.

Rez came out of the Zoom Room wearing a top hat and tails. He grinned at my raised eyebrows.

"I'm the master of ceremonies."

I nodded at him. "Well played. You'll own the spotlight."

The excitement had my stomach in knots. I wanted a good turnout. But the thought of the bar packed with people made me queasy. For the first time, I sympathized with Raylynn's fear of crowds.

"You're playing tonight, right?" Rez motioned toward the Zoom Room.

I shook my head fast and furious. "No. I'm handling the bar."

Rez's eyes widened, and his face went slack. "Jade. You have to play. You've come the closest to kicking the Python's gold-scaled butt."

"But I need to—"

"Play the game, Jade," Marjorie called from her setup. A blingy base-ball hat perched atop her bouffant hairdo. She wore hot pink lipstick and a matching boa that muffled her neck. She reminded me of one of the Muppets. "You deserve to play after all the hard work you've put in."

"Maybe." I hadn't really considered playing, but a small part of me really wanted to beat the Python and reveal him to the world.

"Not maybe. I saved a slot for you in the Zoom Room." Rez tipped his hat in my direction.

"Rez, that's a paid spot."

"It's your spot."

Theo rounded the corner. "There's a line of people around the building. Snakes clear past the coin laundry."

"What?" I ran to the window. Theo was right. The line wrapped around the building, and the parking lot had cars, lots of them.

Theo leaned over my shoulder. "I've never seen so many folks in the lot."

"I can do this." I could raise the money to buy the bar. I was ready to jump in with both feet. Give it my all. Chase my dream. My heart did a beautiful swan dive off the high board. I only wished Luke was here to see it.

"Look who I found at the back door." Ed came in, followed by Raylynn and Jean-Claude.

"It's a madhouse out there. We had to park three blocks away." Raylynn flipped a swooping dark bang away from her eyes, a result of the most recent makeover, and looked all goo-goo-eyed at Jean-Claude.

I rolled my eyes at Raylynn and turned toward Jean-Claude. His pasty-white pallor had a pop of pink. And a sunburned nose from a day spent at the shore with Raylynn. He'd switched out his prior black-on-black attire for a pair of designer jeans and a polo shirt. It looked good on him. "I thought you had a meeting in San Diego?"

"I postponed it." He glanced at Raylynn, and when she beamed back at him, my heart melted. "Besides." He patted the case tucked under his arm. "I wouldn't miss the opportunity to expose the Python."

"What is that?"

"It's my new SCUF controller." He grinned like a schoolboy with a new lunchbox. "I've purchased a seat at the head gaming table."

"I...I...I..." was dumbfounded. I had no idea Jean-Claude played video games. Actually, I had no idea he did anything other than eat unsuspecting authors for breakfast. It never occurred to me that he might have a hobby. Or, that he might do something for...fun.

Raylynn giggled. "Surprised me too, but he's really good."

"Maybe I'm the Python." Jean-Claude narrowed his eyes. "Maybe my rousting the Python on my blog was a ruse. And maybe I'm here to win the whole enchilada and shove it in your faces."

I chewed my lower lip. Could it be? Nah, no way was he the Python. But one could hope.

He wiggled his eyebrows at me, and I laughed with Raylynn. Maybe I could forgive Jean-Claude, but could Luke?

"OK, guys, this is it. The moment we've been waiting for." Rez made a swooping ringmaster motion with his arm.

I turned toward Theo. "Open the door to the masses. Let the gaming begin."

"**W**atch out. There's a minion behind you." Jean-Claude's voice rang in my headset. His avatar, a robust, green female troll with braided pigtails resembling a combination of Shrek and Laura Ingalls from Little House on the Prairie, pointed toward a slimy serpent.

I turned to fight off the serpent that guarded the entrance to the next level. While I was battling it out with him, I heard Rez cry out stats from the player board and announce the first break. Our avatars retreated to their safe zones.

I stood and stretched my arms up over my head. The Zoom Room was standing room only. Most of the watchers had a signature drink in their hands. I walked into the bar area. Gray-haired gamers bent their heads alongside rainbow-haired gamers, discussing their next moves. Others sat at the gaming table munching on fries, laptops open, waiting for Dragontoon to resume.

The cocktail tables were crowded with patrons, and every stool at the bar held a butt, and many others stood in the available spaces. The servers bustled with orders. Both bartenders rattled Boston cocktail shakers, mixing the Python Killer.

I sighed. If only he were here. And then I realized I meant Luke, not the Python.

Marjorie looked up from her laptop and gave me a wave.

I walked over and gave a sad smile. "The Python's a no-show."

"It's only been two hours. Maybe he's waiting to hack in and steal our thunder." She pounded her fist on the table. Gold bangles encircling her wrist clinked together like ice into a glass.

"How are you doing?" I bent down and looked at Marjorie's screen.

"Not too bad. My troll is on level three." She sipped her Python Killer and made the *Mmmmm* sound. "You've outdone yourself with these drinks. They're delicious."

"Don't drink too many of them. They're powerful." Stewart leaned in from the next chair. "I'll give her a ride home. My drink's a virgin. I'm the DD tonight."

"That's good, Stewart. Thanks."

"I see your avatar has made it to level five." Ed sat back in his chair and pointed at a giant flat-screen live streaming the competition and each player's stats.

"Yeah. I found a back door." I smiled, remembering how Luke taught me that trick.

Rez passed the table and paused. "No sign of the Python yet?"

"No. If he's using a different avatar, he's being sneaky." I glanced at Jean-Claude. Could his troll morph into a gold dragon? I had watched him take on a castle guard and a three-headed dog. He had skill, but he lacked the finesse of the Python. Still, Jean-Claude was known to be sly. I'd keep him on my radar.

I went behind the bar and grabbed a glass of water. "How's it going?"

Amy, one of the bartenders, wiped her brow with the back of her hand. "We've sold all the glasses with Dragontoon Clings, and people are still buying the signature drinks."

"Then we need more glasses." I looked around the room for empties.

"Don't worry." She waved a hand toward the kitchen. "My kiddo's home from college. He's been picking up the empties and running them through the dishwasher."

"Great. Thanks." I placed a hand over my heart. "I honestly didn't think it would be this big a deal."

"Really?" She poured the bourbon mixture into the glass in front of her. "Revealing the Python is all my kid's talked about since he's been home."

I gulped down my water and swallowed hard. If the Python didn't show, I'd be a Worldwide Flub.

Rez called for round two. I forced a watery smile, sat at my station, and put on my headphones. After an hour, I was climbing the mountain to the next level. I defeated a powerful wizard and leveled up. Still no Python.

"It's him. It's the Python." Marjorie's squeal escalated in my ear, a falsetto giddiness that flatlined quickly. "I'm dead. He got me."

"Me too." Came another voice. Stewart.

"Sorry, I didn't have your back, Stewie. I got tied up with a dwarf minion, and then there he was." Marjorie gushed like she'd just met her favorite movie star. "All gold and gorgeous."

"I sent a poisonous potion his way," Ed, not gushing in the slightest, explained. "That son-of-a-dragon drank it and leveled up, but not until after he sent a dragon's scale to pierce my heart."

I stole a glance at the gaming screen. I saw the gold dragon making his way up the levels, destroying everything in its path. I also saw Jean-Claude's troll. He wasn't the Python.

One by one, gamers stopped leaning into their screens. The sound of clicking controllers slowed until only a few remained in the room. The Python continued up the levels, kicking any gamers he met to the curb.

"Green Dragon, check your pouch. You're running low on ammo." Jean-Claude's voice boomed through my headset, causing my ears to ring.

"Crap on a Kahlúa Cappuccino!" I was so busy fighting the Centaur, I hadn't paid attention. I had one last weapon. A silver dragon scale. And I was saving it for the finale.

I moved through a secret passage, trying to gain as many gold coins as possible to buy more fireballs. After securing enough ammo to feel competent, I turned in time to see the Python enter my level.

The squeaky Bugs Bunny voice of the Python laughed into my headset. "Hello, Green Dragon. Good to see you again."

Good to see you? Was he being polite? Was that a new technique? Be nice, and then *Whamo! You're dead.*

"Where are you hiding?" My avatar took a step back, out of fireball range.

"I'm right here. Waiting for you." He flicked his forked Python tongue, licking his lips, a taste for victory.

I glanced up at Rez. "He's here. Find. Him."

Rez hopped down from the makeshift stage and walked casually behind gamers, searching for the Python.

"So, you've come to destroy me?" I didn't hide behind a voice alternator. My words rang loud and clear.

"No. I'm hungry for trolls today."

Wait. "What?"

Jean-Claude's troll leveled up through a secret passage. He threw a fireball at the Python. Missed. Jean-Claude's curse came through the headset.

I fought against a two-headed Ogre, all while keeping an eye on the battle between Jean-Claude's troll and the Python. Jean-Claude ducked into a secret passage.

Rez came back a few minutes later, shaking his head.

"He has to be here." I didn't look at Rez. I kept glued to my screen, fighting my way up another level.

"He's hacked in somehow." Rez clicked the keyboard on the master computer.

"I thought that was impossible." My heart sank. If the Python hacked in, we couldn't expose him. If he won the competition, I'd be a laughingstock. "We're on a closed system."

"I'm on it." Rez's fingers flew over the keyboard. "Somehow, he's here. He's on our network."

"He's here to ruin me." My stomach lurched. Keep it together. If he's hacked in, I may not be able to expose him, but I can sure as hell beat him.

I didn't look up at Rez, but I heard him huff. "I'll do another sweep of the remaining gamers."

I advanced to the final level along with another player, whose avatar was a cute little blue squirrel. The Python advanced too.

"Oh, nuts! He's targeting me. He's targeting me." Blue Squirrel scurried away from the Python, screeching and hopping on the screen.

"Not on my watch." I threw a fireball at the Python. He ducked. Shit.

The Python whipped a double blaster from his bag of tricks and sent fireballs in two directions. One hit me in the side. My avatar went down.

A healer appeared. It was the troll. He pushed his power into my dragon. My dragon glowed green, stood, bright and alive.

Jean-Claude's troll dropped to one knee and went down to the ground. "Go get him, Jade."

Applause broke out around me. I couldn't believe it. Jean-Claude had given me his last life.

The Python stared at the dead troll. "Unfucking believable."

"Believe it, you game-hacking scumbag. You're going down." I waited until he moved closer to me.

The room began chanting. "Python killer. Python killer."

"Where are you?" My tone threatened.

"Come and find me." The Python almost...begged.

A familiar noise whirred in the background when the Python spoke. I couldn't put my finger on it. And I thought I heard a dog bark.

Damn. I knew there weren't any dogs in the bar. The Python had found a way to hack into the system. Maybe he did have magic powers.

"You're too chicken to come out and show the world your true self." I poked, hoping Rez would find him.

"Why come out when other people do it for you?" He moved closer.

A pang of guilt tightened in my gut. I was trying to expose the Python the same way Jean-Claude exposed Luke—by force, not by choice. I shouldn't have advertised we were going to expose him. It was wrong, and I felt immediate remorse for doing it. It was the reason he found a way to hack in. To show me that forcing someone wasn't the right way. I should have asked.

His squeaky voice startled me out of my guilt trip. "Go ahead. Try to beat me. Make your move, Dragon Slayer."

"I'll make you a deal. If I beat you, show yourself and quit hacking the games." I prayed he'd agree with my new plan.

"Deal. And if I win?"

I hadn't thought of his victory. "What do you want?"

"To meet you in person."

I stared at my screen. Did I hear the squeaky voice correctly? Did he want to meet me?

"Deal." One more step, and I'd have him. The crowd stilled. Everyone, including me, held their breath, waiting for him to make his move.

He took the chance, and I wielded my silver dragon's scale at him.

His scaly torso improbably contorting in an unconventional limbo. One of those Matrix-dodging moves. My sharp scale only nicked his arm.

"Holy Tequila Sunrise!" The Python's voice vibrated in my ear. "That was underhanded."

My body froze, suspended in time, as my mind focused like a high-powered telescope searching for the outer rim. I yanked off my headphones. "Rez, finish my game."

"Whaaaat?" His face went pale under his brown skin. "You're winning. I'm afraid I can't beat the Python."

"In the words of the great Yoda, 'Fear is the path to the Dark Side.'" I shoved the headphones at him and ran for the door.

I'd heard that familiar noise again, and this time, I recognized it.

Chapter Forty-Three

Luke

Jesus. What was I doing? I should have walked into the bar and told Red how much I loved her. By the time I arrived, it was a packed house. Good for Red. She'd make the money. Buy the place. Bad for me. I couldn't Romeo her with the speech I'd practiced for the last eight hours.

Maybe my tardiness could work in everyone's favor. The Python needed to make a grand entrance, but not too early. He should give the audience time to worry he wouldn't show. Time to buy more drinks, play more games, spend more money.

What better way to end his life than struck down by the woman, or in this case, the dragon, he loved?

Only a few people stared at me as I lugged my load inside. They didn't look like the gaming types. They were here to take care of business and get on with their night. I claimed a table. Set up my laptop. "OK, Red. Game on."

It took me over an hour to level up fighting nymphs and castle guards and medieval creatures. When I surfaced for air, the locals that were here earlier had left me to the chaos on my screen.

I was alone.

My childhood fear of being alone and unwanted surfaced with a shiver down my spine.

Then, there she was. At least, her avatar. Her beautiful smoky voice came through my headset. And I didn't feel alone anymore.

A blue squirrel said something funny, and she laughed. Man, I loved her laugh. I almost hated taking out the little guy just to hear her laugh. But I had to throw a shuriken at Blue Squirrel to level up and give Red her finale.

"You jerk," Red cursed at me. I had to do it. Only one could win, so taking out Blue Squirrel was inevitable.

Now, it was only me and Red. The last two avatars standing in the kingdom of Dragontoon. I was ready to say goodbye to the Python. And then, it hit me like a deadly dragon scale. I wanted to tell her. Right here. Right now. In my squeaky voice. I had to tell her before she was gone. Before she disappeared from my life, again.

I moved closer. Spread my wings to breathe my words of truth, passion, love.

She shot a silver scale at my dragon. Instead of letting her slay me, I dodged.

"Holy Tequila Sunrise, that was underhanded." My voice-synthe-sized microphone squeezed my words into the tone of a comical chipmunk. Underhanded and unexpected. I intended to die, but before I let her win, not that she couldn't kick my ass from here to Kansas, I wanted to tell her I was sorry. Tell her I was here. And tell her that I hated using the Python as my medium.

Tell her I love her.

"I've got no way out. No way to level up. No way to win this game without you." I accidentally spoke my feelings into the headset instead of my predrilled declamation.

"Are you hitting on me, dude?" It was a guy's voice. The young guy that ran the gaming competition.

I looked down at the mound of fluff currently lying on my sneakers. "I might have screwed up." He looked up at me with woeful brown eyes, tapping his tail on the tile floor. His leg bound in a cast that I'd sketched Cronman on and signed.

"Woof!"

His reaction wasn't at my admission of failure but at the jingle of the door to the coin laundry held open by Red. Her face showed surprise, but her eyes flamed fire. The same green flame she wore after I broke her Iron Man costume the first time I met her. The time I fell in love with her.

"You found me." I sent her a nervous smile.

"You're the Python?" Her brows crowded over the bridge of her nose.

"I am."

"All this time?"

"I enjoy the challenge of hacking into the game, and it turns out, I'm good at it." She wasn't running into my arms like the movie in my head. It was, after all, only a movie. I shrugged it off. "It became a thing."

She walked over, knelt, and held a handout to Dog. The lame name I had started calling him. With Dog's approval, she ran hand over his thick fur. "Who's this?"

"Dog. I met him on the way here. Some asshole ran him over. It's the reason I was late."

Her face softened instantly. The anger gone in the spin of the dryer. She made cooing sounds to Dog, telling him what a good boy he was and how sorry she was that had happened to him. She scratched his belly. Dog rolled onto his back, relishing in his good fortune.

I laughed at the look of love in Dog's eyes, reflecting the same in my own.

She shot me a green lasered you're-not-off-the-hook look.

Dog sat up, gave a pitiful whine, and held up his injured paw.

"Poor baby." She scratched behind his ears.

Suck-up.

She stood and crossed her arms over her chest. "Luke, why are you here?"

I took a deep breath and began the speech I'd practiced in the car all the way to Sacramento. "One week is not enough time for a rational person to fall in love. I—"

She held up both hands, stopping me mid perfectly practiced speech. "I understand. You have commitments in San Diego." She ticked a finger. "Sacramento is a long, long way from San Diego." She ticked a second finger. "You don't do long-distance relationships."

I cringed at my own words.

She ticked the third finger. "You've moved on. I get it. It was kind of you to come all this way to help with my gaming competition."

She'd sabotaged my speech. I looked down at Dog. If Dog could roll his eyes, that's what Dog did. I waved my hand in the Luke Skywalker Jedi mind trick move to stop her politely dismissing me.

Her breath caught. "Did you just Jedi mind trick me?"

I grinned. "I wasn't finished with my speech."

Her mouth pressed shut. Her eyes narrowed at me. She motioned for me to go ahead. "Let's hear it."

"You're right. I don't do long distances, so I'm moving to Sacramento." Her mouth opened, but I held a finger at her to hold on. I wasn't finished. "As I said before, one week is not enough time for a rational person to fall in love. But who said we were rational?"

"You're moving here?" She grinned wide, then faltered. "What about your store?" She snapped her hands to her hips. "What about the blonde?"

"Blonde?"

"I saw you in the hotel bar after the awards ceremony."

I shook my head. Now it made sense. Her avoiding me at the panel. Her anger. Her quick retreat from the Con. "You saw a drunk woman trying to sit on my lap and me sending her away."

"I did?"

"Yes." I looked down at my hands, then up into her bright Jade eyes. Eyes that pierced my heart like a lightsaber. Eyes I wanted to wake up to every morning. "I'm sorry I didn't tell you I wrote that blog."

"I'm sorry I didn't tell you I wasn't R.D. Sayer."

"You never told me you were either. You told me you were Red, and that's exactly who I want you to be."

She dug in her pocket, pulled out a quarter, and handed it to me.

"Maybe when your whites are done, you can come next door, and I'll buy you a drink."

"With a little umbrella?"

"No. No umbrellas." Her cute little pucker smile made me want to take her here, on the folding table. "Only drinks with substance are allowed in my bar."

I pushed the coin at her. "I don't need your money. The coin laundry is free."

"Free?" She snorted. "Since when?"

"Since I bought it."

"You bought the coin laundry?"

"I did. I've been thinking San Diego was getting a little too big and lonely for me. I'm considering branching out, having some satellite stores. So, the coin laundry is free until I convert it into a comic bookstore. One that hopefully attaches to the best bar in Sacramento."

"What would you do if I didn't forgive you?" She splayed her hands wide. "What if I don't make enough money to buy the bar?"

I loved watching her fidget. I lifted a shoulder. "I'd be the owner of a free coin-operated laundry?"

"How?" She returned her hands to her hips and stared down at me. "Why?"

"Asking for help wasn't so hard after all. My dads invested in my business. I bought the store from Jean-Claude." I chuckled, remembering how excited my dads were to loan me the money, correction, invest in my business, and play a part in my dream. "My dads want me to open comic bookstores across California. I told them I'd start with one more store. See how things go."

"Sounds like you've leveled up to me." Red smiled, tender and warm, a proud smile. I'd give all the lives I had stored in my life pack to have her look at me that way forever.

"And the why..." I stood and moved toward her, pulling her hesitantly into my arms. Her citrus scent wrapped me, and for the first time in my life, the fear of letting someone get close wasn't there. "Because I love you."

"I love you, too. Luke Walker." Her lips pressed to mine in a kiss that ruined me. She invaded my space, my soul, my heart.

She broke free of my arms. Worry lines formed across her forehead. "I understand how hard it is to ask for help. Raylynn's cosigning my loan if I can raise enough money for the down payment. And everyone helped me put this gaming night together. Raylynn, Rez, the Barflies, my staff, even Jean-Claude. I just hope it all wasn't for nothing. I hope I can help make your dreams come true."

"You already have."

"I've only begun to develop my world. But without Iron Man, it seemed pointless. Now that the Python, and other villains, have been defeated. Let's build it together."

"Well, Captain, you might have a little problem with your re-entry. There's been a lot of turbulence lately, but if you come in nice and slow, you may not explode on impact." Her lips twisted in a playful challenge.

I chuckled at the reference from our first date in the escape room. I was thinking those same thoughts. "You're right. I am the captain of my world, and I'd like to experience Sacramento in a much more personal way. I should start with a date."

"A date?"

"Yeah, a lunch date. How about it, Red? You willing to put your coin in and risk your credits on me?"

"Well. You do have a dog." She stared at Dog for a minute.

"Dog?" I looked down at the furball. He lifted his head and smiled at me. "How would you like to live in Sacramento?"

Dog's tail thumbed in time with the dryer. "I think that's a yes." I tilted my head toward her. "It's a yes for me too. Are you in?"

Red leaped into my arms, murmuring yes through pressed kisses.

I glanced down at my laptop. "Looks like the Python died a majestic death." I turned the screen so she could see my avatar lying on the ground and her dragon taking its victory bows. The live streaming showed the fans circling Rez, clapping him on the back.

"C'mon." I held out my hand to her. "Let's introduce the world to the defeated Python."

She paused. "Why don't we keep him a secret? I mean, in the words of the great Obi-Wan Kenobi, 'Strike me down, and I will become more powerful than you could possibly imagine.'"

"Man, I loved that Jedi. Almost as much as I love you."

She nuzzled me with her perfect nose. "I love you too, Python."

CHAPTER 44

Epilogue

The bar looked amazing for Mom's birthday party. She'd gone an entire year without an episode and we were here to celebrate her. I'd made enough money the night of the *Shadycade beat the Python* extravaganza I was able to make the down payment on the bar, and with Raylynn's help, secured the loan. With all the hoopla from the event and the free social media provided by Jerry, Shadycade had been doing fine.

Theo was like a proud papa when he handed me the keys and took off on his motorcycle to, according to him, a place with a beach, bikinis, and a swim-up bar.

Ed and Stewart sat at the mahogany bar helping me cut up lemons, oranges, and limes.

"Hey, you're eating the oranges. They're for the drinks." Stewart shook an accusatory finger at Ed.

"Am not." Ed huffed and popped a cherry in his mouth. "I'm eating the cherries."

I chuckled as the two men continued to banter over the garnish tray and gave a silent thank you that they weren't having the argument at Applebee's.

"Hey, Jade." Amy had become a full-time bartender since, in my condition, I had to decrease the time I spent on my feet. "That banner you wanted is ready to be hung in the Zoom Room. It's waiting on your approval."

"Thanks. I'll take a look." I pushed off the barstool and waddled my way through an ocean of balloons and into the Zoom Room. Luke and his dad Steve stood on bookended stepladders holding a banner above the ginormous gaming screen that read "Happy Twenty-First Birthday."

"Making your mom's wish to be twenty-one forever has been a hoot." Steve grinned at me.

"It has, hasn't it?" I chewed my lip. "A little higher on your end, Luke."

Luke moved the banner into the perfect position.

"That's it. Thanks guys." I gave them two thumbs-up. "After you hang the banner, will you help me with the streamers and balloons?"

"Can you at least sit down when you're giving out orders?" Luke gave a chin lift toward the gaming chair to my left.

"She's pregnant, not incapacitated." Marjorie strolled into the room wearing a cheetah scarf over her bouffant that matched her dress. She pressed a virgin Python Killer into my hand. "Back in my day, we had babies in the oil fields, no medication, no fuss, then went back to work that very evening."

Luke's face turned a light shade of grasshopper. A thing that had begun with the mere mention of giving birth. I rolled my eyes at the smug look on Marjorie's face. She was messing with Luke and enjoyed every moment.

The three of them hung streamers and I tied balloons together for the balloon arch. Luke didn't want me up on the ladder so I handed them to him and with Steve's help, formed the balloon arch that would frame the photo area. Marjorie brought in a basket of hats and props to use.

Dog, renamed R2 because every Jedi Knight needs his wing droid, strutted in the room and sat at my feet. His tail slapped happy on the tile.

Both men removed the ladders and returned them to our new storeroom. The one we shared with the comic bookstore.

Rez hosted a gaming competition once a month at each of our locations. The Python hadn't returned after his announcement of love for the green dragon and his embarrassing demise. Now, there was a new hacker, the Joker, a multicolored dragon ranking high score and kicking butt on Dragontoon.

Luke had moved to Sacramento a month after the Python's defeat. We had lunch dates, dinner dates, and lots of sexy time. He asked me to marry him six months later in an escape room date. Now, a year and a half later, we were partners in a vintage gaming bar, four California-based comic bookstores, and had our own little Padawan on the way.

"How are you feeling?" Luke snaked an arm around me and kissed the top of my head.

"Fine. Happy." I slurped my drink and gave him a cheeky grin. "Baby Yoda's been kicking me in the ribs all day. He's going to be an extreme gamer."

"Leia's going to be an extreme gamer." Luke smiled down at me.

"Marjie's the perfect name for the babe, but if it's not to your liking, I'll work on your sister." Marjorie gave an exaggerated *humpf* and went in search of someone else to torment.

Luke pulled out a chair and I obliged him and sat. My ankles weren't getting any smaller by standing up. "Paul offered to pick up your mom. Raylynn's on deadline and won't be here until right before we yell, 'Surprise!'"

"What did you tell Mom she was doing tonight?" I asked.

Luke's sexy dimple sunk further into his chin. "I lied and told her we were playing mini golf."

"No joke, you lied?" I arched an eyebrow at him. "To your own mother-in-law. And here I thought you'd reformed from your wicked ways."

"I never lied. That was your thing."

"Ha!" I gave him a slug to the bicep. "I never lied, only imperson-ated. OK, maybe that one time to Jean-Claude. I mean John." I was still having trouble calling him by his real name.

"Speaking of wicked, do you think Jerry would let you borrow the Harley Quinn tonight? I'm feeling like the Joker needs his woman." His mouth pulled into my favorite smile.

"I think I'll go check on the cake," Steve said, making a quick exit.

Luke laughed as his dad hightailed it out of the room. "He's excited to be a grandpops, but prefers he doesn't know the details of how it happened."

Jean-Claude entered the room carrying a package. "Here it is, everyone." He pulled out a copy of Luke's first graphic novel written all by himself. "I must say, I read a blog about it today, and it gave five-star reviews."

Luke's eyebrows shot up. "You reviewed my book?"

"Of course, since I'll be away on my honeymoon during its release date, I reviewed it early. An ARC reader, if you will."

"I might have given him a copy." I shrugged off the pinch Luke attempted to my arm. "The poor guy's about to marry my sister."

Jean-Claude's fiasco at the Con had gone viral and made him even more famous. Go figure, right? He made a fortune with his self-help books. He hosted a podcast, had a YouTube channel, and made appearances on well-known talk shows.

I'd made peace with Raylynn, but she was still a picky, bossy neat freak and habitually hardheaded. She had refused to marry Jean-Claude even though he'd asked her half a dozen times. After the release of her next book, she'd moved in with Jean-Claude and gotten pregnant not long after me. I told her it was a very twin thing to do.

She finally agreed to marry Jean-Claude. "He's knocked me up, I feel inclined to make it legal," Raylynn had said to me flashing a huge diamond ring. "And I love the guy, word warts and all."

I laid my hand on Luke's muscular shoulder. All things felt right in my world. The Con-Flict turned into a Con-nection. It was the best and worst game I'd ever played, but I came out a winner. High score in love, in life, and in everything in between. Not to mention, I get to play with Luke's lightsaber whenever I want.

Lucky Long Island Iced Tea!

The End

If you loved *Love at First Con-flict* please leave a review on Amazon.com

The Python Killer

Ingredients:
Grenadine (Enough to coat the bottom of a glass)
1 shot Rum
2 oz. Cranberry Juice
1 shot Bourbon
1 shot Fireball
4 oz Peach Nectar

Directions:
Coat the bottom of the glass with grenadine. Add ice.
In a cocktail shaker add 2 counts of rum, 2 counts of cranberry juice, and a small cup of ice. Shake it until the ice is melty.
Pour it gently into the glass to avoid mixing with the grenadine.
In the cocktail shaker, combine a shot of Fireball, one shot of bourbon, and 4 ounces of peach nectar into the cocktail shaker. Give it a few shakes. Pour gently into the glass.
Skewer orange slices, cherries, and a few Hot Tamale candies for the final garnish.
Enjoy, Jade

About the Author

Award winning author Janet Leigh writes snarky time-travel romance and romantic comedy novels. She decided to take her love of storytelling and her archive of crazy family stories and write her own novel. Janet published her literary debut, The Shoes Come First, in 2015.

Today, she is a full-time chiropractor and acupuncturist who splits her time between seeing patients and working on her next Rom-Com and Jennifer Cloud novels.

Visit Janetleighbooks.com for updates, excerpts and all that extra stuff!

Follow me!

f facebook.com/janetleighbooks

instagram.com/Janetleighbooks

BB bookbub.com/authors/janet-leigh